IRONSIDE

Also by Holly Black:

THE MODERN FAERIE TALES

Tithe
Valiant
Ironside

THE CURSE WORKERS

White Cat
Red Glove
Black Heart

The Poison Eaters: And Other Stories

Zombies vs. Unicorns
with Justine Larbalestier

Doll Bones

THE SPIDERWICK CHRONICLES

The Field Guide
The Seeing Stone
Lucinda's Secret
The Ironwood Tree
The Wrath of Mulgarath

BEYOND THE SPIDERWICK CHRONICLES

The Nixie's Song
A Giant Problem
The Wyrm King

A MODERN
FAERIE TALE

IRONSIDE

HOLLY BLACK

MARGARET K. McELDERRY BOOKS
New York London Toronto Sydney New Delhi

MARGARET K. McELDERRY BOOKS

An imprint of Simon & Schuster Children's Publishing Division

1230 Avenue of the Americas, New York, New York 10020

This book is a work of fiction. Any references to historical events, real people, or real places are used fictitiously. Other names, characters, places, and events are products of the author's imagination, and any resemblance to actual events or places or persons, living or dead, is entirely coincidental.

Text © 2007, 2019 by Holly Black

"The Lament of Lutie-Loo" © 2019 by Holly Black

Cover photo-illustration © 2020 by Rhett Podersoo

Cover design © 2020 by Simon & Schuster, Inc.

Interior designs by Kathleen Jennings

All rights reserved, including the right of reproduction in whole or in part in any form.

MARGARET K. McELDERRY BOOKS is a trademark of Simon & Schuster, Inc.

For information about special discounts for bulk purchases, please contact Simon & Schuster Special Sales at 1-866-506-1949 or business@simonandschuster.com.

The Simon & Schuster Speakers Bureau can bring authors to your live event.

For more information or to book an event, contact the Simon & Schuster Speakers Bureau at 1-866-248-3049 or visit our website at www.simonspeakers.com.

Also available in a Margaret K. McElderry Books hardcover edition

The text for this book was set in ITC Galliard Std.

The illustrations for this book were rendered in pen and ink.

Manufactured in the United States of America

This Margaret K. McElderry Books paperback edition October 2020

10 9 8 7 6 5 4 3 2 1

Library of Congress Cataloging-in-Publication Data

Names: Black, Holly, author. Title: Ironside / Holly Black.

Description: New York : Margaret K. McElderry Books, 2020. | Series: The modern faerie tales ; book 3 | Audience: Ages 14 up. | Audience: Grades 10-12. | Summary: As the possessor of Roibin's true name, sixteen-year-old Kaye returns to Faerieland to try and complete a nearly impossible quest that will release him from the spell of the faery queen who holds him in thrall.

Identifiers: LCCN 2020023598 (print) | LCCN 2020023599 (ebook) | ISBN 9781534484559 (hardcover) | ISBN 9781534484542 (paperback) | ISBN 9781416979449 (ebook)

Subjects: CYAC: Supernatural—Fiction. | Fairies—Fiction. | Magic—Fiction.

Classification: LCC PZ7.B52878 Iro 2020 (print) | LCC PZ7.B52878 (ebook) | DDC [Fic]—dc23

LC record available at https://lccn.loc.gov/2020023598

LC ebook record available at https://lccn.loc.gov/2020023599

To my parents, Rick and Judy,
for not sticking a hot poker down
my throat or otherwise attempting
to trade me back to the faeries

PROLOGUE

Through the mosses bare,
They have planted thorn-trees
For pleasure here and there.
If any man so daring
As dig them up in spite,
He shall find their sharpest thorns
In his bed at night.
—WILLIAM ALLINGHAM, "THE FAIRIES"

Despite her casting him down to this place, despite the fresh bruises on his skin and the blood under his nails, Roiben still loved Lady Silarial. Despite the hungry eyes of the Unseelie Court and the gruesome tasks its Queen Nicnevin set him. Despite the many ways he'd been humiliated and the things he wouldn't let himself think on while he stood stiffly behind her throne.

If he concentrated hard, he could remember the flame of *his* Queen's copper hair, her unreadable green eyes, the strange smile she'd given him as she'd pronounced his fate just three months past. Choosing him to leave her Bright Court and be a servant among the Unseelie was an honor, he told himself once more. He alone loved her enough to remain loyal. She trusted him above her other subjects. Only his love was true enough to endure.

And he did love her still, he reminded himself.

"Roiben," said the Unseelie Queen. She had been eating her dinner off the back of a wood hob, his green hair long enough to serve as a tablecloth. Now she looked up at Roiben with a dangerous sort of smile.

"Yes, my Lady," he said automatically, neutrally. He tried to hide how much he loathed her, not because it would displease her. Rather, he thought it would please her too well.

"The table trembles too much. I am afraid my wine will spill."

The hollow hill was almost empty; what courtiers remained to amuse themselves beneath garlands of hairy roots did so quietly as the Queen took her supper. Only her servants were close by, all of them grim as ghosts. Her chamberlain cleared his throat.

Roiben stared at her dumbly.

"Fix it," she commanded.

He took a step forward, unsure of what she wanted him to do. The hob's wizened face looked up at him, pale with terror. Roiben tried to smile reassuringly, but that seemed to only make the little man tremble further. He wondered if binding would make the hob steadier, and then was disgusted with himself for the thought.

"Chop his feet so they're even with his hands," a voice called, and Roiben looked up. Another knight, hair dark as his coat, strode toward Nicnevin's throne. A dull circlet sat on his brow. He smirked broadly. Roiben had seen him only once before. He was the knight that the Unseelie Court had sent up to the Seelie as their symbol of peace. Roiben's twin in servitude, although he could only suppose this knight's thralldom was easier than Roiben's own. At the sight of him Roiben's heart leaped with an impossible hope. Could the exchange be done with? Was it possible he would be sent home at last?

"Nephamael," the Queen said, "has Silarial tired of you so quickly?"

He snorted. "She sends me as a messenger, but the message is of little consequence. I rather think she doesn't like me, but you seem better pleased with the trade."

"I could not stand to part with my new knight," Nicnevin said, and Roiben bowed his head. "Will you do what Nephamael suggests?"

Roiben took a deep breath, struggling for a calm he didn't feel. Every time he spoke, he was half afraid he would snap and say what he really thought. "I doubt his plan's efficacy. Let me take the hob's place. I will not spill your wine, Lady."

Her smile widened with delight. She turned to Nephamael. "He asks so prettily, doesn't he?"

Nephamael nodded, although he looked less amused than she had. His yellow eyes seemed to take Roiben's measure for the first time. "And no concern for dignity. You must find that refreshing."

She laughed at that, a laugh that seemed startled from her throat and as cold as ice breaking over a deep lake. Somewhere in the vast, dim cavern, a harp began to play. Roiben shuddered to think what it might be strung with.

"Be my table, then, Roiben. See to it that you do not

tremble. The hob will suffer for any failing on your part."

Roiben took the place of the little faerie easily, barely count-ing it as a humiliation to get down on his hands and knees, to bow his head and let the silver plates and warm dishes be set gingerly on his back. He did not flinch. He remained still, even as Nephamael seated himself on the floor beside the throne, resting yet another goblet on the curve of his spine. The man's hand rested on his ass, and Roiben bit his lip to avoid flinching in surprise. The stench of iron was overwhelming. He won-dered how Nicnevin could bear it.

"I've grown bored," Nephamael said. "Although the Seelie Court is lovely, certainly."

"And there is nothing to amuse you there? I find that hard to believe."

"There are things." Roiben thought he could feel the smile in those words. The hand slid across the hollow of his back. He stiffened before he could help himself, and heard the goblets tinkle together with his movement. "But my delight is in find-ing weakness."

Nicnevin didn't so much as reprimand Roiben. He doubted it was out of any generosity on her part.

"Somehow," she said, "I wonder if you are speaking to me at all."

"It is you I am speaking to," Nephamael said. "But not you I am speaking about. Your weaknesses are not for me to know."

"A charming, ingratiating answer."

"But take your knight here. Roiben. I know his vulnerability."

"Do you? I would think that would be rather obvious. His love of the solitary fey has him on his knees even now."

Roiben steeled himself not to move. That the Queen of

Filth spoke about him as though he were an animal didn't surprise him, but he found that he was more afraid of what Nephamael might say. There was something hungry in the way that Nephamael spoke, a hunger Roiben wasn't sure what might sate.

"He loves Silarial. He declared himself to her. And the quest she gave him was this—to be your servant in exchange for peace."

The Queen of the Unseelie Court said nothing. He felt a goblet lifted from his back and then replaced.

"It is delightfully cruel, really. Here he is, being loyal and brave for a woman who used him poorly. She never loved him. She's forgotten him already."

"That's not true," Roiben said, turning, so that silver dishes crashed around him. He leaped to his feet, uncaring of the gaping courtiers, the spilled wine, the hob's frightened cry. He didn't care about anything right then but hurting Nephamael, who'd stolen his place—his home—and dared gloat over it.

"Stop!" Nicnevin called. "I command you, Roiben, by the power of your promise to cease moving."

Against his will, he froze like a mannequin, breathing hard. Nephamael had twisted out of his way, but the half smirk Roiben expected to find on his face was missing.

"Kill the hob," the Unseelie Queen commanded. "You, my knight, will drink his blood like wine, and this time you will not spill a drop."

Roiben tried to open his mouth to say something to stay her hand, but the command forbade even that movement. He had been stupid—Nephamael had been goading him in the hope of just such a mistake. Even the Queen's lack of rebuke earlier had probably been planned. Now he had made a spectacular fool of himself and cost an innocent creature its life. Self-loathing gnawed at his belly.

Never again, he told himself. No matter what they said or did or made him do, he would not react. He would become as indifferent as stone.

The grim servants were quick and efficient. Within moments they had prepared a warm goblet and raised it to his unmoving lips. The corpse was already being cleared away, open eyes staring at Roiben from beyond death, damning him for his vanity.

Roiben could not stop himself from opening his mouth and gulping the warm, salty liquid. A moment later, he gagged and retched on the dais.

The flavor of that blood stayed with him through the long years of his service. Even when a pixie accidentally set him free, even when he'd won the Unseelie crown. But by then he could no longer remember whose blood it was, only that he had grown used to the taste.

*I prefer winter and fall, when you feel the bone
structure in the landscape—the loneliness of it—the
dead feeling of winter. Something waits beneath it—
the whole story doesn't show.*
—Andrew Wyeth

Human girls cry when they're sad and laugh when they're happy. They have a single fixed shape rather than shifting with their whims like windblown smoke. They have their very own parents, whom they love. They don't go around stealing other girls' mothers. At least that's what Kaye thought human girls were like. She wouldn't really know. After all, she wasn't human.

Fingering the hole on the left side of her fishnets, Kaye poked at the green skin underneath as she considered herself in the mirror.

"Your rat wants to come," Lutie-loo said. Kaye turned toward the lidded fish tank, where the doll-size faerie had her thin, pale fingers pressed against the outside of the glass. Inside,

Kaye's brown rat, Armageddon, sniffed the air. Isaac was curled in a white ball in the far corner. "He likes coronations."

"Can you really understand what he's saying?" Kaye asked, pulling an olive skirt over her head and wriggling it onto her hips.

"He's just a rat," Lutie said, turning toward Kaye. One of her moth wings dusted the side of the cage with pale powder. "Anyone can talk rat."

"Well, I can't. Do I look too monochromatic in this?"

Lutie nodded. "I like it."

Kaye heard her grandmother's voice calling from downstairs. "Where are you? I made you a sandwich!"

"Be there in a second!" Kaye shouted back.

Lutie kissed the glass wall of the cage. "Well, can the rat come or not?"

"I guess. Sure. I mean, if you can get him to not run away." Kaye laced up one thick-soled black boot and limped around the room looking for its mate. Her old bed frame was in pieces in the attic, her old dolls were dressed in punk-rock finery, and above the new mattress on the floor Kaye had painted a mural where a headboard might have been. It was half finished—a tree with deep, intricate roots and gilded bark. Although she'd thought it would, the decorating still hadn't made the room feel like hers.

When he'd seen the mural, Roiben had remarked that she could glamour the room into looking any way she wanted, but a magical veneer—no matter how lovely—still didn't seem real to her. Or maybe it seemed too real, too much a reminder of why she didn't belong in the room at all.

Shoving her foot into the other boot, she tugged on her

jacket. Leaving her hair green, she let magic slide over her skin, coloring and plumping it. There was a slight prickling as the glamour restored her familiar human face.

She looked at herself a moment longer before pocketing Armageddon, scratching behind the ears of Isaac, and walking toward the door. Lutie followed, flying on moth wings, keeping out of sight as Kaye jogged down the stairs.

"Was that your mother on the phone before?" Kaye's grandmother asked. "I heard it ring." She stood at the kitchen counter, pouring hot grease into a tin can. Two peanut butter and bacon sandwiches sat on chipped plates; Kaye could see the brown meat curling past the edges of the white bread.

Kaye bit into her sandwich, glad that the peanut butter glued her mouth shut.

"I left her a message about the holidays, but can she bother to call me back? Oh no, she's much too busy to talk. You'll have to ask her tomorrow night, although why she can't come down here to see you instead of insisting you go visit her at that squalid apartment in the city, I will never know. It must really gall her that you've decided to stay here instead of following her around like a little shadow."

Kaye chewed, nodding along with her grandmother's complaints. In the mirror beside the back door, she could see, beneath the glamour, a girl with leaf green skin, black eyes without a drop of white in them, and wings as thin as plastic wrap. A monster standing beside a nice old lady, eating food intended for another child. A child stolen away by faeries.

Brood parasites. That's what cuckoos were called when they dropped their eggs in other birds' nests. Parasitic bees, too, leaving their spawn in foreign hives; Kaye had read about them in one of the moldering encyclopedias on the landing. Brood parasites didn't bother raising their own babies. They left them to be raised by others—birds that tried not to notice when their offspring grew huge and hungry, bees that ignored that their progeny did not collect pollen, mothers and grandmothers who didn't know the word "changeling."

"I have to go," Kaye said suddenly.

"Have you thought more about school?"

"Gram, I got my GED," Kaye said. "You saw it. I did it. I'm done."

Her grandmother sighed and looked toward the fridge, where the letter was still tacked with a magnet. "There's always community college. Imagine that—starting college before the rest of your class even graduates."

"I'll go see if Corny is outside yet." Kaye started toward the door. "Thanks for the sandwich."

The old woman shook her head. "It's too cold out there. Stand on the porch. He should know better than to ask a young girl to wait outside in the snow. I swear, that boy has no manners at all."

Kaye felt the whoosh of air as Lutie flew past her back. Her grandmother didn't even look up. "Okay, Gram. Bye, Gram."

"Stay warm."

Kaye nodded and used the sleeve of her coat to turn the knob of the door so that she could avoid touching the iron. Even the smell of it burned her nose when she got close. Walking through the porch, she used the same trick on the screen door and stepped out into the snow. The trees on the lawn were encased in ice. Hail from that morning had stuck to whatever it had touched, freezing into solid sparkling skins that covered branches and flashed against the dull gray sky. The slightest breeze sent the limbs jangling against one another.

Corny wasn't coming, but her grandmother didn't need to know that. It wasn't lying. After all, faeries couldn't lie. They only bent the truth so far that it snapped on its own.

Above the doorway, a swag of thorn wrapped in green marked the house as watched over by the Unseelie Court. A gift from Roiben. Each time Kaye looked at the branches, she hoped that being protected by the Unseelie Court included being protected *from* the Unseelie Court.

She turned away, walking past a ranch house with aluminum siding hanging off in patches. The woman who lived there raised Italian ducks that ate all the grass seed anyone in the neighborhood planted. Kaye thought of the ducks and smiled. A trash can rolled in the street, bumping up against plastic bins of beer bottles set out for recycling. Kaye crossed over the parking lot of a boarded-up bowling alley, where a sofa rested near the curb, cushions hard with frost.

Plastic Santas glowed on lawns beside dried grapevine reindeer wrapped with fiber-optic lights. A twenty-four-hour convenience store piped screechy carols that carried through the quiet streets. A robotic elf with rosy cheeks waved endlessly next to several snowman windsocks fluttering like ghosts. Kaye passed a manger missing its baby Jesus. She wondered if kids had stolen him or if the family had just taken him in for the night.

Halfway to the cemetery, she stopped at a pay phone outside a pizza place, put in quarters, and punched in Corny's cell number. He picked it up after the first ring.

"Hey," Kaye said. "Did you decide about the coronation? I'm on my way to see Roiben before it starts."

"I don't think I can go," Corny said. "I'm glad you called, though—I have to tell you something. I was driving past one of those storage places. You know the kind with the billboards that have quotes on them like 'Support Our Troops' or 'What Is Missing in C-H-blank-blank-C-H? U-R.'"

"Yeah," Kaye said, puzzled.

"Well, this one said 'Life Is Like Licking Honey from a Thorn.' What the fuck is that?"

"Weird."

"No shit, it's weird. What is it supposed to mean?"

"Nothing. Just don't dwell on it," Kaye said.

"Oh, right. Don't dwell. That's me. I'm so good at not dwelling. It's my skill set. If I was going to take one of those tests to see what job I was best suited for, I would rate a perfect ten for 'not dwelling on shit.' And what job do you think that would qualify me for exactly?"

"Storage unit manager," Kaye said. "You'd be the one to put up those sayings."

"Ouch. Right between the legs." She could hear the smile in his voice.

"So, you're really not coming tonight? You seemed so sure it was a good idea for you to face your fears and all that."

There was a long silence on the other end of the line. Just as she would have spoken, he said, "The problem with facing my *fears* is that they're my fears. Not to mention that a fear of megalomaniacal, amoral fiends is hard to rationalize away." He laughed, a brittle, strange cackle. "Just once I'd like them to finally give up their secrets—tell me how to really protect myself. How to be safe."

Kaye thought of Nephamael, the last King of the Unseelie

Court, choking on iron, and Corny stabbing him again and again.

"I don't think it's that simple," Kaye said. "I mean, it's almost impossible to protect yourself from people, forget faeries."

"Yeah, I guess. I'll see you tomorrow," Corny said, and ended the call.

"Okay." She heard him hang up the phone.

Kaye walked on, drawing her coat more tightly around her. She stepped into the cemetery and started up the snowy hill, muddy and grooved by the sleds that had gone over it. Her gaze strayed to where she knew Janet was buried, although from where Kaye stood, the polished granite stones looked the same with their plastic garlands and wet red bows. She didn't need to see the grave for her steps to slow, weighed down by the memory like sodden clothes must have weighed down Janet's drowning body.

She wondered what happened when the baby cuckoo realized it wasn't like its brothers and sisters. Maybe it wondered where it had come from or what it was. Maybe it just pretended nothing was wrong and kept on gulping down worms. Whatever that bird felt, though, it wasn't enough to keep it from pushing the other chicks out of the nest.

Cornelius Stone closed his cell phone against his chest and stood still for a moment, waiting for the regret to ebb. He wanted to go to the coronation, wanted to dance with the terrible and beautiful creatures of the Unseelie Court, wanted to gorge on faerie fruit and wake up on a hillside, scourged and sated. He bit his cheek until he tasted blood, but the yearning only rose with the pain.

He sat down in the library aisle on carpeting so new it had a clean, chemical smell that was probably evaporating formaldehyde. Opening the first of the books, he looked at woodcuts and turn-of-the-century line art. He saw pictures of ponies with flippers that looked nothing like the kelpie that had murdered his sister. He leafed to an illustration of a ring of tiny cherubic faeries with red cheeks and pointy ears dancing in a circle. *Pixies,* he read. None of them resembled Kaye in the least.

He tore each page carefully out of the binding. They were bullshit.

The next book was no better.

As he started ripping apart the third, an elderly man looked down the aisle.

"You shouldn't be doing that," he said. He was holding a fat hardback western in one hand and squinted at Corny as though, even with his glasses, he couldn't see him very clearly.

"I work here," Corny lied.

The man looked at Corny's scuffed biker jacket and his shaggy almost-a-mullet hair. "Your job is to rip apart perfectly good books?"

Corny shrugged. "National security."

The guy walked away muttering. Corny shoved the rest of the books into his backpack and walked out the doors. Disinformation was worse than no information at all. Alarms clanged behind him, but he didn't worry. He'd been to other libraries. The alarms didn't do anything but make a pretty sound, like a church bell from the future.

He started in the direction of the coronation hill. No, he

wasn't going to party with Kaye and her prince-of-darkness boyfriend, but that didn't mean he had to stay home. None of those books could help with what he had planned, but he'd expected that. If he wanted answers, he was going to have to go right to the source.

The servants didn't like to let Kaye into the Palace of Termites. She could tell by the way they looked at her, as though she were only the scuff of her shoes, the dirt under her fingernails, the stench of coffee and cigarettes that clung to her clothes. They spoke grudgingly, eyes never meeting hers, and they led her through passageways as though their feet were made of lead.

Here was the place to which she ought to belong, but instead the grim and fabulous court, the cold halls, and the ferocious denizens made her uneasy. It was all very lovely, but she felt self-conscious and awkward against such a backdrop. And if she did not belong here and she didn't belong with Ellen, then she couldn't think of any place left to belong.

It had been nearly two months since Roiben had assumed the title of Unseelie King, but a formal coronation could only occur on the darkest day of winter. After tonight he would be the true Lord of the Night Court, and with the title would come the resumption of the endless war with the Seelie fey. Two evenings past he'd woken Kaye by climbing a tree, tapping against her bedroom window, and drawing her out to sit on the frozen lawn. "Stay Ironside for a time after I'm crowned," he'd told her. "Lest you be dragged into more danger." When she'd tried to ask him for how long or how bad he thought it was going to get, he'd kissed her quiet. He'd seemed restless, but wouldn't say why. Whatever the reason, his restlessness had been infectious.

She followed the shuffling feet of a hunchbacked steward to the doors of Roiben's chambers.

"He will be with you soon," the steward said, pushing open the heavy door and stepping inside. He lit several fat candles along the floor before retreating silently. A tufted tail dragged behind him.

Roiben's rooms were largely unfurnished, the walls an expanse of smooth stone broken up by stacks of books and a bed covered in a brocade throw. There were a few other things, farther inside—a jade bowl of washing water, a wardrobe, a stand with his armor. The chamber was formal, austere, and forbidding.

Kaye dropped her coat onto the end of the bed and sat down beside it. She tried to imagine living here, with him, and failed. The idea of putting a poster on the wall was absurd.

Reaching over, she pulled a bracelet from one of the pockets of her coat, cupping it in her hand. A thin braid of her own green hair, wrapped in silver wire. She'd hoped to surprise him before the ceremony started, hoped that even if she couldn't see him for a while, he'd keep it with him, like storybook knights wore their ladies' tokens when they rode into battle. Lutie and Armageddon had even gone ahead to the hall so that she'd have a moment alone in which to present it.

Next to the grandeur of the room, though, her gift now seemed ugly and homemade. Not worthy of a King.

There was a sound like the clatter of hooves in the hall and Kaye stood, pushing the bracelet back into the pocket of her coat, but it was only another glowering servant, this one bringing a glass of spiced wine as thick and red as blood.

Kaye took the glass and sipped at it politely, then set it down on the floor as the servant left. She flipped through a few books in the flickering candlelight—military strategy, *Peasepod's Ballads*, an Emma Bull paperback she'd loaned him—and waited some more. Taking another sip of wine, she stretched out at the end of the bed, wrapping the brocade cloth around her.

She woke suddenly, a hand on her arm and Roiben's impassive face above her. Silvery hair tickled her cheek.

Embarrassed, she sat up, wiping her mouth with the back of her hand. She had slept restlessly, and the coverlet was half on the floor, soaking up spilled wine and melted candle wax. She didn't even remember closing her eyes.

A scarlet-clad servant bearing a long cloak with black opal clasps stood in the center of the room. Roiben's chamberlain, Ruddles, was near the door, his mouth overfull of teeth in a way that made him seem as though he wore an unpleasant grin.

Roiben frowned. "No one told me you were here."

She wasn't sure if that meant that he wished someone had or that he would have preferred her not to be there at all. Kaye slung her coat over her arm and stood up, her cheeks hot with shame. "I should go."

He stayed seated on the wreckage of his bed. The scabbard on his hip touched the floor. "No." He gestured to the servant and Ruddles. "Leave us."

With shallow bows, they departed.

Kaye remained standing. "It's late. Your thing is going to start soon."

"Kaye, you have no idea what time it is." He stood and reached for her arm. "You've been asleep."

She stepped back, clasping her hands together, pressing her nails into her palm to keep calm.

He sighed. "Stay. Let me beg your forgiveness for whatever it is I've done."

"Stop it." She shook her head, talking faster than she was thinking. "They don't want you to be with me, do they?"

His mouth curved into a bitter smile. "I am forbidden nothing."

"No one wants me here. They don't want me near you. Why?"

He looked startled, ran a hand through silver hair. "Because I'm gentry and you're . . . not," he finished awkwardly.

"I'm low class," she said dully, turning her back to him. "Nothing new there."

Roiben's boots tapped against the stone as he walked behind her and pulled her against his chest. His head rested in the crook of her neck, and she felt his breath as he spoke, his lips moving against her skin. "I have my own thoughts on the subject. I care nothing for the opinions of others."

For a moment, she relaxed into his touch. He was warm and his voice was very soft. It would be easy to crawl back under the coverlet and stay. Just stay.

But Kaye turned in his arms instead. "What's the big deal about you slumming?"

He snorted, one of his hands lingering on her hip. He was no longer looking at her; his stare focused on the cold stone floor, the same gray as his eyes. "It is a weakness. My affection for you."

She opened her mouth to ask another question, and closed it again, realizing he'd answered more than she'd asked. Perhaps that was the reason that the servants didn't like her, perhaps it was the reason that courtiers sneered at her, but it was also what he believed. She could see it in his face.

"I really should go," she said, pulling away. She was relieved to find that her voice didn't catch. "I'll see you out there. Break a leg."

He released her from the cradle of his arms. "You cannot stand on the dais during the ceremony nor walk in the procession. I do not want you to be taken for part of my court. Above all, you must not swear fealty. Promise me, Kaye."

"So, I'm supposed to act like I don't know you?" The door was only a few steps across the floor, but she was conscious of each one. "Like you don't have any *weaknesses*?"

"No, of course not," he said, too quickly. "You are the only thing I have that is neither duty nor obligation, the only thing I chose for myself." He paused. "The only thing I want."

She let a small teasing smile creep onto her face. "Really?"

He snorted, shaking his head. "You think I'm being absurd, don't you?"

"I think you're trying to be nice," said Kaye. "Which is pretty absurd."

He walked to her and kissed her smiling mouth. She forgot about his sullen servants and the coronation and the bracelet she hadn't given him. She forgot about anything but the press of his lips.

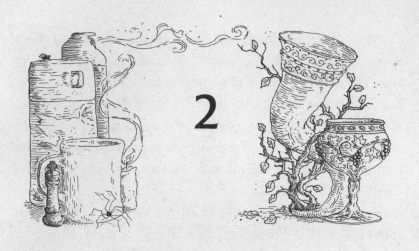

2

There shall be plates a-plenty,
And mugs to melt the chill
Of all the grey-eyed people
Who happen up the hill.
—Edna St. Vincent Millay, "Tavern"

Silarial had not openly moved against Roiben these two long months between Samhain and Midwinter's Eve, and he began to wonder what she intended. The dark, cold months were considered an unlucky time for the Seelie Court to strike, so perhaps she only waited for the ice to melt into spring, when she would have every advantage. Still, he could occasionally believe that she had considered renewing the truce between the Bright and the Night Courts. Even with her greater numbers, war was still costly.

"The envoy from the Seelie Court is here, my Lord," Dulcamara repeated, the silver soles of her boots ringing with each step. Roiben heard "Lord" echo off the walls again and again, like a taunt.

"Send him in," Roiben said, touching his mouth. He wondered if Kaye was already in the hall, if she was alone.

"If I might presume to inform, the messenger is a she."

Roiben looked up with sudden hope. "Send her in, then."

"Yes, my Lord." The envoy stepped out of the way, letting the faerie woman come forward. She was dressed in glacial white cloth, with no armor whatsoever. When she looked up at him, her silver eyes gleamed like mirrors, reflecting his own face.

"Welcome, little sister." The words seemed to steal his breath as he spoke them.

Her hair was cropped close, a white halo around her face. She bowed and did not lift her head.

"Lord Roiben, my Lady sends you her greetings. She is saddened that she must fight against one of her own knights and bids you reconsider your rash position. You could even now renounce all this, surrender, and return to the Bright Court."

"Ethine, what happened to your hair?"

"For my brother," she said, but still did not look at him as she spoke. "I cut it when I lost him."

Roiben just stared at her.

"Have you any message?" Ethine inquired.

"Tell her I will not reconsider." His voice was clipped. "I will not step down and I will not surrender. You may say to your mistress that having tasted freedom, her service no longer tempts me. You may tell her that nothing about her tempts me."

Ethine's jaw clenched as though she were biting back words. "I am instructed to remain for your coronation. With your leave, of course."

"I am always glad of your company," he said.

She left the hall without waiting for his dismissal. As his chamberlain walked into the room wearing a wide and toothy grin, Roiben tried not to see it as an ill omen that of late he was better at pleasing those he hated than those he loved.

Cornelius leaned back against the rough bark of an elm tree just inside the cemetery. He tried to concentrate on something other than the cold, something other than the iron poker clutched in one bare hand or the fishing wire in the other. He had turned his white clothes inside out just in case some of the shit from the books worked, and he'd rubbed himself down with pine needles to disguise his smell. He hoped, in the gray and starless night, it would be enough.

No matter how ready he had told himself he was, hearing faeries shuffling through the snow filled him with panic. He didn't really think the poker was much of a defense against the legions of the Unseelie Court. All he could do now was hold his breath and try not to shiver.

They were gathering for the first coronation in more than a century. Everyone who was anyone in Faerie would be there. Corny wished Kaye were crouched in a snowbank with him tonight, not under the hill at the faerie ball. She always made crazy plans seem like they were going to work, made it seem like you could figure out the un-figure-outable. But to get Kaye to come, he would have had to tell her what he was doing, and there was no way that would have gone well. Sometimes he forgot she wasn't human, and then she would look at him with something alien in her eyes, or smile with a smile far too wide and too hungry. Even though she'd become his best friend, she was still one of *them*. He was better off working alone.

Corny repeated that thought to himself silently as the first of the faerie processional passed. It was a group of trolls, their lichen green limbs as long and gnarled as branches. They kicked up snow as they passed, growling to one another softly, hooked noses scenting the air like hounds'. Tonight they did not bother with disguises.

A trio of women followed, all dressed in white, their hair blowing around them even though there was no wind. They smiled secret smiles at one another. As they passed, oblivious of him, he saw that their curved backs were as hollow and empty as eggshells. Despite the filmy gowns they wore, they appeared to not mind the cold.

Horses wound their way up the hill next, their riders solemn and quiet. Corny's eye caught on the shock of red berries encircling dark hair. He could not stop himself from staring at the rich and strange patterns of the clothes, the shining locks, and the faces, so handsome that just looking made him ache with longing.

Corny bit his lip hard and forced his eyes shut. His hands were trembling at his sides and he was afraid that the clear plastic fishing wire would pull up through the snow. How many times would he be caught off guard like this? How many times could he be made a fool?

Keeping his eyes closed, Corny listened. He listened for the snap of branches, the scrunching of snow, the whispered snatches of conversation, the laughter that was as lilting as any flute. He listened for them to pass, and when they had, he opened his eyes at last. Now he just had to wait. He was betting that no matter what the party was for, there were always latecomers.

It took only a few more minutes for a troop of short gray-clad elves to come up the hill. Hissing impatiently at one another, they waded through the snow. Corny sighed. There were too many for him to be able to do what he'd planned, and they were too large, so he waited till they passed.

A smallish faerie tramped behind them, hopping in the long footfalls of the trolls. Clad in scarlet with a half-pinecone hat, its black eyes glittered like an animal's in the reflected light. Corny clutched the handle of the poker tighter and took a deep breath. He waited for the little faerie to take two hops more, then Corny stepped out of the trees and in one swift movement thrust the poker against the faerie's throat.

It shrieked, falling prone in the snow, hands flying to cover where the iron had touched it.

"Kryptonite," Corny whispered. "I guess that makes me Lex Luthor."

"Please, please," the creature wheedled. "What does it want? A wish? Surely a little thing like myself would have too small wishes for such a mighty being."

Corny jerked hard on the thin fishing wire. An aluminum crab trap snapped together around the faerie.

The little creature screeched again. It scrambled from side to side, breathing hard, clawing at any small gaps, only to fall back with a yowl. Corny finally permitted himself to smile.

Working quickly, he twisted four thin steel wires into place, fixing the trap closed. Then he hefted the cage in the air and ran down the hill, slipping in the ankle-deep snow, careful to take a different path from the one the faeries had come up. He stumbled to where he'd parked his car, the trunk still open, the spare tire within dusted with a fine layer of white.

Dropping the cage there, he slammed the trunk shut and hopped into the front of the car, turning the ignition. The heat came on full blast and he just sat there a moment, letting himself enjoy the warmth, letting himself feel the beat of his heart, letting himself glory in the fact that now, finally, he would be the one making the rules.

Kaye tipped back her goblet, drinking it to the dregs. The first sip of mushroom wine had been foul, but afterward she had found herself touching her tongue to her teeth, searching for more of the earthy, bitter flavor. Her cheeks were hot to the press of her own palms and she felt more than slightly dizzy.

"Don't—that isn't good to eat," Lutie-loo said. The little faerie was perched on Kaye's shoulder, one hand clutching a silver hoop earring and the other holding on to a lock of hair.

"Better than good," Kaye said, drawing her fingers across the bottom of the goblet, sifting the sediment, then licking it from her hand. She took an experimental step, trying to spin, and catching herself moments before she crashed into a table. "Where's my rat?"

"Hiding like we should be. Look," Lutie said, but Kaye couldn't see what she was gesturing at. It could have been anything. Trolls skulked among the tables next to selkies without their skins, while hollow-backed dopplers danced and whirled. There was at least one kelpie—the stench of brine was heavy in the air—but there were also nixies, sprites, brownies, bogies, phookas, a shagfoal in the corner, will-o'-the-wisps zipping among stalagmites, grinning spriggans, and more.

Not just the local denizens either. Folk had traveled from distant courts to witness the coronation. There were envoys from more courts than Kaye had known existed, some Seelie, some Unseelie, and others that claimed those distinctions were meaningless. Even the High Court, to which the Court of Termites was not pledged, sent their own representative, a prince who appeared delighted by the flowing wine. All of them here to watch the Night Court pledge fealty to its new master. They smiled at her, smiles full of thoughts Kaye could not decipher.

The tables were spread with dark blue cloths and set with platters of ice. Branches and holly berries rested beside sculptures composed of frozen blocks of greenish water. A black-tongued monster licked at a chunk containing a motionless minnow. Bitter acorn cakes frosted with a sugary blackberry paste were stacked near pinned and roasted pigeon feet. Slushy black punch floated in an enormous copper bowl, the metal sweating and cloudy with cold. Occasionally someone dipped a long-stemmed icicle cup into it and sipped at the contents.

Kaye looked up as the hall went silent.

Roiben had entered the room with his courtiers. Thistle-down, the Unseelie herald, ran in front of the procession, long golden hair streaming from his wizened head. Then came the piper, Bluet, playing her lilting instrument. Next marched Roiben with his two knights, Ellebere and Dulcamara, following him at an exact three paces. Goblins held up the edges of Roiben's cloak. Behind them were others—his chamberlain, Ruddles, a cupbearer holding a winding goblet of horn, and several pages clutching the harnesses of three black dogs.

Roiben mounted a moss-covered dais near a great throne of woven birch branches and turned toward the crowd, going to his knees. He leaned his head forward and his hair, silver as a knife, fell like a curtain over his face.

"Will you take the oath?" Thistledown asked.

"I will," Roiben said.

"The endless night," Thistledown intoned, "of darkness, ice, and death is ours. Let our new Lord be also made from ice. Let our new Lord be born from death. Let our new Lord commit himself to the night." He lifted a crown woven of ash branches, small broken stubs of twigs forming the spires, and set it on Roiben's head.

Roiben rose.

"By the blood of our Queen which I spilled," he said. "By this circlet of ash placed upon my brow I bind myself to the Night Court on this, Midwinter's Eve, the longest night of the year."

Ellebere and Dulcamara knelt on either side of him. The court knelt with them. Kaye crouched awkwardly.

"I present to you," called the herald, "our undoubted Lord, Roiben, King of the Unseelie Court. Will you humble yourselves and call him sovereign?"

A great joyful shrieking and screaming. The hair stood up along Kaye's arms.

"You are my people," Roiben said, his hands extended. "And as I am bound, you are lashed to my bidding. I am naught if not your King."

With those words, he sank into the chair of birch, his face blank. Folk began to stand again, moving to make their obeisance to the throne.

A spriggan chased a tiny winged faerie under the table, making it tremble. The ice bowl sloshed and the tower of cubes collapsed, tumbling into disarray.

"Kaye," Lutie squeaked. "You're not looking."

Kaye turned to the dais. A scribe sat cross-legged next to Roiben, recording each supplicant. Leaning forward from his throne, the Lord addressed a wild-haired woman dressed in scarlet. As she moved to kneel, Kaye glimpsed a cat's tail twitching from a slit in her dress.

"What am I not looking at?" Kaye asked.

"Have you never seen a declaration, pixie?" sneered a woman with a necklace of silver scarabs. "You are the Ironside girl, aren't you?"

Kaye nodded. "I guess so." She wondered if she stank of it, if iron leaked from her pores from long exposure.

A lissome girl in a dress of petals came up behind the woman, resting slim fingers on her arm and making a face at Kaye. "He's not yours, you know."

Kaye's head felt as though it were filled with cotton. "What?"

"A declaration," the woman said. "You haven't declared yourself." It seemed to Kaye that the beetles paced a circle around the woman's throat. Kaye shook her head.

"She doesn't know." The girl snickered, snatching an apple off the table and biting into it.

"To be his consort," the woman spoke slowly, as though to an idiot. An iridescent green beetle dropped from her mouth. "One makes a declaration of love and asks for a quest to prove one's worth."

Kaye shuddered, watching the shimmering beetle scuttle

up the woman's dress to take its place at her neck. "A quest?"

"But if the declarer is not favored, the monarch will hand down an impossible expedition."

"Or a deadly one," the grinning petal girl supplied.

"Not that we think he would send you on a quest like that."

"Not that we think he meant to hide anything from you."

"Leave me alone," Kaye said thickly, her heart twisting. Lurching forward through the crowd, she knew that she'd gotten far drunker than she had intended. Lutie squeaked as Kaye shoved her way past winged ladies and fiddle-playing men, nearly tripping on a long tail that swept the floor.

"Kaye!" Lutie wailed. "Where are we going?"

A woman bit pearl-gray grubs off a stick, smacking her lips in delight as Kaye passed. A faerie with white hair cropped close enough to her head that it stuck up like the clock of a dandelion looked oddly familiar, but Kaye couldn't place her. Nearby, a blue-skinned man cracked chestnuts with his massive fists as small faeries darted to snatch up what he dropped. The colors seemed to blur together.

Kaye felt the impact of the dirt floor before she even realized that she had fallen. For a moment she just lay there, gazing across at the hems of dresses, cloven feet, and pointed-toed shoes. The shapes danced and merged.

Lutie landed close enough to Kaye's face that she could barely focus on the tiny form.

"Stay awake," Lutie said. Her wings were vibrating with anxiety. She tugged on one of Kaye's fingers. "They'll get me if you go to sleep."

Kaye rolled onto her side and got up, carefully, wary of her own legs.

"I'm okay," Kaye said. "I'm not asleep."

Lutie alighted on Kaye's head and began to nervously knot locks of hair.

"I'm perfectly okay," Kaye repeated. With careful steps she approached the side of the dais where Lord Roiben, newly anointed King of the Unseelie Court, sat. She watched his fingers, each one encircled in a metal band, as they tapped the rhythms of an unfamiliar tune on the edge of his throne. He was clad in a stiff black fabric that swallowed him in shadow. As familiar as he should have been, she found herself unable to speak.

It was the worst kind of stupid to be pining after someone who cared for you. Still, it was like watching her mother onstage. Kaye felt proud, but was half afraid that if she went up, it wouldn't turn out to be Roiben at all.

Lutie-loo abandoned her perch and flew to the throne. Roiben looked up, laughed, and cupped his hands to receive her.

"She drank all the mushroom wine," Lutie accused, pointing to Kaye.

"Indeed?" Roiben raised one silver brow. "Will she come and sit beside me?"

"Sure," Kaye said, levering herself up onto the dais, unaccountably shy. "How has it been?"

"Endless." His long fingers threaded through her hair, making her shiver.

Only months ago she'd thought of herself as weird, but human. Now the weight of gauzy wings on her back and the green of her skin were enough to remind her that she wasn't. But she was still just Kaye Fierch and no matter how magical or clever, it was hard to understand why she was allowed to sit beside a King.

Even if she had saved that King's life. Even if he loved her.

She couldn't help but recall the beetle-woman's words. Did the dreadlocked girl with the drum intend to make a declaration? Ask for a quest? Had the girl with the cat tail already done so? Were the fey laughing at her, thinking that because she had grown up with humans, she was ignorant of faerie customs?

She wanted to make things right. She wanted to make a grand gesture. Give him something finer than a ragged bracelet. Swaying forward, Kaye went down on both her knees in front of the new King of the Unseelie Court.

Roiben's eyes widened with something like panic and he opened his mouth to speak, but she was faster.

"I, Kaye Fierch, do declare myself to you. I . . ." Kaye froze, realizing she didn't know what she was supposed to say, but the heady liquor in her veins spurred her tongue on. "I love you. I want you to give me a quest. I want to prove that I love you."

Roiben gripped the arm of his throne, fingers tightening on the wood. His voice sank to a whisper. "To allow this, I would have to have a heart of stone. You will not become a subject of this court."

She knew that something was wrong, but she didn't know what. Shaking her head, she stumbled on. "I want to make a declaration. I don't know the formal words, but that's what I want."

"No," he said. "I will not allow it."

There was a moment's hush around her and then some scattered laughter and whispering.

"I have recorded it. It has been spoken," said Ruddles. "You must not dishonor her request."

Roiben nodded. He stared off into the brugh for a long

moment, then stood and walked to the edge of the platform. "Kaye Fierch, this is the quest that I grant. Bring me a faerie that can tell an untruth and you shall sit beside me as my consort."

Shrieking laughter rose from the throng. She heard the words: *Impossible. An impossible quest.*

Her face heated, and suddenly she felt worse than dizzy. She felt sick. She must have gone white or her expression must have turned alarming, because Roiben jumped off the platform and caught her arm as she fell.

Voices were all around her but none of them made sense.

"I promise that if I find who put this idea in your head, they will pay for it with their own."

Her eyes blinked heavily. She let them close for a moment and slipped down into sleep, passing out cold in Faerieland.

3

I shall have peace, as leafy trees are peaceful
When rain bends down the bough;
And I shall be more silent and cold-hearted
Than you are now.
—Sara Teasdale, "I Shall Not Care"

The little hob shivered in the corner of the cage as Corny heaved it out of the trunk. Dumping the wire box into the backseat, he got in next to it and slammed the door. Dry heat pumped from vents as the engine idled.

"I'm a powerful being . . . a *wizard*," Corny said. "So don't try anything."

"Yes," said the little faerie, blinking black eyes rapidly. "No. Try nothing."

Corny turned those words over in his head, but the possible interpretations seemed too varied and his mind kept getting tangled. He shook the thoughts out of his head. The creature was caged. He was in control. "I want to keep myself from being charmed, and you're going to tell me how to do it."

"I weave spells. I don't lift spells," it chirped.

"But," Corny said, "there has to be a way. A way to keep from being happily led off the side of a pier or craving the honor of being some faerie's footstool. Not just some herb. Something permanent."

"There is no leaf. No rock. No chant to keep you completely safe from our charms."

"Bullshit. There must be something. Is there any human who is resistant to being enchanted?"

The little faerie hopped to the edge of its cage, and when it spoke, its voice was low. "Someone with True Sight. Someone who can see through glamours. Perhaps a geas."

"How do you get True Sight?"

"Some mortals are born with it. Very few. Not you."

Corny kicked the back of the passenger-side seat. "Tell me something else then, something I'd want to know."

"But such a powerful wizard as yourself—"

Corny shook the crab trap, sending the little faerie sprawling, its pinecone hat falling out through one of the holes in the aluminum cage to land on the floor mat. It yowled, a moan rising to a shriek.

"That's me," Corny said. "Very freaking powerful. Now, if you want out of here, I suggest that you start talking."

"There is a boy with the True Sight. In the great city of exiles and iron to the north. He's been breaking curses on mortals."

"Interesting," Corny said, holding up the poker. "Good. Now tell me something else."

That morning, while the slumbering bodies of faeries still littered the great hall of the Unseelie Court, Roiben met with his councillors in a cavern so cold his breath clouded. Tallow candles burned atop rock formations, the melting fat stinking of clove. *Let our King be made from ice.* He wished it too, wished for the ice that encased the branches out on the hill to freeze his heart.

Dulcamara drummed her fingers against the polished and petrified wood of the table, its surface as hard as stone. Her small wings, the membranes torn so that only the veins remained, hung from her shoulders. She regarded him with pale pink eyes.

Roiben looked at her and he thought of Kaye. Already he could feel the lack of her, like a thirst that is bearable until one thinks of water.

Ruddles paced the chamber. "We are overmatched." His wide, toothy mouth made him look as though he might suddenly take a bite out of any of them. "Many of the fey who were bound to Nicnevin fled when the Tithe no longer tied them to the Unseelie Court. Our troops are thinned."

Roiben watched a flame gutter, flaring brightly before going out. *Take this from me,* he thought. *I do not want to be your King.*

Ruddles looked pointedly at Roiben, closed his eyes, and rubbed just above the bridge of his nose. "We are further weakened as several of our best knights died by your own hand, my Lord. You do recall?"

Roiben nodded.

"It vexes me that you do not seem to expect an imminent attack from Silarial," said Ellebere. A tuft of his hair fell over one eye, and he brushed it back. "Why should she hesitate now that Midwinter's Eve is past?"

"Perhaps she is bored and lazy and sick of fighting," said Roiben. "I am."

"You are too young." Ruddles gnashed those sharp teeth. "And you take the fate of this court too lightly. I wonder if you would have us win at all."

Once, after the Lady Nicnevin had whipped Roiben—he could no longer recall why—she had turned away, distracted by some new amusement, leaving Ruddles—her chamberlain, then—free to indulge in a moment's mercy. He had dribbled a stream of water into Roiben's mouth. He still remembered the sweet taste of it and the way it had hurt his throat to swallow.

"You think that I don't have the stomach to be Lord of the Night Court." Roiben leaned across the petrified wood table, bringing his face so close to Ruddles's that he could have kissed him.

Dulcamara laughed, clapping her hands together as if anticipating a treat.

"You are correct," said Ruddles, shaking his head. "I *don't* think you have the stomach for it. Nor the head. Nor do I think you even truly want the title."

"I have a belly that craves blood," said Dulcamara, tossing her sleek black hair and stepping so that she was behind the chamberlain. Her hands went to his shoulders, her fingers resting lightly at his throat. "He need not hurt anyone himself. *She* never did."

Ruddles went stiff and still, perhaps realizing how far he had overstepped himself.

Ellebere looked between the three of them as if judging

where his best alliance might be made. Roiben had no illusions that any one of them was in the least part loyal beyond the oath that bound them. With one lethal word Roiben could prove he had both the stomach and the head. That might cultivate something like loyalty.

"Perhaps I am no fit King," Roiben said instead, sinking back into the chair and relaxing his clenched hands. "But Silarial was once my Queen, and while there is breath in my body, I will never let her rule over me or mine again."

Dulcamara pouted exaggeratedly. "Your mercy," she said, "is my mischance, my King."

Ruddles's eyes closed with relief too profound to hide.

Long ago, when Roiben was newly come to the Unseelie Court, he had sat in the small cell-like chamber in which he was kept, and he had longed for his own death. His body had been worn with ill-use and struggle, his wounds had dried in long garnet crusts, and he'd been so tired from fighting Nicnevin's commands that remembering he could die had filled him with a sudden and surprising hope.

If he were really merciful, he would have let Dulcamara kill his chamberlain.

Ruddles was right; they had little chance of winning the war. But Roiben could do what he did best, what he had done in Nicnevin's service: *endure*. Endure long enough to kill Silarial. So that she could never again send one of her knights to be tortured as a symbol of peace, nor contrive countless deaths, nor glory in the appearance of innocence. And when he thought of the Lady of the Bright Court, he could almost feel a small sliver of ice burrow its way inside him, numbing him to what would come. He didn't need to win the war, he just needed to die slowly enough to take her with him.

And if all the Unseelie Court died along with them, so be it.

Corny knocked on the back door of Kaye's grandmother's house and smiled through the glass window. He hadn't had much sleep, but he was flushed and giddy with knowledge. The tiny hob he'd captured had talked all night, telling Corny anything that might make him more likely to let it go. He'd uncaged it at dawn, and true knowledge seemed closer to him now than it ever had before.

"Come in," Kaye's grandmother called from inside the kitchen.

He turned the cold metal knob. The kitchen was cluttered with old cooking supplies; dozens of pots were stacked in piles, cast iron with rusted steel. Kaye's grandmother couldn't bear to throw things away.

"What kind of trouble did the two of you get into last night?" The old woman loaded two plates into the dishwasher.

Corny looked blank for a moment, then forced a frown. "Last night. Right. Well, I left early."

"What kind of gentleman leaves a girl alone like that, Cornelius? She's been sick all morning and her door's locked."

The microwave beeped.

"We're supposed to go to New York tonight."

Kaye's grandmother opened the microwave. "Well, I don't think she's going to be up to it. Here, take her this. See if she can keep something down."

Corny took the mug and bounded up the stairs. Tea sloshed

as he went, leaving a trail of steaming droplets behind him. In the hall outside Kaye's door, he stopped and listened for a moment. Hearing nothing, he knocked.

There was no response.

"Kaye, it's me," he said. "Hey, Kaye, come on and open the door." Corny knocked again. "Kaye!"

He heard shuffling and a click, then the door swung open. He took an involuntary step backward.

He'd seen her faerie form before, but he hadn't been prepared to see it here. The grasshopper green of her skin looked especially strange when contrasted with a white T-shirt and faded pink underwear. Her shiny black eyes were rimmed with red, and the room beyond her smelled sour.

She lay back on the mattress, bundling the comforter around her and smothering her face against the pillow. He could see only the tangled green of her hair and the overly long fingers that pulled the fabric against her chest as though it were a stuffed toy. She seemed like a cat resting, more alert than it looked.

Corny came and sat down on the floor near her, leaning back on a satiny tag-sale pillow.

"Must have been a great night," he whispered, experimentally, and her ink black eyes did flicker open for a second. She made a sound like a snort. "Come on. It's the ass crack of noon. Time to get up."

Lutie swooped down from the top of the bookshelves, the suddenness startling Corny. The faerie alighted on his knee, her laughter so high that the sound reminded him of chimes. He resisted the urge to recoil.

"Roiben's chamberlain, Ruddles himself, along with a bogan

and a puck, carried her back. Imagine a bogan gently tucking a pixie into bed!"

Kaye groaned. "I don't think he was that gentle. Now, can everyone be quiet? I'm trying to sleep."

"Your grandma sent up this tea. You want it? If not, I'll drink it."

Kaye flipped over onto her back with a groan. "Give it to me."

He handed over the mug as she shifted into a sitting position. One of her cellophane-like wings rubbed against the wall, sending a shower of powder down onto the sheets.

"Doesn't that hurt?"

She looked over her shoulder and shrugged. Her long fingers turned the tea cup, warming her hands against it.

"I take it we're not going to make it to your mother's show."

She looked up at him and he was surprised to see that her eyes were wet.

"I don't know," she said. "How am I supposed to know? I don't know much about anything."

"Okay, okay. What the hell happened?"

"I told Roiben I loved him. Really loudly. In front of a huge audience."

"So, what did he say?"

"It was this thing called a declaration. They said—I don't know why I even listened—that if I didn't do it someone would beat me to it."

"And they are . . . ?"

"Don't ask," Kaye said, taking a sip of the tea and shaking her head. "I was so drunk, Corny. I don't ever want to be that drunk again."

"Sorry . . . Go on."

"These faeries told me about the declaration thing. They were kind of—I don't know—bragging, I guess. Anyway, Roiben told me I had to stay in the audience for the ceremony, and I kept thinking about how I didn't fit in and how maybe he was disappointed, you know? I thought that maybe he secretly wished I knew more of their customs—maybe he wished I would do something like that before he had to send someone else on a quest."

Corny frowned. "What? A quest?"

"A quest to prove your love."

"So dramatic. And you did this declaration thing? You declared."

Kaye turned her face, so that he couldn't read her expression. "Yeah, but Roiben wasn't happy about it, as in not at all." She put her head in her hands. "I think I really fucked up."

"What's your quest?"

"To find a faerie that lies." Her voice was very low.

"I thought faeries couldn't lie."

Kaye just looked at him.

Suddenly, horribly, Corny understood her meaning. "Okay, hold on. You are saying that he sent you on a quest that you can't possibly complete."

"And I'm not allowed to see him again until I do complete it. So basically, I'm not going to see him ever again."

"No faerie can tell an untruth. That is why it is one of the nice quests given to put off a declarer—no endless labor," said Lutie suddenly. "There are others, like 'Siphon all the salt from all the seas.' That's a nasty one. And then there are the ones that seem impossible, but might not be, like 'Weave a coat of stars.'"

Corny moved onto the bed next to Kaye, dislodging Lutie from his knee. "There has to be a way. There has to be something you can do."

The little faerie fluttered in the air, then settled in the lap of a large porcelain doll. She curled up and yawned.

Kaye shook her head. "But, Corny, he doesn't *want* me to finish the quest."

"That's bullshit."

"You heard what Lutie just said."

"It's still bullshit." Corny kicked at a stray pillow with his toe. "What about seriously stretching the truth?"

"That's not lying," Kaye said, taking a deep swig out of the mug.

"Say that the tea is cold. Just try. Maybe you can lie if you push yourself."

"The tea is . . . ," Kaye said, and stopped. Her mouth was still open, but it was as though her tongue were frozen.

"What's stopping you?" Corny asked.

"I don't know. I feel panicked and my mind starts racing, looking for a safe way to say it. I feel like I'm suffocating. My jaw just locks. I can't make any sound come out."

"God, I don't know what I would do if I couldn't lie."

Kaye flopped back down. "It's not so bad. You mostly can make people believe things without actually lying."

"Like how you made your grandmother believe I was with you last night?"

He noticed that she wore a small smile as she took the next sip from the cup.

"Well, what if you said you were going to *do* something and didn't? Wouldn't that be lying?"

"I don't know," Kaye said. "Isn't that like saying something that you think is true, but turns out not to be? Like something you read in a book, but the book turns out to be wrong."

"Isn't that still lying?"

"If it is, I guess I'm in good shape. I sure have been wrong about things."

"Come on, let's go to the city. You'll feel better when you get out of town. I know I always do."

Kaye smiled, then sat bolt upright. "Where's Armageddon?"

Corny glanced at the cage, but Kaye was already shuffling toward it on her knees.

"He's there. Oh, jeez. They're both there." She sighed deeply, her whole body relaxing. "I thought he might still be under the hill."

"You brought your rat?" Corny asked, incredulous.

"Can we just not talk any more about last night?" Kaye asked, pulling on a pair of faded green camouflage pants.

"Yeah, sure," Corny said, and yawned. "Want to stop for breakfast on the way? I'm feeling like pancakes."

With a queasy look, Kaye began to gather up her things.

On the drive up, Kaye put her head down on the ripped plastic seat, gazing out the window at the sky, trying not to think. The strips of sound-insulating forest cushioning the highway gave way to industrial plants spouting fire and billowing white smoke that blew up until it blended into clouds.

When they got to the part of Brooklyn her mother claimed was still Williamsburg, but was probably actually Bedford-Stuyvesant, the traffic grew less congested. The roads were riddled with potholes, the asphalt cracked and pitted. The streets were deserted and the sidewalks heaped with banks of dirty snow. Only a few cars were parked on the sides of the road, and as soon as Corny pulled up behind one, Kaye opened the door and stepped out. It was strangely lonely.

"You okay?" Corny asked.

Kaye shook her head, leaning over the gutter in case she vomited. Lutie-loo's tiny fingers dug into Kaye's neck as the little faerie tried to keep perched on Kaye's shoulder. "I don't know which part of feeling like shit is from riding for two hours in an iron box and which part is from a wicked hangover," she said, between deep breaths.

Bring me a faerie that can tell an untruth.

Corny shrugged. "No more driving for the whole visit. All you have to ̶d̶o̶ ̶n̶o̶w̶ ̶i̶s̶ put up with riding on the subway."

Kaye groaned, but she was too tired to smack him on the arm. Even the streets stank of iron. Beams of it propped up every building. Iron formed the skeletons of the cars that congested the roads, clogging them like slow-moving blood through the arteries of a heart. Gusts of iron seared her lungs. She concentrated on her own glamour, making it heavier and her senses duller. That managed to push away the worst of the iron sickness.

You're the only thing I want.

"Can you walk?" Corny asked.

"What? Oh, yeah." Kaye sighed, shoving her hands into the pockets of her purple plaid overcoat. "Sure." Everything felt as if it were happening in slow motion. It took effort to concentrate on anything but the memories of Roiben and the taste of iron in her mouth. She pressed her nails into the flesh of her palm.

It is a weakness. My affection for you.

Corny touched her shoulder. "So, which building?"

Kaye checked the number she'd written on the back of her hand and pointed to an apartment complex. Her mother's apartment cost twice as much as one they'd lived in three months ago in Philadelphia. Ellen's promise to Kaye that she'd commute to New York so they could stay in New Jersey had lasted until the first huge fight between Ellen and *her* mother. Typical. But this time Kaye hadn't moved with her.

They walked up the steps to the apartment entrance and leaned on the button. A buzzer droned and Kaye pushed inside, Corny right behind her.

The door to Kaye's mother's apartment was covered in the same dirty maple veneer as the others on the eighteenth floor. A gold plastic nine stuck to the wood just beneath the peephole. When Kaye knocked, the number swung on its single nail.

Ellen opened the door. Her hair was freshly hennaed the same rootless red as her thin eyebrows, and her face looked freshly scrubbed. She was wearing a black spaghetti-strapped tank and dark jeans.

"Baby!" Ellen hugged Kaye hard, swaying back and forth, like the number on the door. "I've missed you so much."

"I missed you, too," Kaye said, leaning against her mother's shoulder heavily. It felt weirdly, guiltily good. She imagined what Ellen would do if she knew that Kaye wasn't human. Scream, of course. It was hard to think beyond the screaming.

After a moment, Ellen looked over Kaye's shoulder. "And Cornelius. Thanks for driving her up. Come on in. Want a beer?"

"No thanks, Ms. Fierch," Corny said. He carried his gym sack and Kaye's garbage bag of overnight things into the room.

The apartment itself was white-walled and small. A queen-size bed filled up most of the room, pushed up against a window and covered in clothing. A man whom Kaye didn't know sat on a stool and strummed a bass.

"This is Trent," Ellen said.

The man stood up and opened his guitar case, settling his instrument delicately inside. He looked like most of the guys Ellen liked: long hair and the stubbly beginnings of a beard, but unlike most, his were streaked with gray. "I got to get going. See you down at the club." He glanced at Corny and Kaye. "Nice to meet you."

Kaye's mother pulled herself onto the counter of the kitchenette, picking up her cigarette from where it scorched a plate. The strap of her tank slid off one shoulder. Kaye stared at Ellen, finding herself looking for some resemblance to the human changeling she'd seen in the thrall of the Seelie Court—the girl whose life Kaye had stolen. But all Kaye saw in her mother's face was a resemblance to her own familiar human glamour.

With a quick wave, Trent and his bass guitar swept out into the hall. Lutie took that moment to dislodge herself from Kaye's neck and fly to the top of the refrigerator. Kaye saw her settle behind an empty vase in what appeared to be a bowl of take-out menus.

"You know what you need?" Ellen asked Corny, picking up the half-empty beer beside her and taking a pull, washing down a mouthful of smoke.

He shrugged, grinning. "Direction in life? Self-esteem? A pony?"

"A haircut. You want me to do it for you? I used to cut Kaye's hair when she was a little girl." She hopped down and headed for the tiny bathroom. "I think I have some scissors around here somewhere."

"Don't let her bully you into it." Kaye raised her voice so she was sure her mother could hear her. "Mom, stop bullying Corny into things."

"Do I look bad?" Corny asked Kaye. "What I'm wearing— do I look bad?" There was something in the way he hesitated as he asked that gave the question weight.

Kaye gave him a sideways look and a grin. "You look like you."

"What does that mean?"

Kaye gestured to the camo pants she'd pulled off the floor that morning and the T-shirt she'd slept in. Her boots were still unlaced. "Look at what I'm wearing. It doesn't matter."

"You're saying I look terrible, aren't you?"

Kaye tilted her head and studied him. His skin had cleared up away from so much exposure to gas station fumes and it wasn't like he'd ever been bad looking. "No one in their right mind would *choose* a mullet as a hairdo unless they were trying to give the world the finger."

Corny's hand traveled self-consciously to his head.

"And you have a collection of wide-wing collared polyester button-downs in colors like orange and brown."

"My mom buys them at flea markets."

Picking up her mother's makeup case off of a mound of clothes by the bed, Kaye pulled out a stick of glittery black liner. "And you wouldn't look like you without them."

"Okay, okay. I get it—what if I didn't want to look like me anymore?"

Kaye paused for a moment, looking up from smudging her eyelid. She heard a longing in his voice that troubled her. She wondered what he would do with a power like hers, wondered if he wondered about it.

Ellen came out of the bathroom with a comb, scissors, a small set of clippers, and a water-stained paper box. "How about some hair dye? I found a box that Robert was going to use before he decided to bleach. Black. Would look cute on you."

"Who's Robert?" Kaye asked.

Corny glanced at his reflection in the greasy door of the microwave. He turned his face to the side. "I guess I couldn't look any worse."

Ellen blew out a thin stream of blue smoke, tapped off the ash, and set her cigarette firmly on her lip. "Okay, sit on the chair."

Corny sat down awkwardly. Kaye pulled herself up onto the counter and finished off her mother's beer. Ellen handed her the cord for the clippers.

"Plug that in, sweetheart." Draping a bleach-stained towel around Corny's shoulders, Ellen began to buzz off the back of his hair. "Better already."

"Hey, Mom," Kaye said. "Can I ask you something?"

"Must be bad," Ellen said.

"Why do you say that?"

"Well, you don't usually call me 'Mom.'" She abandoned the clippers, took a deep drag on her cigarette, and started chopping at the top of Corny's hair with manicuring scissors. "Go ahead. You can ask me anything, kiddo."

The smoke burned Kaye's eyes. "Have you ever thought

about me not being your daughter? Like if I was switched at birth." As the words came out of her mouth, her hand came up involuntarily, fingers curving as if she could snatch the words out of the air.

"Wow. Weird question."

Kaye said nothing. She just waited. She wasn't sure she could bring herself to say anything else.

"It's funny. There was this one time." Running her fingers through Corny's hair, Ellen found stray pieces and cut them. "God, you were not even two, toddling around. I'd stacked up a bunch of books on a chair so you could sit at the table when we visited your grandmother's house. It wasn't real safe, but I wasn't real smart, either. Anyway, I go out to the kitchen, and when I come back, you're on the floor and the pile of books is all over the place. I mean, clearly you fell and clearly I am a terrible mother. But you're not crying. Instead, you have one of the books open and you're reading out of it—clear as a bell. And I thought: My child is a genius. And then I thought: This is not my child."

"Huh," Kaye said.

"And you were so honest—nothing like me as a kid. You'd bend the truth, sure, but you'd never outright lie."

My life is a lie. It was such a relief not to say it. It was a relief to just let the moments slide by until the subject got changed and the awful galloping of her heart slowed again.

"So did you ever imagine what things would be like if you were secretly adopted?" Ellen asked.

Kaye froze.

Ellen mixed the black dye in a chipped cereal bowl with a round metal spoon. "When I was a kid, I used to pretend I was a baby from a circus, and the fire-swallowers and jugglers and tightrope-walkers would come back for me and I'd have my own caravan and I'd tell people their fortunes."

"If you weren't my mother, who would give my friends fabulous makeovers?" As she said the words, Kaye knew she was a coward. No, not a coward. She was greedy. She was that cuckoo chick unwilling to give up the comforts of a stolen nest.

It was amazing how deceptive she could be without lying outright.

Corny reached up to touch the sudden spiky shortness of his hair. "I used to pretend that I was from another dimension. You know, like the mirror-universe Spock with the goatee. I figured, in that other dimension my mom was really the monarch of a vast empire or a wizard in exile or something. The downside was that she probably had a goatee too."

Kaye snickered. The cigarette smoke combined with the chemical stink of the hair dye turned her laughter to choking.

Ellen spooned a glop of black goop onto Corny's head and smeared it with a comb. Flecks stained the back of her hand, and her bracelets jangled together.

Dizzily, Kaye crossed the tiny room and pushed open the window. She could hear the paint crack as it came unstuck. Gulping in lungfuls of cold air, she looked out at the street. Her eyes stung.

"It's just going to be another minute," Ellen said. "Then I'll plastic-wrap his hair and toss this shit out."

Kaye nodded, although she wasn't sure her mother was looking. Out on the street, small clusters of people stood together in the snowy landscape, their breath spiraling up like smoke.

The streetlight reflected off strands of long pale hair and for a moment, before one of the figures turned, she thought of Roiben. It wasn't him, of course, but she had to stop herself from calling down anyway.

"Honey, I'm done here," Ellen said. "Look around and see if you can find this boy another shirt. I ruined his, and anyway, he's too skinny to be drowning in that thing."

Kaye turned. Corny's neck was red and splotchy. "Mom, you're embarrassing him!"

"If this was a television show, I would be the one doing the makeovers," Corny said darkly.

Ellen put out her cigarette on a plate. "God help us."

Kaye rummaged around in the stacks of clothing until she came up with a dark brown T-shirt with the black silhouette of a man riding a rabbit and holding a lance.

She held it up for Corny's inspection. He laughed nervously. "It looks tight."

Ellen shrugged. "It's from a book signing at a bar. Kelly something. Chain? Kelly Chain? It'll look good on you. Your jeans are okay and so's the jacket, but those sneakers aren't working. Double up your socks and you can wear Trent's Chucks. I think he left a pair over by the closet."

Corny glanced up at Kaye. Black dye ran in rivulets down the back of his neck, staining the collar of his T-shirt. "I'm going to retreat to the bathroom now."

As the water in the shower started, filling the tiny apartment with vapor, Ellen sat down on the bed. "While we're primping, how about you do my eyes? I can't manage that smoky thing you do."

Kaye smiled. "Sure."

Ellen lay back on the bed, while Kaye leaned over, carefully painting her mother's lids in shining silver, shadowing and out-lining the edge of her lashes in black. This close, Kaye saw the gentle crow's-feet at the corners of her eyes, the enlarged pores in her nose, the slight purplish discoloration below her lashes. When she brushed her mother's hair out of the way, the shim-mer of some strands revealed where the red dye covered gray. Kaye's fingers shook.

Mortal. This is what it means to be mortal.

"I think I'm done," Kaye said.

Ellen pushed herself into a sitting position and kissed Kaye on the cheek. Kaye could smell the cigarettes on her mother's breath, could smell the decay of teeth and the faint traces of sugary gum. "Thank you, baby. You're a real lifesaver."

I'm going to tell her, Kaye assured herself. *I'm going to tell her tonight.*

Corny emerged from the bathroom in a gust of steam. It was odd to see him in the new clothes with the shorter and darker hair. It shouldn't have made as much of a difference as it did, but the hair made his eyes shine and the tight shirt turned his scrawniness into slenderness.

"You look good," Kaye said.

He plucked self-consciously at the fabric and rubbed at his neck as though he could feel the stain of the dye.

"What do you think?" Ellen asked.

Corny looked back toward the bathroom, as though remembering his reflection. "It's like I'm hiding in my own skin."

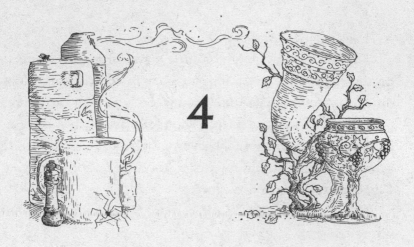

4

Bread does not nourish me, dawn disrupts me, all
      day
I hunt for the liquid measure of your steps.
—PABLO NERUDA, "LOVE SONNET XI"

The ride on the subway was awful. Kaye felt the iron all around her, felt the weight of it and the stink pressing down, suffocating her. She gripped the aluminum pole and tried not to breathe.

"You look kind of pale," Corny said as they climbed the concrete steps to the street.

She could feel her glamour being eaten away, weakening with each moment.

"Why don't you kids walk around awhile?" Ellen's lips shone with gloss and her hair was sprayed so thickly that it didn't move when the breeze hit it. "It'd be boring watching us set up."

Kaye nodded. "Also, if I would just see how cool New York was, I would move up here instead of wasting my time cooling my heels in Jersey?"

Ellen smiled. "And that."

Kaye and Corny walked a little ways through the streets on the edge of the West Village. They passed clothing shops displaying ruffled hats and plaid shorts, tiny record stores promising imports, and a fetish shop featuring a vinyl ball/gag mask with cat ears against a backdrop of holiday red-and-white velvet. A guy in a torn army jacket stood near a corner playing Christmas carols on a nose flute.

"Hey," Corny said. "Coffee shop. We can sit down and warm up."

They walked up the stairs and through the gold-stenciled door.

Café des Artistes was a series of rooms leading one into another through large passageways. Kaye walked past the counter and through a doorway into a chamber that featured a mantel covered in melted white candles, like a monstrous sandcastle eroded by waves. Dimly lit by black chandeliers that hung from a black tin ceiling and reflected in the glass of the aged prints and gilt mirrors, the rooms felt shadowy and cool. A faint and reassuring smell of tea and coffee in the air made her sigh.

They sat down in ornate gilt armchairs, worn so that white molded plastic showed on the hand rests. Corny picked at a golden swirl, and a small piece chipped off with his fingernail. Kaye idly opened the drawer of the small cream-colored table in front of her. Inside, she was surprised to find a collection of paper—notes, postcards, letters.

A waitress walked over and Kaye pushed the drawer shut. The woman's hair was blond on top and a glossy black underneath. "What can I get you?"

Corny picked up a menu off the middle of the table and read from it, as though he were picking things at random. "An omelet with green peppers, tomatoes, and mushrooms, a cheese plate, and a cup of coffee."

"Coffee for me, too." Kaye grabbed the paper out of his hands and ordered the first thing she saw. "And a piece of lemon pie."

"Real well-balanced diet," Corny said. "Sugar and caffeine."

"There might be meringue," Kaye said. "That's eggs. Protein."

He rolled his eyes.

As the waitress walked away, Kaye opened the drawer again and picked through the cards.

"Look at these." Girlish handwriting described a trip to Italy: *I couldn't stop thinking about Lawrence's prediction that I would meet someone in Rome.* A card with a hastily drawn mug in one corner had words written in blocky print with a pencil: *I spit into my coffee and then switched with Laura's boyfriend so that he would taste me in his mouth.* Kaye read the words out loud and then asked, "Where do you think these came from?"

"Garage sales?" Corny said. "Or maybe these are notes people never mailed anywhere. You know, like if you want to write something down, but don't want to let the person it was intended for read it. You leave it here."

"Let's leave something," Kaye said. She fumbled with her bag and pulled out two scraps of paper and an eyeliner pencil. "Be careful. It's soft and it smears."

"So, what, you want me to write down a secret? Like, how about I always wanted a comic book villain for a boyfriend, and after Nephamael, I'm not sure a nice guy is ever going to do it for me."

A couple at another table looked up as though they had caught a few of the words, but not enough to make any sense of what he'd said.

Kaye rolled her eyes. "Yeah, why would one sadistic lunatic put you off sadistic lunatics in general?"

Smirking, Corny took the piece of paper and wrote on it, pressing hard enough that the letters were fat and smudgy. He spun the slip in her direction. "'Cause I know you're going to read it anyway."

"I won't if you say not to."

"Just read it."

Kaye picked up the paper and saw the words: *I would do anything not to be human.*

She took the eye pencil and wrote hers: *I stole someone else's life.* She turned it toward Corny.

He slid them both into the drawer without comment. The waitress came with silverware, coffee, and cream. Kaye busied herself making her coffee as light and sweet as she could.

"You thinking about the quest?" Corny asked.

She'd been thinking about what he'd written, but she said, "I just wish I could talk to Roiben one more time. Just hear him *say* that he doesn't want me. It feels like I got broken up with in a dream."

"You could send him a letter or something, couldn't you? That's not technically seeing him."

"Sure," Kaye said. "If he got mail that wasn't, like, acorn-based."

"There's stuff you still don't understand about faerie customs. Everything that happened—it might not mean what you think it means."

Kaye shook her head, shaking off Corny's words. "Maybe it's good that we split up. I mean, as boyfriends go, he was always busy working. Running an evil court takes a lot of time."

"And he's too old for you," Corny said.

"And moping around all the time," Kaye said. "Too emo."

"No car, either. What's the point of an older boyfriend with no car?"

"Hair longer than mine," Kaye said.

"I bet he takes longer to get ready, too."

"Hey!" Kaye punched him on the arm. "I get ready fast."

"I'm just saying." Corny grinned. "You know, though, dating supernatural creatures is never easy. Admittedly, being supernatural yourself should make it easier."

Across the room, a group of three men looked up from their cappuccinos. One said something and the other two laughed.

"You're freaking them out," Kaye whispered.

"They just think we're plotting out a really bizarre book," Corny said. "Or roleplaying. We could be LARPing, you know." He crossed his arms over his chest. "Now I'm obfuscating, and you have to pay for my dinner."

Kaye caught the eye of a girl hunched over a table. The tips of her stringy hair trailed in her coffee and she was bundled in a series of coats, one layered over another, until it seemed like her back was hunched. When the girl saw Kaye looking, she held up a slip of paper between two fingers and slipped it into a drawer in front of her. Then, with a wink, she slugged back the last of her coffee and got up to leave.

"Hold on," Kaye said to Corny, rising and crossing to the

table. The girl was gone, but when Kaye opened the cabinet, the paper was still there: "The Queen wants to see you. The Fixer knows the way. Page him: 555-1327."

Corny and Kaye walked over to the club just as it started to snow again. The building had a brick front, papered over with posters in tattered layers worn by rain and dirt. Corny didn't recognize any of the bands.

At the front door, a woman in black jeans and a zebra-print coat took the five-dollar cover charge from a short line of shivering patrons.

"ID," the woman said, tossing back tiny braids.

"My mom's playing," Kaye said. "We're on the list."

"I still need to see ID," said the woman.

Kaye stared, and the air around them seemed to ripple, as if with heat. "Go right in," the woman said dreamily.

Corny stuck out his hand to be stamped with a sticky blue skull and walked toward the door. His heart thundered against his chest.

"What did you do to her?" he asked.

"I love this smell," Kaye said, smiling. He wasn't sure if she hadn't heard his question or if she'd just decided not to answer it.

"You have got to be kidding." The inside of the club was painted flat black. Even the piping high above their heads had been sprayed the same matte tone so that all the light in the room seemed to be absorbed by the walls. A few multicolor lights strobed over the bar and across the stage, where a band wailed.

Kaye shouted over the music. "No, really. I love it. Stale beer and cigarette residue and sweat. It burns my throat, but after the car and the subway ride, I barely care."

"That's great," he shouted back. "Do you want to say hi to your mom?"

"I better not." Kaye rolled her eyes. "She's a bitch when she's getting ready. Stage fright."

"Okay, let's grab a seat," Corny said, weaving his way toward one of the tiny tables lit with a red electric votive that looked like a bug light.

Kaye went to get drinks. Corny sat and observed the crowd. An Asian boy with a shaved head and fringed suede chaps gestured to a girl in a knitted wool dress and tarantula-print cowboy boots. Nearby, a woman in a moiré coat slow danced with another woman up against a black support pole. Corny felt a wild surge of excitement fill him. This was a real New York club, an actual cool place to which he should have been forbidden according to the rules of nerd-dom.

Kaye came back to the table as the other band cleared off the stage and Ellen, Trent, and the other two members of Treacherous Iota strode on.

Moments later, Kaye's mother was bent over, raking the strings of her guitar. Kaye watched in rapt fascination, the pools of her eyes wet as she chewed on a plastic stirrer.

The music was okay—candy punk with some messed-up lyrics. Kaye's mom didn't look like the faded middle-aged woman Corny had seen a couple of hours ago, though. This Ellen looked fierce, like she might lean out and eat up all of the little girls and boys gathered around the stage. Even though they weren't biologically related, as she screeched through the first song, Corny thought he could see a lot of Kaye in her.

Watching her transformation made him uncomfortable, especially because his fingers were still stained with black dye from his own. He looked around the room.

His gaze ran over the beautiful boys and the insect-slender girls, but it stopped on a tall man leaning against the far wall, a messenger bag slung over his shoulders. Just looking at him made gooseflesh bloom on Corny's arms. His features were far too perfect to belong to a human.

Looking at that stiff, arrogant posture, Corny thought it was a glamoured Roiben come to beg Kaye's indulgence. But the hair was the color of butter, not salt, and the tilt of the jaw was not like Roiben's at all.

The man stared at Kaye, so fixedly that when a girl in pigtails stopped in front of him, he moved to the left to continue watching.

Corny stood up without really meaning to. "Be right back," he said to Kaye's questioning look.

Now that he was walking in the man's direction, Corny was no longer sure what to do. His heart beat against his rib cage like a ricocheting rubber ball until he thought he might choke. Still, as he got closer, more details added to Corny's suspicions. The man's jaw and cheekbones were too sharp. His eyes were the color of bluebells. He was the most poorly disguised faerie Corny had ever seen.

Onstage, Ellen bellowed into the mic, and the drummer went into a solo.

"You're doing a crap-ass job of blending in, you know that?" Corny shouted over the rhythmic pounding.

The faerie narrowed his eyes. Corny looked down at his

borrowed sneakers, suddenly remembering that he could be charmed.

"Whatever do you mean?" The man's voice was soft. It showed none of the anger that had been in his face.

Corny ground his teeth together, ignoring his longing to look into those lovely eyes again. "You don't look human. You don't even talk human."

A smooth, warm hand touched Corny's cheek, and Corny jumped. "I feel human," the faerie man said.

Without meaning to, Corny leaned into the touch. Desire flared in him, so sharp it was almost pain. But as his eyes drifted closed, he saw his sister's face disappearing under briny water, saw her screaming great gulps of sea as a beautiful kelpie-turned-boy dragged her down. He saw himself crawling through the dirt to bring a pulpy fruit to drop at a laughing faerie knight's feet.

His eyes snapped open. He was so furious his hands shook. "Don't flirt," Corny said. He wasn't going to be weak again. He could do this.

The faerie watched him with arched eyebrows and a smile filled with mockery.

"I'll bet you want Kaye," Corny said. "I can get her for you."

The faerie frowned. "And you would betray another of your kind so easily?"

"You know she's not my kind." Corny took him by the elbow. "Come on. She might see us. We can talk in the bathroom."

"I beg your pardon."

"Keep begging," Corny said, grabbing the faerie's arm and

leading him through the crowd. A glance back told him that Kaye was preoccupied with the performance onstage. Adrenaline flooded him, narrowing his focus, making rage and desire seem suddenly indistinguishable. He swept into the bathroom. The single stall and two urinals were empty. On a dark purple wall, beside a hand-lettered sign promising decapitation to employees failing to wash their hands, hung a shelf piled with toilet paper and cleaning supplies.

An utterly unpleasant idea occurred to Corny. He had to fight not to smile.

"The thing is," he said, "that's not how human guys dress at all. It's not sloppy enough. Roiben always makes the same mistake."

The fey man's lip curled slightly, and Corny tried to keep his face blank, as though he had missed that rather interesting tell.

"Look at yourself. Fix your glamour so that you look more like you're wearing what I'm wearing, okay?"

The faerie looked Corny over. "Repugnant," he said, but unshouldered his messenger bag, leaning it against the wall.

Corny grabbed a can of Raid off the shelf. If Kaye couldn't even have a cigarette anymore, the effects of a concentrated insect poison should be impressive. He didn't need to speculate long. As the faerie turned, Corny sprayed him full in the face.

The blond choked and fell immediately to his knees, glamour dropping from him, revealing dreadful, inhuman beauty. Corny reveled for a moment in the look of him convulsing on the filthy floor, then he pulled the lace out of his sneaker and used it to tie the creature's hands behind its back.

The faerie squirmed as the knots went tight, trying to twist away as he coughed. Corny scrambled for the can and hit the faerie with it as hard as he could.

"I swear to fucking God, I will spray you again," Corny said. "Enough of this shit will kill you."

The faerie went still. Corny stood up, straddling the faerie's body, fingering the nozzle on the Raid can. He caught his own gaze in the mirror, saw his short dyed dark hair and his borrowed clothes, how pathetic they were. He still looked painfully, disappointingly human.

Thin, strong fingers wound around Corny's calves, but Corny pressed the sole of his sneaker against the faerie's neck and squatted down over him. "Now you're going to tell me a whole bunch of things I've always wanted to know."

The creature swallowed.

"Your name," Corny said.

The blue eyes flashed. "Never."

Corny shrugged and slid his foot off of the faerie, suddenly uncomfortable. "Fine. Something I can call you, then. And not some stupid 'me myself' bullshit. I read."

"Adair."

Corny paused, thinking of the paper in the drawer. "Are you the Fixer? Did you slip Kaye a note?"

The man looked puzzled, then shook his head. "He's a human, like you."

"Okay. Adair, if you're not the Fixer, what do you want with Kaye?"

The faerie was silent for a long moment. Corny slammed the can into the side of the creature's head.

"Who told you to come here?"

Adair shrugged and Corny hit him again. Blood stained his mouth.

"Silarial," he gasped.

Corny nodded with satisfaction. He was breathing hard, but each breath came out like a laugh. "Why?"

"The pixie. I'm to take her to the Seelie Court. Many of my Lady's subjects are seeking her out."

Corny sat down on Adair's stomach and fisted his hand in the golden hair. "Why?"

"Queen wants to talk. Just talk."

A man with a fauxhawk opened the door, blanched, and then shut it with a slam. The faerie twisted himself around, pushing upright.

"Tell me something else," Corny said. His clenched fingers shook. "Tell me how to protect—"

At that moment the bathroom door swung open again. This time it was Kaye. "Corny, they're—" she said, then seemed to focus on the scene in front of her. She blinked her eyes rapidly and coughed. "This is so not what I expected to see when I walked in here."

"Silarial sent him," Corny said. "For you."

"The bartender's calling the cops. We have to get out of here."

"We can't let him go," Corny said.

"Corny, he's *bleeding*." Kaye coughed again. "What did you do? I feel like my lungs are on fire."

Corny started to stand, to explain.

"I curse you." The faerie rolled onto his side and spat a reddish gob of spittle onto Corny's cheek. It ran like a tear. "Let everything that your fingers touch wither."

Corny staggered back, and as he did so, his hand brushed the wall. The paint under his fingers buckled and flaked. Stopping, he looked at his palm, the familiar lines and grooves and calluses seemed, suddenly, to form a new and horrible landscape.

"Come on!" Kaye grabbed him by the sleeve, steering him toward the door.

The metal of the knob tarnished at the stroke of his skin.

5

Hell is oneself,
Hell is alone.
—T. S. Eliot

Afaun with bloodstained claws sank into a low bow before Roiben's throne. They had come, each of his vassals, to boast of their usefulness, to tell him of their service to the crown, to win his favor and the promise of better tasks. Roiben looked out at the sea of them and had to fight down panic. He gripped the arms of his throne hard enough that the braided wood groaned.

"In your name," said the creature, "I have killed seven of my brethren and kept their hooves." He emptied out a sack with a clatter.

"Why?" Roiben asked before he thought better of it, his eye drawn to the jagged chopped bone of the ankles, the way the gore had dried black. The mortar that grooved the floor of the audience chamber was already discolored, but this gift freshened the ruddy stains.

The faun shrugged. Brambles snarled the fur of his legs. "It was a token that often pleased Lady Nicnevin. I sought only to ingratiate myself with you."

Roiben closed his eyes tightly for a moment, then opened them again and took a deep breath, schooling himself to indifference. "Right. Excellent." He turned to the next creature.

A delicate fey boy with tar-black wings curtsied. "I am pleased to report," he said in a soft, shivery voice, "I have led nearly a dozen mortal children off of rooftops or to their deaths in marshes."

"I see," Roiben said with exaggerated reasonableness. For a moment, he was afraid what he might do. He thought of Kaye and what she would think of this; he thought of her standing on her own roof in the T-shirt and underwear she wore to bed, swaying forward drowsily. "In my name? I think you amuse only yourself. Perhaps you could find something more vicious than children to torment now that the war has begun."

"As my Lord commands," said the winged faerie, scowling at his feet.

A small hunched hob came forward. With gnarled hands, he unrolled a hideous cloth and spread it over the floor.

"I have killed a thousand mice, keeping only their tails and weaving those together into a rug. I present it now as a tribute to your magnificence."

For the first time he could recall, Roiben had to bite the inside of his cheek to keep from laughing. "Mice?" He looked at his chamberlain. Ruddles raised a single brow.

"Mice," said the hob, puffing out his chest.

"This is quite an effort," said Roiben. His servants rolled up the rug as the hob walked away, looking pleased with himself.

A silky made a bobbing bow, her tiny body clothed only in her pale yellow-green hair. "I have caused fields of grapes to wither on the vine, becoming black and heavy with poison. The wine from their juice will harden the hearts of men."

"Yes, because the hearts of men aren't nearly hardened enough." Roiben frowned. His diction sounded human. He didn't have to guess where he had picked up those phrases.

The silky did not appear to notice the sarcasm. She smiled as though he were offering her great praise.

And so they came, a parade of deeds and gifts, each more grisly than the last, all of them done in the name of Roiben, Lord of the Unseelie Court. Each hideous feat laid before him as a cat drops the bird it has finally killed, once all possible amusement has been wrung from toying with it.

"In your name," each one said.

In his name. The name that no one living knew in full, save for Kaye. His name. Now that it belonged to all these others to conjure and to curse by, he wondered who had the greater claim to it.

Roiben gritted his teeth and nodded and smiled. Only later, in his chambers, sitting on a stool in front of his mouse-tail rug, did he allow himself to be filled with loathing. For all those of the Unseelie Court, who cut and slit and gutted everything they touched. For himself, sitting on a throne in a court of monsters.

He was still staring at the gifts when a terrible, thunderous crash made the walls shake. Dirt rained down on him, stinging his eyes. A second shock reverberated through the hill. He raced out of the room, toward the noise, and passed Bluet in the hallway. Dust covered her, and the long twisted spikes of her hair nearly obscured a fresh cut on her shoulder. Her lips were the color of a bruise.

"My Lord!" she said. "There has been an attack!"

For a moment, he just stared at her, feeling foolish, not quite able to understand. For all his hatred of Silarial, he couldn't quite accept that he was at war with those he had loved, those whom he still considered his people. He couldn't accept that they'd struck first.

"Attend to yourself," he told her dazedly, moving on toward the sound of screams. A handful of faeries darted past him, silent and covered in dirt. One, a goblin, stared at him with wet eyes before rushing on.

The great hall was on fire. The top was cracked open like an egg, and a portion of one side was missing. Gusts of greasy black smoke rose up to the starry sky, devouring the falling snow. At the center of the brugh was a truck—a semi—its iron body burning. The chassis was twisted, the cab crushed under heaps of dirt and rock, as red and gold flames licked upward. A sea of burning oil and diesel fuel spread to scorch everything it touched.

He stared, stunned. There, under the debris, were dozens upon dozens of bodies: his herald, Thistledown; Widdersap, who had once whistled through a blade of grass to make a serving girl dance; Snagill, who'd carefully limned the ceiling of the feasting room in silver. The hob who'd woven the mouse-tail rug screamed, rolling around in fire.

Ellebere pushed Roiben to the side, just as a granite tombstone fell from above, cracking on the floor of the hall. "You must leave, my Lord," he shouted.

"Where is Ruddles?" Roiben demanded. "Dulcamara?"

"They don't matter." Ellebere's grip on Roiben tightened. "You are our King."

Through the smoke, figures appeared, chopping at the fallen and the injured.

"Get the fey in the hallways to safety." Roiben wrenched his arm free. "Take them to the Kinnelon ruins."

Ellebere hesitated.

Two bolts flew through the rancid smoke to embed themselves in what remained of the earthen wall. Thin shafts of glass that Seelie knights used for arrows— so fine that you could barely feel them as they pierced your heart.

"As you said, I *am* your King. Do it now!" Roiben pushed his way through the choking brume, leaving Ellebere behind.

The same faun who had brought Roiben the hooves of his fellows was trying to dig another faerie out from beneath a mound of earth. And nearby lay Cirillan, who loved tears so much that he saved them in tiny vials that cluttered up his room. His aqua skin was smeared with dusty blood and silver burrs that had been shot from Bright Court slings.

As Roiben watched, the faun gasped, his body arched, and he fell.

Roiben drew his curved sword. All his life he had been in service to battle, but he had never seen the like of what was happening all around him. The Bright Court had never fought so *inelegantly*.

He dodged just before the tines of a golden trident caught him in the chest. The Seelie knight swung again, her teeth bared.

He slammed his sword into her thigh and she faltered. Grabbing her trident at the base, he sliced her throat, quick and clean. Blood sprayed his face as she fell to her knees, reaching for her own neck in surprise.

He didn't know her.

Two humans rushed at him from either side. One held up a gun, but he cut off the hand that held it before the mortal had a hope of firing. He stabbed the other through the chest. A human boy—perhaps twenty, with a Brookdale College T-shirt and rumpled hair—slumped over Roiben's hooked sword.

For a moment, the boy reminded him of Kaye.

Kaye. Dead.

There was a shout and Roiben turned to see a shower of silver pinecones burst just short of where he stood. Through the smoke he saw Ruddles, taking a bite out of the side of a Seelie fey's face, Dulcamara dispatching two others with knives. One of Roiben's pages, Clotburr, slammed a burning harp into another faerie.

Here, in his once majestic hill, human corpses still held their iron weapons in stiffening hands as they slumped beside more than a dozen unmoving Unseelie troops in shining armor. The fire lit the bodies, one by one.

"Quickly," Dulcamara said. Choking black smoke was everywhere. Somewhere in the distance, Roiben could hear sirens wailing. Above them, the mortals came to pour water on the burning hill.

Clotburr coughed, slowing, and Roiben lifted him up, settling the boy against his shoulder.

"How did she do this?" asked Dulcamara, her fingers clenched white-knuckled around the hilt of her blade.

Roiben shook his head. There were protocols to faerie battles. He could not imagine Silarial putting decorum aside, especially when every advantage was hers. But too, who of her people would know what she had done this day? Only those few she had sent to command the mortals. Most were dead. One cannot dishonor oneself before the dead. It occurred to him then that he'd misunderstood Dulcamara's question. She didn't want to know how Silarial could be so hideously inventive; she was puzzling out how it had been accomplished.

"Mortals," Roiben said, and now that he considered it, he had to admit a grudging awe for so radical and terrible a stratagem. "Silarial's Folk are charming humans instead of leading them off roofs. She's making troops of them. Now we are more than overmatched. We are lost."

The weight of the soot-smeared faerie in his arms made him think of all of the Folk of the Night Court, all those he had sworn to be sovereign over. All those lives he'd been willing to accept in trade for Silarial's death. And he wondered in that moment what he might have accomplished if he'd done more than just endure. Whom he might have saved.

As though catching his thoughts, Ruddles turned toward him with a frown. "What now, my King?"

Roiben found himself wanting to win the unwinnable war.

He had known only two rulers, both great and neither good. He did not know how to be any kind of King nor how to win, other than to be even more ruthless than they. But in that moment, he wondered what might happen if he bent his will to finding out.

Kaye pushed Corny ahead of her, through the crowd near the door of the club, out past the ID-check woman, who still looked giddy with enchantment. He held his hands above his head, as in surrender, and when people came close, he flinched. They walked like that for several blocks, past people in their heavy coats shuffling through the slush. Kaye watched the heels of a woman's ostrich-leather boots stab through an icy mound of snow. The woman stumbled.

Corny turned toward her, dropping his hands so that they now hung in front of him. He looked like a zombie lurching toward its next victim.

"I know where," Kaye said, taking deep breaths of the acrid iron air.

She crossed several blocks, Corny behind her. The streets were a maze of names and bodegas, similar enough for her to get easily turned around. She found her way back to Café des Artistes, though, and from there to the fetish shop.

Corny looked at her in confusion.

"Gloves," she told him firmly as she steered him inside.

The scent of burning patchouli thickened the air in the Irascible Peacock. Leather corsets and thongs hung from the walls, their metal buckles and zippers gleaming. Behind the desk a bored-looking older man read the paper, not even glancing up at them.

In the back of the store, Kaye could see the restraints, floggers, and whips. The hollow eyes of masks watched her as she threaded her way toward a pair of elbow-length rubber gloves.

She grabbed them, paid the bored clerk with five glamoured leaves, and bit off the plastic tag with her teeth.

Corny stood next to a marble table, fingers pressed to a stack of flyers advertising a fetish ball. The paper yellowed in widening circles, aging beneath his hands. Withering. A slow smile curved on his mouth, as though watching it gave him pleasure.

"Stop that," Kaye said, holding out the gloves.

Corny started, looking at her as though he didn't know her. Even as he slid on the gloves, he did so numbly, and then stared at his rubber-encased arms in puzzlement.

Walking out, the shine of a pair of chromed handcuffs lined in mink caught Kaye's eye and she picked them up, running her thumb over the soft pelt. Years of shoplifting instincts made her slip them into her pocket before she hit the door.

"I can't believe you jumped some guy in a bathroom," Kaye said as soon as they'd crossed the street.

"What?" Corny glowered. "*I* can't believe you just stole a pair of fuzzy handcuffs, klepto. Anyway, he wasn't *some guy*. He was from the Seelie Court. He was one of them."

"One of *them*? A faerie? Like I'm one of them?"

"He was there to get you. He said he was supposed to bring you to Silarial," Corny yelled at her, and the name seemed to carry through the cold night air.

"And for that you almost kill him?" Kaye's voice rose, sounding shrill even to her own ears.

"I hate to break this to you," Corny said nastily, "but Silarial hates you. You're the one who screwed up her plan to take over the Unseelie Court, plus you've been screwing her ex-boyfriend—"

"Will you stop with the—"

"Right, I know. Impossible quest. Look, I'm sure I could list more things about you she hates, but I think you get my point. Whatever she wants, we want the opposite."

"I don't care about her or her messengers!" Kaye shouted. "I care about you, and you're acting crazy."

Corny shrugged and turned away from her, looking through the window of a shop as if he were seeing some other place in the racks of clothing. Then he smiled at himself in the glass. "Whatever, Kaye. I'm right about Adair. They love to hurt people. People like Janet."

Kaye shuddered, guilt over Janet's death too fresh for his words not to feel like an accusation. "I know—"

Corny interrupted her. "Anyway, I got cursed, so I guess I got what I deserved, right? The universe is in balance. I got what I was asking for."

"That's not what I meant," Kaye said. "I don't even know what I mean. I'm just freaked out. Everything's coming apart."

"*You're* freaked out? Everything I touch rots! How am I going to eat food? How am I going to jerk off?"

Kaye laughed despite herself.

"Not to mention I am going to have to dress up in down-market fetish-wear forever." Corny held up a gloved hand.

"Good thing that turns you on," Kaye said.

He rolled his eyes. "Okay, it was dumb. What I did. At least I should have found out what Silarial wanted."

Kaye shook her head. "It doesn't matter. Let's go back to Brooklyn and figure out what to do about your hands."

Corny pointed to a pay phone hanging outside of a bar. "You want me to call your mom's cell? I could tell her we got kicked out of the club for being underage. I can lie like crazy."

Kaye shook her head. "After you beat up someone in the bathroom? I think she knows what we got kicked out for."

"He was hitting on me," Corny said primly. "I had to protect my virtue."

Kaye let herself and Corny into her mother's apartment and threw herself down on the bed. Corny flopped down beside her with a groan.

Looking up at the popcorn of the ceiling, she studied the grooves and fissures, letting her mind drift from Corny's curse and the explanation she didn't have for running out on her mother's show. She thought of Roiben instead, standing in front of the entire assemblage of the Unseelie Court, and of the way they'd bowed their heads. But that made her think of all the children they'd snatched from cradles and strollers and swing sets to replace with changelings, or worse. She imagined Roiben's slender fingers circling flailing, rosy limbs. Looking across the bed, she saw Corny's fingers instead, each one encased in rubber.

"We're going to fix things," Kaye said.

"How are we going to do that, exactly?" Corny asked. "Not that I'm doubting you, mind."

"Maybe I could take the curse off of you. I have magic, right?"

He sat up. "You think you can?"

"I don't know. Let me get rid of my glamour so I can use whatever I've got." She concentrated, imagining her disguise tearing like cobwebs. Her senses flooded. She could smell the crusts of burnt food in the burners of the stove, the exhaust from cars, the mold inside the walls, and even the filthy snow they'd tracked across the floor. And she felt the iron, heavier than ever, eating away at the edges of her power, as clearly as she felt the brush of wings across her shoulders.

"Okay," she said, rolling toward him. "Take off a glove."

He removed one and held out the hand to her. She tried to imagine her magic as she'd been told to, like a ball of energy prickling between her palms. She concentrated on expanding it, despite the iron-soaked air. When it settled over Corny's hands, her skin stung like she clutched nettles. She could change the shape of his fingers, but she couldn't touch the curse.

"I don't know what I'm doing," she said finally, helplessly, letting her concentration lapse and the energy dissipate. Just the attempt had exhausted her.

"That's okay. I heard about a guy who breaks spells. A human."

"Really? How'd you hear about him?" Kaye fumbled with her pocket.

Corny turned his face away from her, toward the window. "I forget."

"Remember the paper that girl gave me? The Fixer? There's a place to start. Fixing sounds like what we're looking for."

Corny yawned and put the glove back on. "Your mom is going to totally make us sleep on the floor, isn't she?"

Kaye turned to him, pressing her face against his shoulder. His shirt smelled like bug spray and she wondered what the faerie who'd cursed him had wanted. She wondered about the other Kaye, still trapped in the Seelie Court. "Do you think I should tell her?" she mumbled into the T-shirt.

"Tell her what? That we want the bed?"

"That I'm a changeling. That she has a daughter who got stolen."

"Why would you want to do that?" He lifted his arm and Kaye ducked under it, pillowing her head on his chest.

"Because none of this is real. I don't belong here."

"Where else would you belong?" Corny asked.

Kaye shrugged. "I don't know. I'm neither fish nor fowl. What's left?"

"Good red herring, I think," he said. "It's a fish."

"At least I'm good and red."

A key rattled in the door.

Kaye jumped up and Corny grabbed her arm. "Okay, tell her."

She shook her head hurriedly. The door opened and Ellen walked into the room, her shoulders dusted with new-fallen snow.

Kaye reached for the shreds of her glamour to make herself human-seeming, but it came to her uneasily. The magic and the iron had eaten up more of her energy than she'd supposed. "It's not working," Kaye whispered. "I can't change back."

Corny looked panicked. "Hide."

"I heard you guys got into some trouble, eh?" Ellen laughed as she dumped her guitar case on top of the paper-covered kitchen table. She tugged off her coat and dropped it on the floor.

Kaye turned her back to her mother, hiding her face beneath her hair. She wasn't sure how much her glamour hid, but at least she could no longer feel her wings.

"He was hitting on me," Corny said.

Ellen raised her eyebrows. "You should learn to take a compliment better."

"Things got out of hand," Kaye said. "The guy was a jerk."

Walking over to the bed, Ellen sat down and started tugging off her boots. "I guess I should be glad you two vigilantes weren't hurt. What happened to you, Kaye? You look like you got a jar of green dye dropped on you. And why are you hiding your face?"

Kaye sucked in her breath so hard that she felt dizzy. Her stomach twisted.

"You know," Corny said. "I think I'm going to walk down to the corner store. I feel a sudden need for cheese curls. Want anything?"

"Some kind of diet drink," Ellen said. "Grab some money out of my coat pocket."

"Kaye?" he called.

She shook her head.

"Okay, I'll be right back," Corny said. Out of the corner of her eye, she saw him give her a look as he unlatched the door.

"I have something to tell you," Kaye said without turning.

She could hear her mother banging in the cabinets. "There's something I want to tell you, too. I know I promised we'd stay in Jersey, but I just couldn't. My mother—she just gets to me, you know that. It hurt me when you stayed behind."

"I—" Kaye started, but Ellen cut her off.

"No," she said. "I'm glad. I guess I always figured that so long as you were happy, then I was an okay mother no matter how strange our lives got. But you weren't happy, were you? So, okay, Jersey didn't work out, but things will be different in New York. This place is mine, not some boyfriend's. And I'm bartending, not just doing gigs. I'm turning things around. I want another chance."

"Mom." Kaye half turned. "I think you should hear what I have to say before you go on."

"About tonight?" Ellen asked. "I knew there was more to

the story. You two would never attack some guy because he—"

Kaye cut her off. "About a long time ago."

Ellen took out a cigarette from a pack on the table. She lit it off of the stove. Turning, she squinted, like she'd just noticed Kaye's skin. "Well? Shoot."

Kaye took a deep breath. She could feel her heartbeat like it was pounding in her brain instead of her chest. "I'm not human."

"What is that supposed to mean?" Ellen frowned.

"Your real daughter has been gone a long time. Since she was really little. Since we were both really little. They switched us."

"What switched you?"

"There are things—supernatural things out in the world. Some people call them faeries, some people call them monsters or demons or whatever, but they exist. When the . . . the faeries took your real daughter, they left me behind."

Ellen stared at her, the ash on her cigarette growing long enough to rain on the back of her hand. "That is complete bullshit. Look at me, Kaye."

"I didn't know until October. Maybe I should have guessed—there were clues." Kaye felt as though her eyes were raw, as though her throat were raw as she spoke. "But I didn't know."

"Stop. This isn't funny and it isn't nice." Ellen's voice sounded torn between being annoyed and being truly frightened.

"I can prove it." Kaye walked toward the kitchen. "Lutie-loo! Come out. Show yourself to her."

The little faerie flew down from the refrigerator to alight on

Kaye's shoulder, tiny hands catching hold of a steadying lock of hair.

"I'm bored and everything stinks," Lutie pouted. "You should have taken me with you to the party. What if you had gotten drunk and fallen down again?"

"Kaye," Ellen said, her voice shaking. "What is that thing?"

Lutie snarled. "Rude! I will tangle your hair and sour all your milk."

"She's my evidence. So that you'll listen to me. *Really* listen."

"Whatever it is," Ellen said, "you're nothing like it."

Kaye took a deep breath and dropped what glamour was left. She couldn't see her own face, but she knew how she looked to Ellen now. Eyes black and glossy as oil, skin green as a grass stain. She could see her hands, folded in front of her, her long fingers, with an extra joint that made them seem curled even when they were at rest.

The cigarette dropped from her mother's fingers. It burned the linoleum floor where it fell, the edges of the melting plastic crater glowing, the center black as ash. Black as Kaye's eyes.

"No," Ellen said, shaking her head and backing away from Kaye.

"It's me," Kaye said. Her limbs felt cold, as though all the blood in her body rushed to her face. "This is what I really look like."

"I don't understand. I don't understand what you are. Where is my daughter?"

Kaye had read about changelings, about how mothers got their own babies back. They heated up iron pokers, threw the faerie infants on the fire.

"She's in Faerieland," Kaye said. "I've seen her. But you *know* me. I'm still me. I don't want to scare you. I can explain everything now that you'll listen. We can get her back."

"You stole my child and now you want to help me?" Ellen demanded.

In pictures Kaye'd been a skinny black-eyed little thing. She thought of that now. Of her bony fingers. Eating. Always eating. Had Ellen ever suspected? Known in that kind of gut-motherly way that no one would have believed?

"Mom . . ." Kaye walked toward her mother, reaching out her hand, but the look on Ellen's face stopped her. What came out of Kaye's mouth was a startled laugh.

"Don't you smile," her mother shouted. "You think this is funny?"

A mother is supposed to know every inch of her baby, her sweet flesh smell, every hangnail on her fingers, the number of cowlicks in her hair. Had Ellen been repulsed and ashamed of her repulsion?

Had she stacked up those books as a seat, hoping that Kaye would fall? Was that why she'd forgotten to stock the fridge? Why she'd left Kaye alone with strangers? Had her mother punished her in little ways for something that was so impossible that it could not be admitted?

"What the fuck did you do with my child?" Ellen shouted.

The nervous giggling wouldn't stop. It was like the absurdity and the horror needed to escape somehow and the only way out was through Kaye's mouth.

Ellen slapped her. For a moment Kaye went completely silent, and then she howled with laughter. It spilled out of her like shrieks, like the last of her human self burning away.

In the glass of the window, she could see her wings, slightly bent, glistening along her back.

With two beats of them, Kaye leaped up onto the countertop. The fluorescent light buzzed above her head. The blackened wings of a dozen moths dusted its yellowed grill.

Ellen, startled, stepped back again, flattening herself against the cabinets.

Looking down, Kaye could feel her mouth grinning wide and terrible. "I'll bring you back your real daughter," she said, her voice full of bitter elation. It was a relief to finally know what she had to do. To finally admit she wasn't human.

And at the very least, it was a quest she might be able to accomplish.

6

All was taken away from you: white dresses,
wings, even existence.

—Czeslaw Milosz, "On Angels"

C orny shivered on the steps of the apartment building. The cold of the cement soaked up through the thin fabric of his jeans as flurries of snow froze in his hair. The hot coffee he had bought at the bodega tasted like ashes, but he grimaced through another sip for the warmth. He tried not to notice that thin hairline cracks had already begun to form at the very tips of his rubber gloves.

He didn't want to think too carefully about the relief he'd felt when Kaye couldn't remove the curse. He'd felt diseased at first, like it was him rotting away and not the things he touched. But it wasn't him withering. Only everything else. He imagined all the things he hated, all the things he could destroy, and found his grip on the cup so tight that the cardboard bent and coffee splashed his leg.

Kaye pushed though the front door with enough force to

nearly send it crashing against the side of the building. Lutie fluttered alongside her, darting out into the safety of the air.

Corny stood up reflexively.

Kaye paced back and forth on the steps. "She pretty much hates me. I guess I should have pretty much expected that."

"Well, then I'm not bringing her a soda," Corny said, popping the tab and taking a swig. He made a face. "Ugh. Diet."

Kaye didn't even smile. She wrapped her purple coat around herself. "I'm going to get back the other Kaye for her. I'm going to switch us back."

"But . . . Kaye." Corny struggled to find the words. "You're her daughter, and that other kid . . . she doesn't even know Ellen. Ellen doesn't know her."

"Sure," Kaye said hollowly. "It might be awkward at first, but they'll work it out."

"It's not that simple—" Corny started.

Kaye cut him off. "It *is* that simple. I'm going to call the number on that piece of paper and go see the Queen. If she wants something from me, then I have a chance of getting the other Kaye back."

"Sure. I bet she'd trade Chibi-Kaye for your head on a platter," Corny said, frowning.

"*Chibi*-Kaye?" Kaye looked as if she didn't know whether to laugh or hit him.

He shrugged. "You know, like in those mangas where they draw the cute, small version of a character."

"I know what a chibi is!" She dug around in her pocket. "Give me your cell phone for a second."

He looked at her evenly. "You know I'm coming with you, right?"

"I don't—" Kaye started.

"I can handle it," Corny said before she could finish. "Just because this is dumb doesn't mean you get to do it alone. And I don't need your protection."

"And I don't want to screw up your life more than I already have!"

"Look," Corny said. "Before, you mentioned that maybe this Fixer guy would know something about my curse. We would have called this person and I would have gone with you anyway."

"Fine, okay, okay. Cell?"

"Let me call," Corny said, holding out his hand.

Kaye sighed, seeming to deflate. She held out the paper. "Fine."

Corny punched in the number, although it took a few tries with the thick gloves. The phone rang once and a computer voice said, *"Hit pound and dial your number."*

"Pager," he said to Kaye's questioning look. "Yeah, your guide to the Seelie Court is totally a dealer."

Lutie settled on Kaye's shoulder and grabbed a clump of green hair, wrapping it around her tiny body like a cloak. "Bitter coldy cold," she said.

"Let's head toward your car. Maybe by the time we get there, he'll call back."

Corny jumped off the steps. "Otherwise, we can sleep in the back covered in fast-food garbage like the brother and sister in 'Babes in the Wood' who got—"

"Lutie," Kaye said, interrupting him. "You can't come. You have to watch over my mom. Please. Just to make sure that she's okay."

"But it smells and I'm bored."

"Lutie, please. Where we're going—it could be dangerous."

The little faerie flew up, wings and clotted cream hair making her seem like a tossed handful of snow. "I'm half sick of iron, but I will stay. For you. For you." She pointed one toothpick-tiny finger down at Kaye as she rose toward the apartment window.

"We'll come for you as soon as we can," Corny called, but he was relieved. Sometimes it was tiring trying not to stare at her delicate hands or her miniature bird-black eyes. There was nothing human about her.

As they crossed the street, Corny's phone rang. He flipped it open. "Hey."

"What you want?" It was a young man's voice, soft and angry. "Who gave you this number?"

"I'm sorry. Maybe I dialed wrong." He made wide eyes at Kaye. "We're looking for a . . . the . . . the Fixer."

The line went quiet, and Corny winced at how stupid he sounded.

"You still haven't told me what you want," the boy said.

"My friend got a note. Said you could help her see the Queen."

"Okay."

"So, wait, you *are* the Fixer?" Corny said. Kaye looked over impatiently.

"Ask him about the curse," she said.

"Yeah, that's me." The boy's tone made it hard for Corny to decide if he was actually offering his services. "And yeah, I'm supposed to take a girl upstate. Tell her to come over here in the morning and we can go. You got paper?"

"Hold on." Corny fumbled for something to write with. Kaye reached into her pockets and came up with a marker. When she held it out, he took it and her arm. "Okay, go."

The boy gave them his address. Riverside Drive on the Upper West Side. Corny wrote it on Kaye's skin.

"I want to leave now," Kaye said. "Tell him. Tonight."

"She wants to leave tonight," Corny repeated into the phone.

"Is that girl crazy?" the boy asked. "It's two in the morning."

Kaye pulled the phone out of Corny's hands. "We just need directions.

"Uh-huh," she said. "Okay." She hung up. "He wants us to head over to the address he gave you."

Corny wondered what it was in Kaye's voice that convinced him.

Corny parked in front of a metered spot, figuring he could move the car later. Out beyond the park, the river glistened, reflecting the lights of the city. Kaye took a deep breath as she stepped out, and he saw human color cover her green cheeks.

They walked back and forth on the street, checking numbers until they came to a short building with a glossy black door.

"This isn't really the place, is it?" Corny asked. "It's kind of really nice. Too nice."

"The address is right." Kaye held up her arm to show him what he'd written.

A woman with red-rimmed eyes and frizzy hair stepped out onto the landing, letting the door swing behind her. Corny stepped out of the way and caught it before it slammed closed.

As she walked down the steps, he thought he saw a swaddled-up bundle of twigs in her arms.

Kaye's gaze followed the bundle.

"Maybe we should think more about this," Corny said.

Kaye pressed the buzzer.

After a few moments, a dark-skinned boy with his hair in thick herringbone cornrows opened the door. One of his eyes was cloudy, the lower part of the pupil obscured by a milky haze. Metal studs threaded through his eyebrow, and a stretch of pale scar tissue on his lower lip seemed to indicate that a ring had once been ripped loose from his mouth, although a new one gleamed next to the scar.

"You're in with the Seelie Court?" Corny asked, incredulous.

The boy shook his head. "I'm as human as you. Now, her, on the other hand." He looked at Kaye. "The Queen never said nothing about a pixie. I don't let Folk in my house."

Corny looked over at Kaye. To him, she seemed glamoured, her wings gone, her skin pink, and her eyes a perfectly average brown. He looked back at the boy in the doorway.

"So what exactly *did* she say?" Kaye asked. "Silarial."

"Her messenger told me that you were a little jumpy around faeries," the boy said, looking at Corny. "That you might feel more comfortable with me."

Kaye poked Corny in the side and he rolled his eyes. Jumpy wasn't exactly how he wanted to be thought of.

"I was supposed to tell you that the Lady Silarial invites you to visit her court." The boy turned his lip ring idly. "She wants you to consider your part in the coming war."

"Okay, that's enough," Corny said. "Let's get out of here."

"No," Kaye said. "Wait."

"She anticipated your hesitation." The boy smiled.

Corny interrupted him. "Let me guess. For a limited time only the Queen offers a free magazine subscription with each forced march to Faerieland. You can choose between *Nearly Naked Nixies* and *Kelpie Quarterly*."

The boy let out a surprised laugh. "Sure. But not just the magazine. She's also offering both of you her protection for the duration of the trip. There and back again."

Corny wondered if it were possible that this guy had just made a Tolkien reference. He really didn't look like the type.

Kaye squinted. "I've seen you before. In the Night Court."

The smile dropped from the boy's face. "I was only there once."

"With a girl," Kaye said. "She dueled one of Roiben's people. You probably don't remember me."

"You're from the Night Court?" the boy demanded. His glance went to Corny and his eyes narrowed.

Corny reminded himself he didn't care what this guy thought of either one of them.

Kaye shrugged. "More or less."

The boy sucked on his teeth. "Not such a nice place."

"And the Bright Court is full of sugar and spice and everything nice?" Kaye asked him.

"Point." The boy slid his hands into the pockets of his oversize coat. "Look, the Lady wants me to take you to her, and I don't have much choice about being her bitch, but you've still got to come back in the morning. I've got someone coming really early, and I've got to take care of him before I head out."

"We can't," Corny said. "We don't have anywhere to sleep."

The boy looked at Kaye. "I can't let her stay here. I do jobs for people—*human* people. They see some faerie and her boy hanging around and think they can't trust me."

"So I guess they don't know that you're Silarial's boy," Corny said. "Then they'd *know* not to trust you."

"I do what I have to do," he said. "Not like you—a little Night Court lackey. Does it bother you when they torture humans, or do you like to watch?"

Corny shoved him, hard, the force of his rage surprising even him. "You don't know anything about me."

The boy laughed, short and sharp, stumbling back. Corny thought of his own hands, deadly inside thin gloves. He wanted to stop the boy's laughing.

Kaye pushed between them. "So if I were to take off my glamour and sit here on your stoop, that would be a problem?"

"You wouldn't do that. Your glamour protects you a lot more than it does me."

"Does it?" Kaye asked.

A pixie. The boy had known right away, not just that Kaye was a faerie, but the *kind* of faerie she was. Corny thought about the little hob and what he'd said: *There is a boy with the True Sight. In the great city of exiles and iron to the north. He's been breaking curses on mortals.* The boy had True Sight. He couldn't tell if she was wearing glamour or not.

He turned to Kaye and widened his eyes slightly in what he hoped would seem like surprise. Then he turned back to the boy and smiled. "Looks like she meant it. Wow, I can never get used to her wings and green skin—so freaky-looking. I guess we'll just be hanging out on your steps now. It's not like we have anywhere else to go. But don't worry—if anyone comes by looking for you, we'll tell them you'll be right out . . . as soon as you're done helping a phooka find his keys."

The boy frowned. Corny put his gloved hand on Kaye's arm, willing her to play along. With a quick glance in his direction, she shrugged her narrow shoulders.

"At least you'll know where to find us in the morning," she said.

"Fine," said the boy, holding up his hands. "Get in here."

"Thanks," Corny said. "This is Kaye, by the way. Not 'the pixie' or 'my Night Court mistress' or whatever, and I'm . . ." He paused. "Neil. Cornelius. People call me Neil."

Kaye looked over at him, and for a terrible moment he thought she was going to laugh. He just didn't want this boy calling him Corny. *Corny*, like he was King of the Dorks, like his very name announced how uncool he was.

"I'm Luis," the boy said, oblivious, opening the door. "And this is my squat."

"You squat *here*?" Kaye asked. "On the Upper West Side?"

Inside, the plaster walls were cracked, and chunks of debris covered the scuffed wooden floors. Wet brown stains soaked the ceiling in rings, and a tangle of wires inside the framing were visible in one corner.

Corny's breath clouded the air as though they were still outside. "More majestic than a trailer," he said. "But also oddly shittier."

"How did you find this place?" Kaye asked.

Luis looked at Kaye. "Remember that faerie my friend Val dueled with in the Unseelie Court?"

Kaye nodded. "Mabry. She had goat feet. Tried to kill Roiben. Your friend killed her."

"This is Mabry's old place." Luis sighed and turned back to her. "Look, I don't want you talking to my brother. Faeries messed him up pretty bad. You leave him alone."

"Sure," Corny said.

Luis led them into a parlor room furnished with over-turned milk cartons and ripped-up sofas. A very thin black boy with locs that stuck up from his head like spikes sat on the floor, eating jelly beans out of a cellophane bag. His features reminded Corny of Luis's, but there was an eerie hollowness around his eyes, and his mouth looked sunken and strange.

Kaye plopped herself onto the mustard plaid couch, sprawling against the cushions. The back was ripped, and stuffing tufted up from the torn cloth beside a stain that looked a lot like blood. Corny sat down next to her.

"Dave," Luis said. "Some people I'm helping out. They're going to stay the night. That doesn't mean we all need to get friendly—" A buzzing interrupted him. He stuck his hand into the pocket, pulling out his beeper. "Shit."

"You can use my cell," Corny volunteered, and immediately felt like a sucker. What was he doing being nice to this guy?

Luis paused for a moment, and in the dim light his clouded eye looked blue. "There's a pay phone at the bodega on—" He interrupted himself. "Yeah, okay. I'd appreciate it."

Corny stared a moment too long, then looked away, fumbling through his pockets. Dave narrowed his eyes.

Dialing, Luis walked out of the room.

Kaye leaned over to Corny and whispered, "What were you doing out there?"

"He sees through glamour," Corny whispered back. "I heard about him—he's been breaking faerie curses."

She snorted. "No wonder he doesn't want humans knowing he's in bed with the Seelie Court. He's playing both sides. When he comes back, you should ask him about your hands."

"What do you mean 'in bed'?" Dave asked. His voice was dry, like rustling paper. "What's my brother doing?"

"She doesn't mean anything," Corny said.

"How come we're not supposed to talk to you?" Kaye asked.

"*Kaye,*" Corny warned.

"What?" Her voice was low. "Luis isn't here. I want to know."

Dave laughed, hollow and bitter. "Always trying to be the big brother. He's trippin' if he thinks he can stop them from killing me."

"Who wants to kill you?" Corny asked.

"Luis and I used to be delivery boys for a troll." Dave dumped a handful of jelly beans into his mouth and talked around the chewing. "Potions. Keep the iron sickness from getting to them. But if a person takes it—you know what you can do?"

Corny leaned forward, intrigued despite himself. "What?"

"Anything," Dave said. "All the shit they can do. All of it."

There was a distant banging, like someone had come to the door. Kaye turned toward the doorway, wide-eyed.

A half-chewed licorice bean fell from Dave's mouth. "Sounds like my brother's going to be busy awhile. Did you know that drinking urine drives out faerie enchantments?"

"Nasty." Kaye made a face.

Dave wheezed with what might have been laughter. "Bet he's pissing in some cups right now."

Kaye scrunched down in the sofa, kicking off her boots and putting her feet on Corny's lap. They smelled like the crushed stems of dandelions and he thought of dandelion milk covering his fingers, sticky and white, on a summer lawn years ago, while he pulled off flower heads and tossed them at his dozing sister. He was abruptly choked by grief.

"So wait," Kaye said. "Why do they want to kill you?"

"'Cause I poisoned a bunch of them. So I'm a dead man, but what good does it do to stay shut up in here while Luis tries to bargain for an extra week or two of boredom? At least I can have some fun with the time I got left." Dave grinned, but it looked more like a grimace, the skin on his cheeks pulled painfully tight. "Luis can tell me what to do all he wants, but he's going upstate this week. While the cat's away, the mouse'll finally get some play."

Corny blinked hard, like the pressure of his eyelids could push back memories. "Wait," he said. "You murdered a bunch of faeries?"

"You think I didn't?" Dave asked.

"Hey!" Luis stood in the doorway. A Latina girl and an older woman stood behind him. "What are you doing?"

Corny circled one of Kaye's ankles with a gloved hand.

"I'll talk to whoever I want, " Dave said, standing up. "You think you're better than me, giving orders."

"I think I *know* better than you," Luis said.

The girl turned toward Corny, and he saw that her arms and face were shadowed by something that looked like vines growing beneath her skin. Tiny smears of dried blood dotted where the points of thorns stuck up through her flesh.

"You don't know anything." Dave kicked a table, sending

it crashing onto its side, and walked out of the room.

Luis turned toward Kaye. "If I hear—if he tells me you came anywhere near him," he shouted. "If you spoke to him—"

"Please," said the woman. "My daughter!"

"I'm sorry," Luis said, shaking his head, glancing at the door.

"What's wrong with her?" Corny asked.

"She sees these boys all the time hanging around the park," the woman told Corny. "They're pretty but they're trouble. Not human. One day they bother Lala and she insults them. Then this. Nothing in the *botánica* is helping."

"You should both go wait in the other room," Luis said, rolling up the sleeves of his coat. "This is about to get messy."

"I'm good here," Corny said, trying to seem unimpressed. He had several different fantasies of himself that he liked to trot out when he was feeling miserable. In one, he was the scary lunatic—the guy who was going to snap one day and bury the bodies of all the people who'd wronged him in a mass grave in the backyard. Then there was the misunderstood genius, the person whom everyone discounted but who triumphed in the end through his superior competence. And the most pathetic fantasy of all—that he had some secret mutant power he was always on the verge of discovering.

"I need her to lie down on the floor." Luis walked over to the tiny kitchen and came back with a crude knife. The woman's eyes never left the blade. "Cold iron."

Luis actually had a secret power and was competent. That pissed Corny off. All he had was cursed hands.

"What's that for?" Lala asked.

Luis shook his head. "I won't cut you. I promise."

The woman narrowed her eyes, but the girl seemed reassured and sank down onto the floor. The vines squirmed under her skin, rippling as they shifted. Lala winced and cried out.

Kaye looked up at Corny and raised her eyebrows.

Luis crouched over Lala, straddling her slender body.

"He knows what to do, yes?" the woman asked Corny.

Corny nodded. "Sure."

Luis reached into his pocket and scattered a white substance—maybe salt—over the girl's body. She bucked, screaming. The vines crawled like snakes.

"He's hurting her!" Lala's mother gasped.

Luis didn't even glance up. He threw another handful, and Lala shrieked. Her skin stretched and rippled away from the salt, up into her neck, choking her.

Her mouth opened, but instead of a sound, thorn-covered branches burst out, winding toward Luis. He slashed at them with his knife. The iron cut through the vines easily, but more came, splitting and curling like tentacles, grabbing for him.

Corny yelled, pulling his legs up onto the couch. Kaye stared in horror. Lala's mother's cries had become one long teakettle scream.

One branch wrapped around Luis's wrist, while others crawled toward his waist and writhed along the floor. The long thorns sank into his skin. Lala's eyes rolled back in her head, and her body convulsed. Her lips shone with blood.

Luis dropped the knife and wrapped his hands around the stems, ripping the brambles even as they coiled around his hands.

Corny lunged forward, grabbing the knife and cutting at the thorns.

"No, you idiot," Luis yelled. A knot of branches suddenly

ripped free of Lala's mouth, wormlike white roots sliding out of her throat, glistening with saliva. The great vine blackened and shriveled.

Lala started to cough. The woman knelt by her, weeping and smoothing back the girl's hair.

Luis's arms were striped with scratches. He stood up and looked away as if dazed.

Lala's mother helped the girl to her feet and began to lead her toward the door. *"Gracias, gracias,"* she muttered.

"Wait," Luis said. "I need to talk to your daughter for a minute. Without you."

"I don't want to," Lala said.

"Can't she come back once she's rested?" the woman asked.

Luis shook his head and after a moment, the woman relented. "You saved her life, so I am trusting you, but be quick. I want her home and away from all of this." She closed the door separating the hall from the room.

Luis looked at Lala. The girl swayed a little and caught herself by bracing her hand against the wall.

"What you told your mother," he asked, "that's not exactly what happened, is it?"

She hesitated, then shook her head.

"One of those boys gave you something to eat—maybe you just ate a little bit? Maybe just one seed?"

She nodded again, not meeting his eyes.

"But now you know better, right?" Luis asked her.

"Yes," she whispered, then fled to join her mother. Luis watched her go. Corny watched him watch her.

"Your pixie talked to my brother, didn't she?" he demanded, nodding to Kaye.

"What do you think?" Corny replied.

Luis yawned. "I think we're out of here as soon as possible. I'll show you where to sleep."

Corny arranged himself on the floor of mattresses spread out over what might have once been a dining room. Dave had already rolled himself into a shroud of blankets against the far wall, beneath what was left of a chair rail. Kaye staggered in from the parlor, curled herself around a throw pillow, and fell immediately into sleep. Luis lay down nearby.

Flexing his fingers, Corny watched the rubber tighten over his knuckles. Already the sheen had gone off the gloves. They might be brittle by morning. Carefully, he slid out one hand and touched the edge of Luis's duvet. The thin fabric tore, threads fraying, bleeding feathers. He watched them blow in the slight draft from the window, dusting everything like snow.

Luis turned in his sleep and feathers caught in his braids. One settled at the very corner of Luis's mouth, fluttering with each breath. It seemed like it would tickle. Corny wanted to brush it out of the way. His fingers twitched.

Luis's eyes slitted. "What are you looking at?"

"You drooling," Corny lied quickly. "It's disgusting."

Luis grunted and rolled over.

Corny pulled his glove back on, heart beating so hard that he felt light-headed.

I like him, he thought in horror, the unfairness of that on top of everything else filling him with unfocused rage. *Shit. I like him.*

Kaye woke to sunlight streaming through large windows. Corny was sprawled beside her, snoring slightly. Somehow he had stolen all her blankets. Both Dave and Luis were gone.

Her mouth tasted stale, and she was so thirsty that she didn't think about where she was or why she was there until she went into the bathroom and gulped down several handfuls of water. It tasted of iron. Iron seemed to be everywhere, bubbling up from the pipes and sifting down from the ceiling.

Padding across the cold floors to try to find something to eat, Kaye heard a strange noise, like a purse upended. The smells of mildew were more intense now and she could feel her glamour being worn away. She looked down at her hand, green as a leaf. Heading in the direction of the noise, she came to the scavenged-sofa room, where a fire blazed in the grate.

A middle-aged man with short curly hair and an overstuffed messenger bag stood near the windows. As Kaye walked in, the man started to speak. But instead of sounds, copper coins fell from his lips to clatter and roll on the worn wooden floorboards.

Luis put his hand on the man's arm. "Did you do what I told you?" he asked, bending to pick up the pennies. "I know the metal tastes like blood, but you just got to do it."

The man nodded and gestured wildly to his mouth.

"I told you, the cure was to eat your words. That means every single coin that came out of your mouth. You're telling me you did that?"

This time the man hesitated.

"You spent some, didn't you? Please, please tell me that you didn't go to CoinStar or some stupid shit like that."

"Ugh," the man said, and pennies scattered.

"Go find the rest. It's the only way you're going to be cured." Luis crossed his arms over his chest, lean muscles showing through the thin fabric of his T-shirt and along his bare arms. "And no more deals with the Folk."

There were so many things Kaye didn't know about faeries.

The man looked like he wanted to say something, probably that he didn't appreciate being ordered around by some kid, but he merely nodded as he took out his wallet. After counting out a stack of twenties, he gathered the coins on the floor and departed without a sign of thanks.

Luis tapped the bills against the palm of one hand as he turned to Kaye. "I told you to stay out of sight."

"Something's happening to me," Kaye said. "My glamour's not working so good."

Luis groaned. "You're telling me that he was looking at a green girl with wings?"

"No," she said. "It's just that it seems so much harder to keep up."

"The iron in the city sucks up faerie magic quick," he said with a sigh. "That's why faeries don't live here if they have a choice. Only the exiled ones, the ones that can't go back to their own courts for whatever reason."

"So why don't they join another court?" Kaye asked.

"Some do, I guess. But that's dangerous business—the other court's as likely to kill them as take them in. So they live here and let the iron eat away at them." He sighed again. "If you really need it, there's Nevermore—a potion—staves off the iron sickness. I can't get you any right now—"

"Nevermore?" Kaye asked. "Like 'quoth the raven'?"

"That's what my brother calls it." Luis shifted uncomfortably, smoothing back his braids. "In humans it bestows glamour—makes us almost like faeries. Gets us high. You're *never* supposed to use it *more* than once a day or *more* than two days in a row or *more* than a single pinch at a time. *Never. More.* Don't let your friend near it."

"Oh. Okay." Kaye thought of Dave's haunted eyes and blackened mouth.

"Good. You ready to go?" Luis asked.

Kaye nodded. "One more question—have you ever heard of a curse where whatever someone touches withers?"

Luis nodded. "It's a King Midas variation. Whatever you touch turns to—fill in the blank. Gold. Shit. Jelly doughnuts. It's a pretty powerful curse." He frowned. "You'd have to be young and rash and really pissed off to toss all that power at a mortal."

"So the King Midas—you know how to cure it?"

He frowned. "Salt water. King Midas walked out into a brackish river and let it wash away his curse. The ocean would be better, but it's basically the same principle. Anything with salt."

Corny walked into the room, yawning hugely. "What's going on?"

"So, Neil," Luis said, his eyes going to Corny's gloves. "What happen? She curse you by accident?"

Corny looked blank for a moment, like the nickname had thrown him completely. Then his eyes narrowed. "Nope," he said. "I got cursed on purpose."

7

Not the sweet, new grass with flowers
Is this harvesting of ours;
Not the upland clover bloom;
But the rowen mixed with weeds,
Tangled tufts from marsh and meads,
Where the poppy drops its seeds
In the silence and the gloom.

—HENRY WADSWORTH LONGFELLOW, "AFTERMATH"

Snow fell lightly around the abandoned Untermeyer estate, dusting the dirt and dead grass with white. The remains of the old fire-blackened mansion showed through the bare branches. A vast fireplace stood like a tower, overgrown with dead vines. Underneath what remained of a slate roof, the gentry of the Unseelie Court had hastily prepared camp. Roiben sat on a low couch and watched as Ethine entered his chambers. She moved gracefully, feet seeming to only lightly touch the ground.

He had composed himself, and when one of his Folk's clawed hands happened to push her, causing her to stumble as she crossed the threshold, he only looked up as though annoyed by her clumsiness. Beside him were bowls of fruit, brought cold from dark caverns; cordials of clover and nettle; and tiny bird hearts still glossy with blood. He bit into a grape, not minding the crack of seeds against his teeth.

"Ethine. Be welcome."

She frowned and opened her mouth, then hesitated. When she spoke, she merely said, "My Lady knows she dealt you a terrible blow."

"I did not realize your Lady liked to brag, even by proxy. Come, have a bite of fruit, take something to cool your hot tongue."

Ethine moved toward him stiffly and perched on the very edge of the lounge. He handed her an agate goblet. She took the shallowest of sips, then set it down.

"It chafes you to be polite to me," he said. "Perhaps Silarial should have taken your feelings into consideration when she chose her ambassador."

Ethine contemplated the earthen ground, and Roiben stood.

"You begged her to let someone else go in your place, didn't you?" He laughed with vindictive certainty. "Perhaps even told her how much it hurt you to see what your brother had become?"

"No," Ethine said softly.

"No? Not in those words, but I'll wager you said it all the same. Now you see how she cares for those who serve her. You are one more thing with which to needle me and nothing more than that. She sent you despite your pleading."

Ethine had closed her eyes tightly. Her hands were clasped in her lap, fingers threaded together.

He took her glass and drank from it. She looked up, annoyed, the way she had once been annoyed when he'd pulled her hair. When they were children.

It hurt him to look at her as an enemy.

"I do not see that you care for my feelings any more than she does," Ethine said.

"But I do." He made his voice grave. "Come, deliver your message."

"My Lady knows she dealt you quite a blow. She further knows that your control of the other faeries in your lands is spotty after the botched Tithe."

Roiben leaned against the wall. "You even sound like her when you say it."

"Don't jest. She wants you to fight her champion. If you win, she will leave your lands unmolested for seven years. If you lose, you will forfeit the Unseelie Court to her." Ethine looked at him with anguished eyes. "And you will *die*."

Roiben barely heard her plea, he was so surprised by the Bright Queen's offer. "I cannot think but that this is either generosity or some cunning beyond my measure. Why should she give me this chance at winning when now I have near none?"

"She wants your lands hale and whole when she takes them, not weakened by a war. Too many great courts have fallen into rabble."

"Do you ever imagine no court at all?" Roiben asked his sister quietly. "No vast responsibilities or ancient grudges or endless wars?"

"We have come to rely on humans too much," said Ethine, frowning. "Once, our kind lived apart from them. Now we rely on them to be everything from farmers to nursemaids. We live in their cast-off spaces and sup off their tables. If the courts fall, we will be parasites with nothing to call our own. This is the last of our old world."

"I hardly think it is as serious as all that." Roiben looked past Ethine. He didn't want her to see his expression. "How about this. Tell Silarial that I will take her insulting and lop-sided bargain with one variation. She must wager something too. She must put up her crown."

"She will never give you—"

Roiben cut her off. "Not to me. To you."

Ethine opened her mouth, but no sound came out.

"Tell her that if she loses, she makes you the Bright Queen of the Seelie Court. If I lose, I will give her both my crown and my life." It felt good to say, even if it were a rash wager.

Ethine rose. "You mock me."

He made a dismissive gesture. "Don't be silly. You know very well that I do not."

"She told me that if you wished to bargain, you must do so with her." She paced the room, gesturing wildly. "Why won't you just come back to us? Pledge yourself to Silarial, ask for her forgiveness. Tell her how hard it was to be Nicnevin's knight. She could not have known."

"Silarial has spies everywhere. I very much doubt that she was ignorant of my suffering."

"There was nothing for her to do! Nothing for any of us to do. She spoke often of her fondness for you. Let her explain. Let her be your friend again. Forgive each other." Her voice dropped low. "You don't belong in a place like this."

"And why is that, dear sister? Why don't I belong here?"

Ethine groaned and slapped one open hand against the wall. "Because you are not a fiend!"

She reminded Roiben so much of his old, innocent self that for a moment he hated her, for a moment he only wanted to shake her and scream at her and hurt her before someone else did. "No? Is it not enough, what I have done? Is it not enough to have cut the throat of a nix that dared laugh too loud or too long before my mistress? Is it not enough to have hunted down a hob that stole a single cake from her table? Is it not enough to have been deaf to their entreaties, their begging?"

"Nicnevin commanded you."

"Of course she did!" he shouted. "Again and again and again she commanded me. And now I am changed, Ethine. This is where I belong if I belong anywhere at all."

"What about Kaye?"

"The pixie?" He gave her a quick look.

"You were kind to her. Why do you want me to think the worst of you?"

"I was not kind to Kaye," he said. "Ask her. I am not kind, Ethine. Moreover, I no longer have any interest in kindness. I mean to win."

"If you were to win," Ethine said, her voice faltering, "I would be the Queen and you would be *my* enemy."

He snorted. "Now don't go casting a pall over my best outcome." He held out the cup to her. "Drink something. Eat. After all, it is natural for siblings to squabble, is it not?"

Ethine took the cup back from him and lifted it to her mouth, but he had left her only a single swallow.

Kaye cradled a large ThunderCats thermos of coffee as she walked to Corny's car. Luis followed, wrapped in a black coat. It hung voluminously from his shoulders, its inner lining torn to pieces. He had taken it out of the back of one of the closets, from a pile strewn with chunks of plaster.

She was glad to keep moving. As long as there was something in front of her, something still to do, things made sense.

"You got a map of Upstate New York?" Luis asked Corny.

"I thought you knew the way," Corny said. "What kind of guide needs a map?"

"Can you two not—" Kaye started, but stopped in front of a newspaper vending machine. There, in a sidebar on the front page of the *Times*, was a picture of the cemetery on the hill by Kaye's house. The hill where Janet was buried. The hollow hill under which Roiben had been crowned. It had collapsed beneath the weight of an overturned truck. The photo showed smoke billowing up from the hill, fallen gravestones scattered like loose teeth.

Corny slid quarters into the machine and pulled out a paper. "A bunch of bodies were found, too burnt to identify. They're looking for dental matches. There was some speculation that maybe people were sledding when the truck hit. Kaye, what the fuck?"

Kaye touched the picture, running her fingers over the ink of the page. "I don't know."

Luis frowned. "All those people. Can't the Folk kill each other and leave us out of it?"

"Shut up. Just shut up," Kaye said, walking to Corny's car and jerking on the handle. Pieces of chrome came off on her singed fingers. She felt sick.

"I've got to unlock it," Corny said, opening the door for her with his keys. "Look, he's okay. I'm sure he's okay."

She threw herself into the backseat, trying not to imagine Roiben dead, trying not to see his eyes dulled with mud. "No, you're not."

"I'm calling my mom," Corny said. He started the car while he dialed, his gloved fingers awkward.

Luis pointed out the turns and Corny drove with the phone cradled against his shoulder. This time Kaye welcomed the iron sickness, welcomed the dizziness that made it hard to think.

"She says Janet's coffin wasn't disturbed, but the stone's gone." Corny pushed his phone closed. "Nobody saw anyone sledding that late, and according to the local paper the truck wasn't even supposed to be making deliveries in the area."

"It's the war," Kaye said, putting her head down on the vinyl seat. "The faerie war."

"What's wrong with her?" she heard Luis ask softly.

Corny's eyes stayed on the road. "She was dating someone from the Unseelie Court."

Luis looked back at her. "Dating?"

"Yeah," Corny said. "He gave her his class ring. It was a whole big thing."

Luis looked incredulous.

"Roiben," Corny said. At the sound of Roiben's name, Kaye closed her eyes, but the dread didn't ebb.

"That's not possible," said Luis.

"Why do you think Silarial wants to see me?" Kaye demanded. "Why do you think it's worth two messengers and a guarantee of protection? If he isn't dead already, she thinks I can help kill him."

"No," said Luis. "You can't *date* the Lord of the Night Court."

"Well, I'm not. He dumped me."

"You can't *get dumped* by the Lord of the Night Court."

"Oh, yes you can. You so completely can."

"We're all on edge." Corny rubbed his face with gloved fingers. "And it's a bad day when I'm the voice of reason. Relax. We're going to be stuck in this traffic for a long time."

They drove upstate while the late afternoon sunlight filtered through the leafless trees and the new-fallen snow melted into slush. They passed strip malls hung with wreaths and garlands, while kicked-up road salt streaked tide lines onto the sides of cars.

Kaye looked out the window, counting silver cars, reading every sign. Trying not to think.

At sunset they finally pulled onto a dirt road and Luis told them to stop.

"Here," he said, and opened the door. In the fading light Kaye could see an ice-covered lake stretching out from a bank just beyond the lip of the road. Mist shrouded the center of the lake from view. Dead trees rose from the water, as though there had once been a forest where the lake now stood. A forest of drowned trees. The fading light turned the trunks to gold.

Wind whipped loose snow into Kaye's face. It stung like chips of glass.

"There's a boat," Luis said. "Come on."

They walked downhill, shoes skidding on the ice.

Corny gasped and Kaye looked up from watching her feet. A young man stood in front of her, half obscured by the branches of a fir tree. She yelped.

He was as still as a statue, in a down jacket and a woolen cap. He stared past the three of them as though they weren't there. His skin was darker than Luis's, but his lips had gone pale with cold.

"Hello?" Luis said, waving his hand in front of the guy's face.

The man didn't move.

"Look," Corny said. He pointed through the evergreen trees to a woman in her fifties standing by herself. Her ginger hair fluttered in the slight breeze. Squinting, Kaye could see other spots of color along the lake. Other humans, waiting at attention for some signal.

Kaye's gaze dropped to the man's chapped fingers. "Frostbite."

"Wake up!" Luis shouted. When that got no response, he slapped the man across one cheek.

The frozen man's gaze shifted suddenly. Without a trace of expression he threw Luis to the ground and stomped on his stomach.

Luis groaned in pain, rolling to his side, his body curling up defensively.

Corny threw himself at the man. They fell backward, cracking through the thin ice of the lake as they splashed into the shallow water.

Kaye rushed forward, trying to pull Corny onto the shore. A hand closed on her arm.

She turned to see a creature, as tall and thin as a scarecrow, shrouded in tattered black fabric that whipped through the air. His eyes were a dead, pupil-less white, and his teeth were clear as glass.

Kaye's scream died in her throat. Her nails scrabbled at the creature's arm and he let her go, pushing past. He moved so nimbly that by the time she'd turned her head, his skeletal hand was on the frozen man's throat.

Corny splashed up onto the bank and collapsed in the snow.

The creature pressed a thumb against the man's forehead and hissed some words that Kaye didn't know. The frozen man moved slowly to resume standing like an indifferent sentry, clothing soaked through and dripping.

"What do you want?" Kaye demanded, taking off her coat and wrapping it around a shivering Corny. "Who are you?"

"Sorrowsap," said the creature, bowing his head. His hair was thin and coiled like the tangle of roots beneath a weed. "At your service."

"Great! That's just fucking great." Luis held his stomach.

Corny shuddered reflexively and pulled the coat tighter.

"*My* service?" Kaye asked. Looking across the forest, she saw the other human figures walk back to their original positions. They had been coming, had been perhaps only moments away from entering the fight.

"The King of the Unseelie Court commands that I guard your steps. I have followed you since you left his court."

"Why would he do that?" Kaye blurted. She thought of Roiben covered in collapsed dirt, his face as pale as a marble tombstone, and she closed her eyes against the image. He should have been protecting himself and been less worried about her.

Sorrowsap tilted his head. "I serve his whims. I need not understand them."

"But how could you stop the frozen people like that?" Luis

asked. "This barrier has to have been created to keep you out more than us."

At the question, Sorrowsap smiled, his clear wet teeth making his mouth look poisonous. He reached into a sack beneath his robes and threw down what at first seemed like green leather lined in red silk. Then Kaye saw the fine hairs dotting the surface and the sticky wetness underneath. Skin. The skin of a faerie.

"She told me," said Sorrowsap.

Luis made a noise in the back of his throat and turned away, like he was going to retch.

"You can't—I don't want—" Kaye said, furious and terrified. "You killed her because of me."

Sorrowsap said nothing.

"Never do that! Never!" She walked up to him, hands fisted. Before she thought better of it, she slapped him. Her hand stung.

He didn't even flinch. "Just because I am to protect you does not give you governance over me."

"Kaye," Luis said stiffly. "It's done."

Kaye looked toward Luis, but he avoided meeting her eyes.

"I'm freezing," Corny said. "As in 'to death.' Let's get where we're going."

"All these people are going to die from the cold," Kaye said, although it seemed that, lately, her trying to make things better had only succeeded in making them worse. "We can't just leave them."

Corny took out his phone. "Let's call the—"

Luis shook his head. "I don't think we should lead more victims out here. That's what you'd be doing if the police came."

"I'm not getting reception anyway," Corny said. "You break curses. Can't you do anything for them?"

Luis shook his head. "This is way beyond what I know how to handle."

"We have to dry this guy off," Kaye said. "Maybe cover his fingers before they get worse. Sorrowsap, can you keep him . . . deactivated?"

"You have no governance over me." Yellow eyes watched her with as little expression as an owl's.

"I didn't think I did," Kaye said. "I'm asking for your help."

"Let them die," said Sorrowsap.

She sighed. "Can't you snap them out of it? Remove whatever enchantment is keeping them like this—remove it permanently? Then they could just go home."

"No," he said, "I cannot."

"I am going to help this guy. If he attacks me, you are going to have to stop him. And if you don't keep him turned off, he's going to attack."

Sorrowsap's face seemed expressionless, but one of his hands curled into a fist. "Very well, pixie-who-has-my-King's-favor." He strode to the frozen man and placed his thumb on the man's forehead once more.

Kaye sat down in the snow and pulled off her own boots as Sorrowsap chanted the unfamiliar words. Taking off her socks, she wrapped them over the man's hands. Luis draped the guy in his coat and ducked out of the way of a swinging arm when the hissing chant faltered.

"It's not going to help," Corny said. "These people are screwed."

Kaye stepped back. The cold felt like razors cutting her

skin. Even wearing her coat, Corny's lips had gone blue. The frozen man would die with all the others.

"The Seelie Court's close," Luis said.

"There I cannot follow," said Sorrowsap. "If you go, you will be without my protection and that would cause my Lord deep displeasure."

"We're going," Kaye said.

"As you say." Sorrowsap bowed his head. "I will wait for you here."

Kaye looked at Corny. "You don't have to come. You'd warm up quickly in the car."

"Don't be an idiot," he told her through chattering teeth.

"The next leg of the journey means getting into that," Luis said, pointing along the shore. For a moment Kaye saw nothing. Then the wind rippled the water, setting something to rock and glisten in the moonlight. A boat, carved entirely from ice, its prow shaped like a swan ready to soar into flight. "The Bright Lady didn't exactly tell me about her frozen zombie sentries, so I'm thinking she's full of surprises."

"Great," Corny said, stumbling over the frozen snow.

Kaye stepped gingerly onto the slippery surface of the boat and sat down. The seat was cold against her thighs. "So, would this water fix Corny's curse?"

Corny got in next to her. "I don't—"

"Corny?" Luis frowned.

"Neil," Kaye said. "I mean fix Neil's curse."

"No," Luis pushed the boat hard and it slid out onto the water. Luis hopped in, making them rock wildly as he sat. He looked over at Corny. "Too still and not salt."

They didn't paddle, but a strange current propelled them

across the lake, past the drowned trees. Beneath the dripping hull of the boat the water was choked with vibrant green duckweed, as though a forest grew underneath the waves.

Green and gold fish darted under the boat, visible through the ice hull. Fish had to keep swimming to breathe, Kaye thought. She knew how they felt. There was nothing safe to think about, not Roiben, not her mother, not all the people slowly dying on the far shore. There was nothing to do but keep going until despair finally froze her.

"Kaye—check it out," Corny said. "It's like from a book."

Through the mist, Kaye saw the outline of an island filled with tall firs. As they got closer, the sky grew lighter and the air became warm. Although there was no sun, the shore was lit bright as day.

Corny glanced at his watch and then held it out to show her. The digital numbers had stopped on December 21 at 6:13:52 p.m. "Bizarre."

"At least it's warmer," Kaye said, rubbing his arms through the coat, hoping she could rub the chill out of him.

"That would be better news if we weren't in a *boat made of ice*."

"I don't know about you all," Luis said. He smiled slightly, almost like he was embarrassed. "But I can't even feel my ass anymore. Swimming might be better."

Corny laughed, but Kaye couldn't smile. She was putting Corny in danger. Again.

The last of the haze blew off and Kaye saw that each tree on the island was white with cocoon silk in place of snow. She thought she could see masses of caterpillars writhing at the peaks of the trees, and she shuddered.

The boat dug into the soft mud. They climbed out, feet sinking slightly so there was a sucking noise with each step across the shore.

Stupid mud, Kaye thought. *Stupid boat. Stupid faerie island.* She found herself suddenly exhausted. Stupid, stupid me.

There was music, distant and faint, accompanied by the sound of laughter. They followed it into a grove of flowering cherry trees, the blooms blue instead of pink, petals falling like a shower of poison with every slight breeze.

She thought of something the Thistlewitch had told her when she had explained to Kaye that she was a changeling: *The child's fey nature becomes harder and harder to conceal as it grows. In the end, they all return to Faerie.*

That couldn't be true. Kaye didn't want it to be true.

Corny shivered once, hard, like his body was shaking off the cold, and toed off his sodden and mud-covered shoes. It was warm, but not hot, on the island—so perfect a temperature, in fact, that it was as though there were no weather at all.

A few of the Bright Folk strolled on the grass. A boy in a skirt of silver scale mesh held the hand of a pixie with wide azure wings. Clouds of tiny buzzing faeries hovered in the air like gnats. A knight in white painted armor looked in Kaye's direction. A singing voice, heartbreakingly lovely, drifted down to where she stood. From the branches of the trees, pointed faces stared down.

A knight with eyes the color of turquoises walked up to meet them and bowed deeply. "My Lady is pleased by your arrival. She asks that you come and sit with her." He glanced at her companions. "Only you."

Kaye nodded, worrying her lip with her teeth.

"Beneath the tree." He gestured toward a massive willow, its drooping branches covered with struggling cocoons. Every now and again one of the silken purses would rip open and a white bird would flutter loose and take flight.

Kaye made herself lift one of the heavy leathery branches and duck underneath.

Light filtered through the leaves to glimmer on the faces of Silarial and her courtiers. The Lady of the Bright Court did not sit on a throne, but rather on a collection of tapestry cushions heaped upon the ground. Other faeries were strewn about like ornaments, some of them horned, others thin as sticks and sprouting leaves from their heads.

Silarial's hair was parted in two soft waves at her brow, the strands shining like copper, and for a moment Kaye thought of the pennies that had fallen from the man's mouth in Luis's apartment. The Bright Lady smiled, and she was so stunning that Kaye forgot to speak, forgot to bow, forgot to do anything but stare.

It hurt to look at her.

Perhaps like great pain, great loveliness must be forgotten.

"Will you have something?" asked Silarial, gesturing to bowls of fruit and pitchers of juice, their surfaces beading from the chill of the contents. "Unless it is not to your taste."

"I'm sure it is very much to my taste." Kaye bit into a white fruit. Black nectar stained her lips dark and ran over her chin.

The courtiers laughed behind their long-fingered hands and Kaye wondered whom exactly she had been trying to impress. She was letting herself be baited.

"Good. Now take off that silly glamour." The Lady turned to the faeries that lounged beside her. "Leave us."

The assemblage rose lazily, lifting their harps and goblets, pillows and books. They made their way out from beneath the tree as haughtily as offended cats.

Silarial turned on the pillows. Kaye sat at the very edge of the pile of cushions and wiped the black juice from her mouth with her sleeve. She let the glamour fall from her, and when she saw her own green fingers, she was surprised by her relief at not having to hide them.

"You mislike me," Silarial said. "Not without reason."

"You tried to have me killed," Kaye said.

"One of my people—any one of my people—was a small price to pay to trap the Lady of the Night Court."

"I'm not one of your people," Kaye said.

"Of course you are." Silarial smiled. "You were born in these lands. You belong here."

Kaye had no answer. She said nothing. She wished she did know who had birthed her and who had switched her, but she didn't want to hear it from the Lady's lips.

Silarial plucked a plum from one of the plates, looking up at Kaye through her lashes. "This war began before I came into the world. Once, there were little courts, each huddled together near a circle of thorn trees or beside a meadow of clover. But as time passed and our places thinned, we drew together in larger numbers. The High Court was making inroads. My mother won Folk to her with the keen edge of her blade and her tongue.

"But not my father. He and his people dwelt here in the mountains and they had no use for her or her kin, at least at first. In time, however, she fascinated even him, becoming his consort, gaining governance over his lands and even bearing two children by him."

"Nicnevin and Silarial," Kaye said.

The Bright Lady nodded. "Each girl as unlike the other as two of the Folk could be. Nicnevin and our mother were of a kind, with their taste for blood and pain. I was as our father, content with less brutal amusements."

"Like freezing a ring of humans to death around a lake?" Kaye asked her.

"I do not find that particularly diverting, merely necessary," Silarial said. "Nicnevin killed our father when he gave a boon to a piper she preferred to torment. I am told our mother laughed when my sister explained how it had been done, but then, death was my mother's meat and drink. I served her a banquet of my grief." The Bright Queen looked upward, into the wriggling shadows of the willow. "I will not let my father's lands fall to my sister's court."

"But they don't want your lands. Your sister's dead."

Silarial looked surprised for a moment. Her fist tightened around the plum. "Yes, dead. Dead before my plan could break her. I spent all the long years of peace between our people building my strategy and biding my time, and she died before my bereavement could be sated. I will not give her court the chance to plan as I planned. I will take her lands and her people and that will be my vengeance. It will secure the safety of all of the Bright Court.

"This is your home, whether you wish it or no, and your war. You must pick a side. I know of your pledge to Roiben—your declaration—and he was right to rebuff you. He went to the Unseelie Court as a hostage for peace. Do you think he wants you to be tied to them as his consort would be? Do you think he wishes you to suffer as he's suffered?"

"Of course not," Kaye snapped.

"I know what it is to give up something you desire. Before Roiben left for the Unseelie Court, he was my lover—did you know that?" She frowned. "Passion made him occasionally forget his place, but oh, do I regret giving him up."

"You forget his place now."

Silarial laughed suddenly. "Let me tell you a story of Roiben when he was in my court. I think of it often."

"Sure," Kaye said. She felt strangled by the things she could not say. She didn't believe Silarial meant anything but harm, but to let the Queen know that would be foolish. And she did want to hear any story about Roiben. The way that Silarial spoke gave her hope he was still alive.

Some of the tension went out of her, some of the dread.

"Once there was a fox that got tangled in a thornbush near our revels. Tiny sprites darted around, trying to free it. The fox didn't understand the faeries were being helpful. It only understood that it was in pain. It snapped at the sprites, trying to catch them in its teeth, and as it moved, the thorns dug deeper into its fur. Roiben saw the fox and went over to keep it still.

"He could have held its muzzle and let it twist its body deeper into the bush. He could have let go of it when it bit him. He did neither of those things. He let the fox bite his hand, again and again until the sprites freed it from the thorns."

"I don't get the point of the story," Kaye said. "Are you saying that Roiben lets himself get hurt because he thinks he's being helpful? Or are you saying Roiben used to be good and kind, but now he's a prick?"

Silarial tilted her head, brushing back a stray lock of her hair. "I am wondering if you aren't like that fox, Kaye."

"What?" Kaye stood up. "I'm not the one who's hurting him."

"He would have died for you at the Tithe. Died for a pixie he'd met only days before. Then he refused to join me when we might have united the courts and forged a real peace—an enduring peace. Why do you think that is? Maybe because he was too busy disentangling you and yours from thornbushes."

"Maybe he didn't see it that way," Kaye said, but she could feel her cheeks go hot and her wings twitch. "There could still be peace, you know. If *you* would just stop biting his hand. He doesn't want to fight you."

"Oh, come now." Silarial smiled and sank her teeth into the plum. "I know you've seen the tapestry of me he slashed to pieces. He doesn't just want to fight me. He wants to *destroy* me." The way she said "destroy," it sounded pleasurable. "Do you know what happened to the fox?"

Kaye snorted. "I'm pretty sure you're going to tell me."

"It ran off, stopping only to lick its cuts, but the next morning it was caught in the bushes again, thorns buried deep in its flesh. All Roiben's pain for nothing."

"What do you want me to do?" Kaye asked. "What did you bring me here for?"

"To show you that I am no monster. Of course Roiben despises me. I sent him to the Unseelie Court. But he can come back now. He is far too biddable to lead them.

"Join us. Join the Seelie Court. Help me show Roiben. Once he gets past his anger, he will see that it would be best if he ceded control of his court to me."

"I can't—" Kaye hated that she was tempted.

"I think you can. Convince him, that is. He trusts you. He gave you his *name*." Silarial's expression didn't change, but something in her eyes did.

"I'm not using that."

"Not even for his own good? Not even for peace between our courts?"

"You mean make him surrender. That's not the same thing as peace."

"I mean convince him to surrender the terrible burden of the Night Court," Silarial said. "Kaye, I am not so vain that I cannot appreciate that you outwitted me once, nor so foolish that I cannot understand your desire to preserve your own life. Let us be at odds no more."

Kaye sank her nails into her palm, hard. "I don't know," she managed to say. It was a seductive thought that the war might not go on, that everything could be so easily resolved.

"Think on it. Should he no longer be the Lord of the Night Court, your pledge would be void. You would never have to complete the impossible quest. Declarations are only made to Lords or Ladies."

Kaye wanted to say that it didn't matter, but it did. Her shoulders slumped.

"Were you willing to help me, I could arrange for you to see him, even to speak with him, despite the declaration. He is on his way here now." Silarial stood. The soft susurrations of her gown were the only sounds under the canopy of branches as she crossed to where Kaye stood. "There are other ways to persuade you, but I do not like to be cruel."

Kaye took a quick breath. He was alive. Now she just had

to do what she'd come for. "I want the human Kaye. Ellen's daughter. The real me. Switch her back. If you do that, I'll think about what you said. I'll consider it."

After all, it wasn't like Kaye was really agreeing to anything. Not really.

"Done," said Silarial, reaching out to stroke her cheek. Her fingers were cool. "After all, you are one of mine. You had only to ask. And, of course, you will have the hospitality of the Bright Court while you consider."

"Of course," Kaye echoed faintly.

8

Forest, I fear you! in my ruined heart
your roaring wakens the same agony
as in cathedrals when the organ moans
and from the depths I hear that I am damned.
—CHARLES BAUDELAIRE, "OBSESSION"

Y ou're a fool," Ellebere said. He looked out of place in the city, though he'd glamoured himself a red pin-striped black suit and a silk tie the color of dried blood.

"Because it's a trap?" Roiben asked. His long wool coat whipped in the breeze from the river. The stench of iron seared his nose and throat.

"It must be." Ellebere turned, so that he was walking backward, facing Roiben. He gestured wildly, ignoring the people who had to veer out of his way. "Just her offer of peace is suspicious, but if she agrees to your absurd demand, then she must have some sure way of killing you."

"Yes," Roiben said, grabbing his arm. "And you're about to walk into a road."

Ellebere stopped, pushing back strands of wine-colored hair from his eyes. He sighed. "Can her knight beat you?"

"Talathain?" Roiben considered that for a moment. It was hard to imagine Talathain—whom he had wrestled with in patches of clover, who had loved Ethine for years before he'd found the courage to bring her a mere bundle of violets—as formidable. But those memories seemed old and unfamiliar, as if they belonged to another person. Perhaps *this* Talathain was another person too. "I think I can win."

"The Bright Queen has a deadly weapon, then, perhaps? Or armor that cannot be pierced? Some way to use iron weaponry?"

"It could be that. I turn it over again and again in my mind, but I have no more answer than you do." Roiben looked at his hand and saw all the throats he had cut in Nicnevin's service. All the pleading eyes and trembling mouths. All the mercy that he could not bestow, least of all on himself. He let go of Ellebere. "I only hope that I am a better murderer than the Bright Lady imagines me."

"Tell me that there is some plan, at least."

"There is some plan," Roiben said, with a twist of his mouth. "Although without knowing what Silarial intends, I know not what good it is."

"You shouldn't have come Ironside yourself. In the mortal world you are vulnerable," said Ellebere, glowering. They crossed the road next to a too-thin mortal pushing an empty stroller and another furiously punching keys on her cell phone. "Dulcamara could have accompanied me. You could have explained what we were to do and sent us off to do it. That's how a proper Unseelie King behaves."

Roiben veered off the sidewalk, ducking under a torn

chain-link fence that singed his fingers and snagged on the cloth of his coat. Ellebere clambered over the top, jumping down with a flourish.

"I'm not sure it's *proper* for a knight to tell a King how to behave," Roiben said. "But come, indulge me a little longer. As you rightly point out, I am a fool and I am about to make a series of very foolish bargains."

The building behind the fence looked like several of the neighboring boarded-up buildings, but this one had a garden on the roof, long tendrils of winter-dead plants hanging over onto the brick sides. On the second floor, the windows were completely missing. Shadows flickered against the inner walls.

Roiben paused. "I would like to say that my time in the Unseelie Court changed my nature. For a long time it was a comfort for me to think so. Whenever I saw my sister, I would recall how I had once been like her, before I was *corrupted*."

"My Lord . . ." Ellebere blanched.

"I am no longer sure if that's true. I wonder if I found my nature instead, where before it was hidden, even from me."

"So what is your nature?"

"Let's find out." Roiben walked across the cracked front steps and knocked against the wood covering the door.

"Will you at least tell me what we're doing here?" Ellebere asked. "Visiting exiles?"

Roiben put a finger to his lips. One of the boards swung open from a nearby window. An ogre stood, framed in the opening, his horns curving back from his head like a ram's and his long brown beard turning to green at the tip. "If it isn't Your Dark Majesty," he said. "I'm guessing you heard about my changeling stock. The best you're like to find. Not carved from logs or sticks, but lovingly crafted from mannequins—some with real glass eyes. Even mortals with a bit of the Sight in them can't see through my work. The Bright Queen herself uses me—but I bet you knew that. Come around the back. I'm eager to make something for you."

Roiben shook his head. "I'm here to make *you* something. An offer. Tell me, how long have you been in exile?"

Kaye rested beside Corny and Luis in a bower of ivy, the soft earth and sweet breeze lulling her to dozing. Night-blooming flowers perfumed the air, dotting the dark with constellations of white petals.

"It's weird." Kaye leaned back against the grass. "It's dark now, but it was night when we got here and it was bright then. I thought it was going to stay eternal day or something."

"That is odd," said Corny.

Luis ripped open his second protein bar and bit into it with a grimace. "I don't know why she's making me stay. This is bullshit. I did everything she told me. Dave is . . ." He stopped.

"Dave is what?" Corny asked.

Luis looked at the wrapper in his hands. "Prone to getting into trouble when I'm not around to stop him."

Kaye watched the petals fall. The human changeling was probably returned to Ellen by now, taking up all Kaye's space in the world she knew. With one quest done and the other impossible, she had no idea what would happen next. She very much doubted the Queen would just let her leave. Keeping Luis at court was both encouraging and discouraging—encouraging because maybe Silarial would let him guide them back at some not-too-distant point, but discouraging because the Seelie Court felt like a web that thrashing would only wrap more tightly around them.

Not that she had anywhere else to go.

Silent hobmen brought a tray of hollowed-out acorns filled with a liquid as clear as water and placed them beside plates of little cakes. Kaye had already eaten three. Lifting a fourth, she offered it to Corny.

"Don't," Luis said when Corny reached for it.

"What?" Corny asked.

"Don't eat or drink anything of theirs. It's not safe."

Music started up somewhere in the distance, and Kaye heard a high voice begin to sing the tale of a nightingale who was really a princess and a princess who was really a pack of cards.

Corny took the cake.

She wanted to put a cautioning hand on Corny's arm, but there was something brittle in his manner that made her hold back. His eyes glittered with banked fire.

He laughed and dropped the confection into his mouth. "There is no safe. Not for me. I don't have True Sight. I can't resist their enchantments, and right now I don't see why I should bother trying."

"Because not trying is stupid," Luis said.

Corny licked his fingers. "Stupid tastes pretty good."

A faerie woman approached, her bare feet silent on the soft earth. "For you," she said, and placed three packets of clothing on the grass.

Kaye reached over to touch the first one. Celery green fabric felt silky under her fingertips.

"Let me guess," Corny said to Luis. "We're not supposed to wear anything of theirs either. Maybe you're going to walk around naked?"

Luis frowned, but Kaye could see that he was embarrassed.

"Stop being a dick," she said, tossing Corny his pile of clothes. Corny grinned as if she'd paid him a compliment.

Ducking behind a bush, she pulled off her T-shirt and slid the dress over her head. She'd been wearing the same camo pants and T-shirt since she'd left Jersey, and she couldn't wait to get out of them. The faerie cloth felt as light as spider silk when she pulled it over her head, and it reminded her of the only other faerie gown she'd worn—the one she'd almost been sacrificed in, the one that had come apart in the sink when she'd tried to wash the blood out of it. Her memories of the averted Tithe were still a shuddersome blur of bedazzlement and terror and Roiben's breath tickling her neck as he'd whispered: *What belongs to you, yet others use it more than you do?*

His name. The name she'd tricked out of him without knowing its worth. The name she'd used to command him and could use still. No wonder his court didn't like her; she could make their King do her bidding.

"I look ridiculous, don't I?" Corny said, stepping out from the branches and causing Kaye to start. He wore a brocaded black and scarlet tunic over black pants, and his feet were bare. He looked handsome and not at all ridiculous. He frowned. "My clothes are soaked, though. At least this is dry."

"You seem like a decadent aristocrat." Kaye turned, letting the thin skirt whirl around her. "I like my dress."

"Nice. All that green really brings out the pink of your eye membranes."

"Shut up." Picking up a twig from the ground, she twisted up her hair with it like she'd done with pencils in school. "Where's Luis?"

Corny pointed with his chin. Turning, Kaye spotted him leaning against a tree, chewing on what was probably the last of the protein bar. Luis glowered as he shoved his hands deeper into the pockets of a long brown jacket, clasped with three buckles at his waist. Kaye's damp purple coat hung from the branch of a tree.

"I guess we're supposed to go to the party like this," Kaye called.

Luis sauntered closer. "They call it a revel."

Corny rolled his eyes. "Let's go."

Kaye headed toward the music, letting her fingers run through the heavy green leaves. She plucked a great white flower down from one of the branches and pulled off one bruised petal after another.

"He loves me," Corny said. "He loves me not."

Kaye scowled and stopped. "That's not what I was doing."

Shapes moved through the trees like ghosts. The laughter and music seemed always a little more distant until suddenly she was among a throng of faeries. Crowds of Folk danced in wide and chaotic circles or diced or simply laughed as though the breeze had carried a joke to their ears only. One faerie woman crouched beside a pool, conversing intently with her reflection, while another stroked the bark of a tree as though it were the fur of a pet.

Kaye opened her mouth to tell Corny something but stopped when her eye was caught by white hair and eyes like silver spoons. Someone threaded through the crowd, cloaked and hooded, but not hooded enough.

There was only one person Kaye knew with eyes like that.

"I'll be right back," she said, already weaving between a damp girl in a dress of woven river grass and a hob on crude mossy stilts.

"Roiben?" she whispered, touching his shoulder. She could feel her heart speeding and she hated it, she hated everything about how she felt at that moment, so absurdly grateful she would have liked to slap herself. "You fucker. You could have told me to go on a quest to bring you an apple from the banquet table. You could have sent me on a quest to tie a braid in your hair."

The figure drew back its hood, and Kaye remembered the other person who would have eyes like Roiben's. His sister, Ethine.

"Kaye," Ethine said. "I had hoped I would happen on you."

Mortified, Kaye tried to back away. She couldn't believe she had just blurted things she wasn't sure, in retrospect, that she wanted even Roiben to hear.

"I have only a moment," Ethine said. "I must bring the Queen a message. But there is something I would know. About my brother."

Kaye shrugged. "We're not exactly speaking."

"He was never cruel when we were children. Now he is brutal and cold and terrible. He will make war on us whom he loved—"

It startled Kaye to think of Roiben as a child. "You grew up in Faerie?"

"I don't have time for—"

"Make time. I want to know."

Ethine looked at Kaye for a long moment, then sighed.

"Roiben and I were brought up in Faerie by a human midwife. She'd been stolen away from her own children and would call us by their names. Mary and Robert. I misliked that. Otherwise, she was very kind."

"What about your parents? Do you know them? Love them?"

"Answer my question, if you please," Ethine said. "My Lady wants him to duel instead of lead the Unseelie Court into battle. It would prevent a war—which the Unseelie Court is too depleted to win—but it would mean his death."

"Your Lady is a bitch," Kaye said before she thought better of it.

Ethine wrung her hands, fingers sliding over one another. "No. She would accept him back. I know she would if he were only to ask her. Why won't he ask her?"

"I don't know," Kaye said.

"You must discern something. He has a fondness for you."

Kaye started to protest, but Ethine cut her off.

"I heard the way you spoke to me when you supposed me to be him. You speak to him as to a friend."

That was not how Kaye would have characterized it. "Look, I did this declaration thing. Where you get a quest. He pretty much told me to fuck off. Whatever you think I know about him or can tell you about him, I just don't think I can."

"I saw you, although I didn't hear the words. I was in the hill that night." Ethine smiled, but her brow furrowed slightly, as though she were puzzling through Kaye's human phrasings. "Still, one must assume the quest was not an apple from a banquet table nor tying a braid in his hair."

Kaye blushed.

"If you thought the King of the Unseelie Court would give you so simple a quest, you must think him besotted."

"Why wouldn't he? He said that I . . ." Kaye stopped, realizing that she shouldn't repeat his words. *You are the only thing I want.* It wasn't safe to say that to Ethine, no matter what had happened.

"A declaration is very serious."

"But . . . I thought it was, like, letting everyone know we were together."

"It is far more immutable than that. There is only ever a single consort, and more often there is none. It joins you both to him and to his court. My brother declared himself once, you know."

"To Silarial," Kaye said, although she hadn't known, not really, not before right then. She remembered Silarial standing in the middle of a human orchard and telling Roiben that he'd proved his love to her satisfaction. How angry Silarial had been when he turned away. "He finished his quest, didn't he?"

"Yes," Ethine said. "He was to stay at the Unseelie Court, as Nicnevin's sworn knight, until the end of the truce. Nicnevin's death ended it. He could be the Bright Lady's consort now if he wanted, if he returned to us. A declaration is a compact and he has fulfilled his side of the bargain."

Kaye looked around at the revelers and felt small and stupid. "You think they should be together, don't you? You wonder what he saw in me—some dirty pixie with bad manners."

"You're clever." The faerie woman did not meet Kaye's gaze. "I imagine he saw that."

Kaye looked down at the scuffed tops of her boots. *Not that clever, after all.*

Ethine looked thoughtful. "In my heart I believe that he

loves Silarial. He blames her for his pain, but my Lady . . . she did not intend for him to suffer so—"

"He doesn't believe that. At best he thinks she didn't care. And I think he very much wanted her to care."

"What quest did he send you on?"

Kaye frowned and tried to keep her voice even. "He told me to bring him a faerie that can tell a lie." It hurt to repeat it, the words a reproach for her thinking he liked her enough to put feelings above appearances.

"An impossible task," Ethine said, still considering.

"So you see," Kaye said, "I'm probably not the best person to answer your questions. I very much wanted him to care too. And he didn't."

"If he doesn't care for you, for her, or for me," Ethine said, "then there is no one else I can think of whom he cares for, save himself."

A blond knight strode toward them, his green armor making his body nearly disappear into the leaves.

"I really do have to go," Ethine said, turning away.

"He doesn't care about himself," Kaye called after her. "I don't think he's cared about himself for a long time."

Corny strolled through the woods, trying to ignore how his heart hammered against his chest. He tried not to make eye contact with any faeries, but he was drawn to their cats' faces, their long noses and bright eyes. Luis's scowl was fixed, no matter what they passed. Even a river full of nixes—cabochons of water beading on their bare skin—did not move him, while it was all Corny could do to look away.

"What do you see?" Corny asked finally, when the silence between them had stretched so long that he'd given up on Luis's speaking first. "Are they beautiful? Is it all illusion?"

"They're not exactly beautiful, but they're dazzling." Luis snorted. "It sucks, when you think of it. They have forever, and what do they do—spend all their time eating and fucking and figuring out complicated ways to kill each other."

Corny shrugged. "I probably would too. I can see myself with bag after bag of Cheetos, downloading porn, and playing *Avenging Souls* for weeks straight if I was immortal."

Luis looked at Corny for a long moment. "Bullshit," he said.

Corny snorted. "Shows what you know."

"Remember that cake you ate before?" said Luis. "All I saw was an old mushroom."

For a moment Corny thought he was joking. "But Kaye ate one."

"She ate, like, *three*." Luis said with such glee that Corny started to laugh, and then they were both laughing together, as easy and silly as if they were going to be friends.

Corny stopped laughing when he realized that he wanted them to be friends. "How come you hate the Folk?"

Luis turned so that his cloudy eye was to Corny, making it hard for Corny to read his expression. "I've had the Sight since I was a little kid. My dad had it and I guess it got passed down to me. It made him crazy; or maybe *they* did." Luis shook his head wearily, as though he were already tired of the story. "When they know you can see them, they fuck with you in other ways. Anyway, my dad got the idea in his head that no one was safe. He shot my mother and my brother; I think he was trying to protect them. If I had been there, he would have shot me, too. My brother made it—barely—and I had to put myself in debt to a faerie to get him better. Can you imagine how things would be without the fey? I can. Normal."

"I should tell you—one of them, a kelpie, killed my sister," Corny said. "He drowned her in the ocean about two months ago. And Nephamael, he did stuff to me, but I still wanted . . ." His words trailed off as he realized that maybe it wasn't okay for him to talk about a guy *that way* in front of Luis.

"What did you want?"

In the clearing ahead, Corny spotted a group of faeries tossing what looked like dice into a large bowl. They were lovely or hideous or both at once. One golden-haired head looked uncomfortably familiar. Adair.

"We have to go," he whispered to Luis. "Before he spots us."

Luis took a quick look over his shoulder as they walked faster and faster. "Which one? What did he do?"

"Cursed me." Corny nodded as they ducked under the curtain of a weeping willow. Neither mentioned that Silarial had promised no harm would come to them. Corny guessed that Luis was as cynical about the parameters of that promise as he was.

A tangle of faeries rested near the trunk of the tree: a black-furred phooka leaning against two green-skinned pixie girls with brownish wings; an elfin boy slumped by a drowsy-looking faerie man. Corny stopped short, surprised. One of them was reciting what seemed to be an epic poem on the subject of worms.

"Sorry," Corny said, turning. "We didn't mean to bother anybody."

"Nonsense," said a pixie. "Come, sit here. You will give us a story too."

"I'm not really—" he started, but a faerie with goat feet pulled him down, laughing. The black dirt felt soft and damp under his hands and knees. The air was heavy with the rich smells of soil and leaf.

"The drake rose up with wings like leather," intoned a faerie. "Its breath set afire all the heather." Perhaps the poem was about *wyrms*.

"Mortals are so interestingly shaped," said the elfin boy, running his fingers over the smoothness of Corny's ears.

"Neil," Luis said.

The phooka reached over to touch the roundness of Corny's cheek, as though fascinated. A faerie boy licked the inside of Corny's arm and he shivered. He was a puppet. They pulled his strings and he danced.

"Neil," Luis said, his voice distant and unimportant. "Snap out of it."

Corny leaned into their caresses, butting his head against a phooka's palm. His skin felt hot and oversensitized. He groaned.

Long fingers tugged at his gloves.

"Don't do that," Corny warned, but he wanted them to. He wanted them to caress every part of him, but he hated himself for wanting it. He thought of his sister, following a dripping kelpie boy off a pier, but even that didn't curb his longing.

"Come, come," said a tall faerie with hair as blue as the feathers of a bird. Corny blinked.

"I'll hurt you," Corny said languorously, and the faeries around him laughed. The laughter wasn't particularly mocking or cruel, but it hurt all the same. It was the amusement of watching a cat threaten the tail of a wolf.

They slid off the gloves. Decayed rubber dust flaked from the tips of his fingers.

"I hurt everything I touch," Corny said dully.

He felt hands at his hips, in his mouth. The soil was cool against his back, soothing when the rest of him was prickling with heat. Without meaning to he reached out for one of the faeries, feeling hair flow across his hands like silk, feeling the shocking warmth of muscled flesh.

His eyes opened with the sudden knowledge of what he was doing. He saw, as from a great distance, the tiny pinholes in cloth where his fingers touched, the blackberry stains of bruises blooming on necks, the brown age spots spreading like smeared dirt across ancient skin. They didn't even seem to notice.

A slow smile spread over his lips. He could hurt them even if he couldn't resist them.

He let the pixies stroke him, arching up and biting at the exposed neck of the elfin boy, inhaling their strange mineral-and-earth scents, letting lust overtake him.

"Neil!" Luis shouted, pulling Corny up by the back of his shirt. Corny stumbled, reaching out to right his balance, and Luis pulled back before Corny's hand could catch him. Corny grabbed Luis's shirt instead, the fabric singeing. Corny stumbled and fell.

"Snap out of it," Luis ordered. He was breathing fast, maybe with fear. "Stand up."

Corny pushed himself onto his knees. Desire made speaking difficult. Even the movement of his own lips was disturbingly like pleasure.

A faerie rested long fingers on Corny's calf. The touch felt like a caress and he sagged toward it.

Warm lips were next to his. "Get up, Neil." Luis spoke softly, against Corny's mouth, as if daring Corny to obey. "Time to get up."

Luis kissed him. Luis, who could do everything that he couldn't, who was smart and sarcastic and the last boy in the world likely to want an awkward geek like Corny. It was dizzying to open his mouth against Luis's. Their tongues slid together for a devastating moment, then Luis pulled back.

"Give me your hands," he said, and Corny obediently held out his wrists. Luis bound them with a shoelace.

"What are you—" Corny tried to make some sense of what was happening, but he was still reeling.

"Thread your fingers together," Luis said in his competent, calm voice and pressed his mouth to Corny's again.

Of course. Luis was trying to save him. Like he saved the man with the mouth full of pennies or Lala with the snaking vines. He knew about cures and poultices and the medicinal value of kisses. He knew how to distract Corny long enough to bind his hands, how to use himself as bait to lure Corny away from danger. He saw right through to Corny's carefully hidden desire, and—worse than using it against him—Luis had used it to rescue him. Exhilaration turned to acid in Corny's stomach.

He stumbled back and staggered toward the curtain of branches. They scraped his face as he passed through.

Luis followed. "I'm sorry," he called after Corny. "I'm—I didn't—I thought—"

"I'm? I didn't? I thought?" Corny shouted at him. His face was suddenly too hot. Then his stomach clenched. He barely had time to turn before retching up chunks of old mushrooms.

Predictably, Luis had been right about the cakes.

An owl's yellow eyes caught the moonlight, making Kaye jump. She'd given up on calling Corny's name and was now just trying to find her way back to the revel. Each time she turned toward the music, it seemed to be coming from another direction.

"Lost?" asked a voice, and she jumped. It was a man with greenish-gold hair and white moth wings that folded across his bare back.

"Kind of," Kaye said. "I don't suppose you could show me the way?"

He nodded and pointed one finger to the left and the other to the right.

"Hilarious." Kaye folded her arms across her chest.

"Both ways would bring you to the revel eventually. One would just take quite a bit longer." He smiled. "Tell me your name and I'll tell you which is better."

"Okay," she said. "Kaye."

"That's not your real name." His smile was teasing. "I bet you don't even know it."

"It's probably safer that way." She looked into a dense copse of trees. Nothing seemed familiar.

"But someone must know it, mustn't they? Someone who gave it to you?"

"Maybe no one gave me a name. Maybe I'm supposed to name myself."

"They say that nameless things change constantly—that names fix them in place like pins. But without a name, a thing isn't quite real either. Maybe you're not a real thing."

"I'm real," Kaye said.

"You know a name that isn't yours, though, don't you? A true name. A silver pin that could stick a King in place."

His tone was light, but the muscles in Kaye's shoulders tensed. "I told Silarial that I wouldn't use it. I won't."

"Really?" He cocked his head to the side, looking oddly like a bird. "And you wouldn't trade it for another life? A mortal mother? A feckless friend?"

"Are you threatening me? Is Silarial threatening me?" She stepped back from him.

"Not yet," he said with a laugh.

"I'll find my own way back," she mumbled, and headed off, refusing to be lost.

The trees were heavy with impossible summer leaves, and the earth was warm and fragrant, but the woods were as still as stone. Even the wind seemed dead. Kaye walked on, faster and faster, until she came to a stream pitted with rocks. A squat figure crouched near the water, the brambles and branches of her hair making her look like a barren bush.

"You!" Kaye gasped. "What are you doing here?"

"I am sure," the Thistlewitch said, her black eyes shining, "you have better questions for me than that."

"I don't want any more riddles," Kaye said, and her voice broke. She sat down on the wet bank, not caring about the water soaking her skirt. "Or eggshells or quests."

The Thistlewitch reached out a long, lanky arm to pat Kaye with fingers that felt as rough as wood. "Poor little pixie. Come and rest your head on my shoulder."

"I don't even know which side you're on." Kaye groaned, but she scooted over and leaned against the faerie's familiar bulk. "I'm not sure how many sides there are. I mean, is this like a piece of paper with two sides or like one of those weird dice that Corny has with twenty sides? And if there are really twenty sides, then is *anyone* on my side?"

"Clever girl," the Thistlewitch said approvingly.

"Come on, that made no sense. Isn't there *anything* you can tell me? About anything?"

"You already know what you need and you need what you know."

"But that's a riddle!" Kaye protested.

"Sometimes the riddle is the answer," the Thistlewitch replied, but she patted Kaye's shoulder all the same.

Fair as the moon and joyful as the light;
Not wan with waiting, not with sorrow dim;
Not as she is, but was when hope shone bright;
Not as she is, but as she fills his dream.
—Christina Rossetti, "In an Artist's Studio"

In the darkness of early dawn, Corny woke to distant bells and the thunderous pounding of hooves. He rolled over, disoriented, sore, and filled with sudden panic. Somehow he'd gotten his leather jacket back on, but the edges of the sleeves looked tattered. His wrists ached and when he inadvertently pulled against the shoelace that tied them, it made them hurt more. His mouth tasted sour.

Realizing he was still in the Seelie Court explained the dread and the discomfort. But when he saw Luis, wrapped in Kaye's purple coat, cheek pillowed against the burl of a nearby blackthorn tree, he remembered the rest. He remembered what an idiot he'd been.

And the agonizing softness of Luis's lips.

And the way Luis had brushed Corny's hair off his face while he puked in the grass.

And the way that Luis had only been being kind.

Shame made his face hot and his eyes burn. His throat closed up at the thought of actually having to talk about it. He rolled onto his knees and stood awkwardly, physical distance the only thing that calmed him. Maybe Kaye was in the direction of the noise. If he could find her, Luis might not say anything. He might act like it had never happened. Corny threaded his way alone through the trees, until he spotted the procession.

Silver-shod horses raced past, their manes streaming and eyes glittering, the faces of the faeries on their backs covered by helms. The first rider was arrayed in dark red armor that seemed to flake like old paint, the next in white as leathery as a snake's egg. Then a black steed galloped toward Corny, only to rear up, front hooves dancing in the air. This rider's armor was as black and shining as crow feathers.

Corny stepped away. The rough bark of a tree trunk scraped his back.

The black-clad rider drew a curved blade that glittered like rippling water.

Corny stumbled, terror making him stupid. The horse trotted closer, its breath hot on Corny's face. He threw up his tied hands in warding.

The sword cut through the shoelace binding his wrists. Corny cried out, falling in the dirt.

The rider sheathed the sword and pulled off a ridged helm.

"Cornelius Stone," Roiben said.

Corny laughed in hysterical relief. "Roiben! What are you doing here?"

"I came to bargain with Silarial," Roiben said. "I saw Sorrowsap on the other side of the lake. Who bound your hands? Where's Kaye?"

"This is, um, for my own good," Corny said, holding up his wrists.

Roiben frowned, leaning forward in the saddle. "Favor me with the story."

Reaching up, Corny touched one of his fingers to a low green leaf. It curled, turning gray. "Pretty nasty curse, huh? Tying me up with the shoelace was supposed to keep me from touching anyone by accident. At least I think that was what it was for—I don't remember everything about last night."

Roiben shook his head, unsmiling. "Leave this place. As quickly as you can. Sorrowsap will get you safely out of the Bright Court lands. Nothing is as it seems now, apparently, not even you. Kaye—she ought—" He paused. "Tell me she's well."

Corny wanted to tell Roiben that he could shove his bullshit pretense of caring up his ass, but he was still a little shaken by the sword so recently swung at his head. "What do you care?" he asked instead.

"I care." Roiben closed his eyes, as though willing himself calm. "Whatever you think of me, get her out of here." He leaned back in the saddle and twitched the reins. The horse stepped back.

"Wait," Corny said. "There's something I've been wanting to ask you: What's it like being a king? What's it like finally being so powerful that no one can control you?" It was sort of a taunt, sure, but Corny really wanted the answer.

Roiben laughed hollowly. "I'm sure I wouldn't know."

"Fine. Don't tell me."

Roiben tilted his head. Corny was disconcerted to suddenly have the faerie Lord's full attention. When he spoke, his voice was grave. "The more powerful you become, the more others will find ways to master you. They'll do it through those you love and through those you hate; they will find the bit and the bridle that fits your mouth and makes you yield."

"So there's no way to be safe?"

"Be invisible, perhaps. Be worthless."

Corny shook his head. "Doesn't work."

"Make them yield first," Roiben said, and the half smile on his lips wasn't quite enough to render the suggestion frivolous. "Or be dead. No one can yet master the dead." He replaced his helm. "Now get Kaye and go."

With a flick of the reins Roiben wheeled the horse around and rode down the path, dust clouding behind the shining hooves.

Corny threaded his way back through the woods, only to find Adair leaning against a tree.

"You're an ill fit among such beauty," said the faerie, pushing back butter blond hair. "It's a mistake you humans often make—being so ugly."

Corny thought of Roiben's words. *Make them yield first.*

"This was a pretty cool gift," he said, letting his hand trail across the bark of a nearby oak, blackening the trunk. "The curse. I should thank you."

Adair stepped back.

"You must have been really pissed off. The curse even withers fey flesh." Corny smiled. "Now I just have to decide what's the best way to express my gratitude. Whatever do you think Miss Manners would advise?"

Kaye tried to keep her face expressionless as Roiben ducked under the canopy of branches that formed Silarial's chamber. His silver hair poured over his shoulders like mercury, but it was sweat-darkened at his neck.

Longing twisted in her gut along with a terrible, giddy anticipation she couldn't seem to quash. The human glamour Silarial had covered her with felt tight and heavy. She wanted to call out to him, to touch his sleeve. It was easy to imagine that there had been some misunderstanding, that if she could just speak to him for a moment, everything would be like it had been before. Of course, she was supposed to stand near the trunk of the massive willow and keep her eyes on the floor the way the human attendants did.

The glamour had seemed clever at first, when Silarial had suggested it. Kaye wasn't supposed to approach Roiben until she'd succeeded in her quest. Since she hadn't, the glamour would make like she wasn't there. Kaye was just supposed to wait until he and Silarial were done talking, and then she was supposed to try to convince him to go along with the Seelie Queen's plan. If she agreed with it, of course. Which she was pretty sure she wouldn't, but at least she would get the smug satisfaction of pissing him off.

It had sounded like a better scenario than it felt now as she stood there, watching him through her lashes as if they were strangers.

Silarial looked up lazily from her cushions. "Ethine tells me that you will not agree to my conditions."

"I do not think you expected me to, m—" He stopped suddenly, and Silarial laughed.

"You nearly called me 'my Lady,' didn't you? That's a habit in need of breaking."

He looked down and his mouth twisted. "Indeed. You have caught me being foolish."

"Nonsense. I find it charming." Smiling, she swept her hand toward where Kaye stood among Silarial's attendants. "You must be parched for a taste of the changeless lands of your youth."

A willowy human in a simple blue shift stepped out of the line as if by some signal Kaye could not discern. The servant leaned into a copper bowl on the table as if she were bobbing for apples. Then, kneeling in front of Roiben, she bent backward and opened her mouth. The surface of the wine shimmered between her teeth.

Kaye was reminded suddenly and terribly of Janet drowning, of how her lips had been parted just like that, of how her mouth had looked filled with seawater. Kaye pressed her fingernails into her palms.

"Drink," said the Bright Lady, and her eyes were full of laughter.

Roiben knelt down and kissed the girl's mouth, cupping her head and tilting her so that he might swallow. "Decadent," he said, settling back onto the cushions. He looked amused and far too relaxed, his long limbs spread out as though he were in his own parlor. "Do you know what I really miss, though? Roasted dandelion tea."

Silarial petted the girl's hair before she sent her back to fetch a mouthful from another bowl. Kaye reminded herself not to stare, to look up only through her lashes, to keep her face carefully neutral. She dug her fingernails deeper into her skin.

"So tell me," said Silarial. "What conditions do you propose?"

"You must risk something if you wish me to risk everything."

"The Unseelie Court has no hope of winning a battle. You ought to take whatever I offer and be grateful for it."

"Nonetheless," Roiben said. "If I lose the duel against your champion, you will become sovereign of the Unseelie Court, and I will be dead. Quite a lot for me to wager against your offer of transient peace, but I do not ask for equal stakes. If I win, I only ask that you agree to make Ethine Queen in your place."

For a moment Kaye thought she saw Silarial's eyes shine with triumph. "Only? And if I don't agree?"

Roiben leaned back on the cushions. "Then war, winnable or no."

Silarial narrowed her eyes, but there was a smile at the corners of her mouth. "You have changed from the knight that I knew."

He shook his head. "Do you recall my eagerness to prove myself to you? Pathetically grateful for even the smallest regard. How tedious you must have found me."

"I admit I find you more interesting now, bargaining for the salvation of those whom you despise."

Roiben laughed, and the sound of it—thick with self-loathing—chilled Kaye.

"But perhaps you despise me even more than they?" Silarial asked.

He looked down at the fingers of his left hand, watching them pluck at the onyx clasps of his other cuff. "I think of the way I longed for you, and it makes me sick." He looked up at her. "But that doesn't mean I've stopped longing. I yearn for home."

Silarial shook her head. "You told Ethine you would never step down from being Lord of the Night Court. You would never reconsider your position. You would never serve me. Is that still true?"

"I won't be as I once was." Roiben gestured to Kaye and to the other girls standing against the wall. Mute servants. "No matter what I long for."

"You have said that nothing about me tempts you," Silarial said. "What of it?"

He smiled. "I told Ethine to tell you that. I never said it."

"And is it so?"

He stood, walked the short distance to where Silarial reclined, and knelt before her. He lifted his hand to her cheek, and Kaye could see his hand tremble. "I am tempted," he said.

The Bright Queen leaned closer and pressed her mouth to his. The first kiss was short and careful and chaste, but the second was not. Roiben's hands cupped her skull and bent her back, kissing her like he wanted to break her in half. When he drew back from Silarial, her lip bled and her eyes were dark with desire.

Kaye's face flamed hot and she could feel her heartbeat even in her cheeks. It seemed to her that Roiben's hand's shaking as he reached for Silarial was worse than the kisses, worse than anything he had said or could say. She knew what it felt like to tremble like that before touching someone—desire so acute that it became despair.

Kaye forced herself to look at the dirt, to concentrate on the winding roots next to her slipper. She tried not to think about anything. She didn't know how much she'd been hoping that he still loved her, until she felt how much it hurt to realize he didn't.

A rustle of clothes made Kaye look up automatically, but it was only Silarial rising from her cushions. Roiben's eyes were wary.

"You must want me to agree to your terms very much," the Bright Queen said lightly, but her voice was unsteady. She brushed a strand of hair away from his face.

"Ethine would very probably give you back your crown were she to win it," Roiben replied.

"If you should defeat my champion . . . ," Silarial began, then paused, looking down at him. She brought one white hand to his cheek. "If you should defeat my champion, you will regret it."

He half smiled.

"But I will grant you your boon. Ethine will be Queen if you win. See that you do not win." She walked to the bowls of liquids, and Kaye saw Silarial's face reflected in all their surfaces. "Of course, all this negotiating matters not at all if you will merely join me. Leave the court of those you detest. Together we can end this war today. You would be my consort—"

"No," he said. "I told you that I won't—"

"There is someone here with the means to convince you."

He stood suddenly, whirling toward the wall of servant girls. His gaze shifted across them and stopped on her. "Kaye." His voice sounded anguished.

Kaye looked around, gritting her teeth.

"How did you guess?" Silarial asked.

Roiben walked to Kaye and put his hand on her arm. She jumped, shifting away from his touch. "I should have guessed sooner. Very clever to glamour her so thoroughly."

Kaye felt sick thinking of the way he'd kissed Silarial. She wanted to slap him. She wanted to spit in his face.

"But how did you choose her from among my other maidens?"

He took Kaye's hand and turned it over so that the Queen could see the reddened half-moons where Kaye's nails had dug into her flesh. "It was that, really. I don't know anyone else with that particular nervous habit."

Kaye looked up at him and saw only a strange human face reflected in his eyes.

She snatched her hand away, rubbing it against her skirt as if she could rub off his touch. "You're not supposed to see me until I can solve your stupid riddle."

"Yes, I deserve whatever scorn you heap on me," he said, voice soft. "But what are you doing here? It's not safe. I told Corny—"

His lips were still kiss-reddened and it was hard not to concentrate on them. "This is where I belong, isn't it? This is where I came from. The other Kaye is home now, like she always should have been. With her mother, Ellen."

He looked momentarily furious. "What did Silarial make you promise for that?"

"It must suck to love her, since you don't trust her at all," Kaye said, tasting bile on her tongue.

There was a silence, in which he looked at her with a kind of terrible desperation, as though he wanted very much to speak, but could not find the words.

"It doesn't matter what he thinks of me or of you," Silarial said, coming close to where Kaye stood. Her words were soft, spoken with great care. "Use his name. End the war."

Kaye smiled. "I could, you know. I really, really could."

He looked very grave, but his voice was as soft as the Bright Queen's. "Will you rule over me, Kaye? Shall I bow to a new mistress and fear the lash of her tongue?"

Kaye said nothing. Her anger was a live thing inside of her, twisting in her gut. She wanted to hurt him, to humiliate him, to pay him back for everything she felt.

"What if I promise that I won't use the name, won't even repeat it?" Silarial said. "He would be yours alone to command. Your toy. I would just advise you how to use him."

Kaye still said nothing. She was afraid of what would come out if she opened her mouth.

Roiben paled. "Kaye, I . . ." He closed his eyes. *"Don't,"* he said, but she could hear despair in his voice. It made her even angrier. It made her want to live down to his expectations.

Silarial spoke so close to Kaye's ear that it made her shiver. "You must command him, you know. If not, I would threaten your mother, that human boy of yours, your changeling sister. You would be persuaded. Don't feel badly about giving in now."

"Say you won't repeat it," Kaye said. "Not just 'if I promise,' the real oath."

Silarial's voice was still a whisper. "I will not speak Roiben's true name. I will not bid him with it, nor will I repeat it to any other."

"Rath Roiben," Kaye said. He flinched and his hand went to the hilt at his belt, but it stayed there. His eyes remained shut. *Rye*. The word was poised on her lips. *Rath Roiben Rye*.

"Riven," Kaye finished. "Rath Roiben Riven, do as I command."

He looked up at her, quickly, eyes widening with hope.

She could feel her smile grow cruel. He'd better do what she said, right then. If he didn't, Silarial would know that Kaye had spoken the wrong name.

"Lick the Queen of the Seelie Court's hand, Rath Roiben Riven," she said. "Lick it like the dog you are."

He went down on one knee. He almost rose before he remembered himself and drew his tongue over Silarial's palm. Shame colored his face.

She laughed and wiped her hand against her gown. "Lovely. Now what else shall we make him do?"

Roiben looked up at Kaye.

She smirked.

"I deserve this," he whispered. "But, Kaye, I—"

"Tell him to be silent," said Silarial.

"Silence," Kaye said. She felt giddy with hate.

Roiben lowered his eyes and went quiet.

"Command him to pledge his loyalty to me, to be forever a servant of the Seelie Court."

Kaye sucked in her breath. That she would not do.

Roiben's face was grim.

Kaye shook her head, but her fury was replaced with fear. "I'm not done with him yet."

The Bright Queen frowned.

"Rath Roiben Riven," Kaye said, trying to think of some command she could give to stall for time. Trying to think of a way to twist Silarial's words or make some objection that the Bright Queen might believe. "I want you to—"

A scream tore through the air. Silarial took a few steps from them, distracted by the sound.

"Kaye—" Roiben said.

A group of faeries pushed their way under the canopy, Ethine among them. "My Lady," a boy said, then stopped as if stunned at the sight of the Lord of the Night Court on his knees. "There has been a death. Here."

"What?" The Queen glanced toward Roiben.

"The human—" one of them began.

"Corny!" Kaye yelled, pushing through the curtain of willow branches, forgetting Silarial, the commands, anything but Corny. She raced in the direction that others were going, ran toward where a crowd gathered and Talathain pointed a weird crossbow. At Cornelius.

The ground where he sat had withered in two circles around his hands, tiny violets turning brown and dry, toadstools rotting, the soil itself paling beneath his fingers. Beside Corny the body of Adair rested, a knife still in his hand, his neck and part of his face shriveled and dark. His dead eyes stared into the sunless sky.

Kaye stopped abruptly, so relieved that Corny was alive that she almost collapsed.

Luis stood nearby, his face pale. Her purple coat hung from his shoulders. "Kaye," he said.

"What happened?" she asked, realizing that Corny still wasn't safe. Kneeling by the body, Kaye slipped Adair's knife up her sleeve, the hilt hidden by the loose cradle of her hand.

"Neil killed him," Luis said finally, his voice low. "The Seelie fey don't like to see death—especially not here, in their court. It offends them, makes them remember that even they will eventually—"

Corny laughed suddenly. "I bet he didn't see that coming. Not from me."

"We have to get out of here," Kaye said. "Corny! Get up!"

Corny looked up at her. He sounded strange, distant. "I don't think they're going to let me leave."

Kaye glanced at the gathering crowd of fey. Silarial stood by Talathain. Ethine watched as Roiben spoke with Ellebere and Ruddles. Some of the Folk pointed at the body in disbelief, others ripped at their garments and wailed.

"You promised Corny would be safe," Kaye told the Queen. She was stalling for time.

"He *is* safe," said Silarial. "While one of my people lies dead."

"We're going." Kaye walked away from Corny. Her hands were trembling and she could feel the sharp edge of the knife against her skin. Just a few more steps.

"Let them go," Roiben said to Silarial.

Talathain turned his crossbow toward Roiben. "Do not presume to command her."

Roiben laughed and drew out his sword, slowly, as if daring Talathain to fire. His eyes were full of rage, but he seemed relieved, as though the clarity of his hate pushed back his shame. "Come," he said. "Let us make another corpse between us two."

Talathain dropped the crossbow and reached for his own blade. "Long have I waited for this moment."

They circled each other as the Folk moved back, giving them room.

"Let me fight him," said Dulcamara, dressed all in red, her hair in looping ropes stitched together with black thread.

Roiben smiled and shook his head. Turning toward Kaye, he mouthed, "Go," then swung at Talathain.

"Stop them," Silarial said to Kaye. "Order him to stop."

Advancing and retreating, they seemed partners in a swift and deadly dance. Their swords crashed together.

Ethine took a step toward her brother and then halted. She turned pleading eyes to Kaye.

"Roiben," Kaye yelled. "Stop."

He went still as stone. Talathain lowered his weapon with what appeared to be regret.

Silarial walked up to Roiben. She ran her hand over his cheek and then looked back at Kaye. "If you want to leave here with your friends," Silarial said, "you know what you must order him to do."

Kaye nodded her head, walking toward them, her heart beating so hard that it felt like a weight inside her. She stopped behind Ethine. There had to be a way to get Luis and Corny and herself free before Silarial figured out that Kaye hadn't used Roiben's true name. She needed something she could bargain with, something she would be willing to trade.

Kaye put Adair's knife to Ethine's neck.

She heard her name echo in half a dozen shocked voices.

"Corny! Get up! Luis, help him!" She swallowed hard. "We're leaving right now."

Silarial was no longer smiling. She looked stunned, her lips white. "There are things I could—"

"No!" Kaye shouted. "If you touch my mother, I'll cut Ethine. If you touch Luis's brother, I'll cut Ethine. I am going to walk out of here with Luis and Corny, and if you don't want her hurt, you and all of yours are just going to let me."

"My Lady," Ethine gasped.

Talathain pointed his sword in Kaye's direction, twisting it like a promise.

"Let the pixie and the humans through," Silarial said. "Although I think she will regret it."

With a wave of Silarial's hand, the glamour was gone. Kaye found herself drinking the air deeply, suddenly tasting the green of the plants and smelling the rich dark earth and the worms crawling through it. She had forgotten the dizzying sensations of being a faerie and the terrible weight of such a powerful glamour; it had been like filling her ears with cotton. She nearly stumbled, but she pushed her nails into her hand and stayed still.

"Not with my sister," Roiben said. "Not my sister, Kaye. I won't let you."

"Rath Roiben Riv—" Kaye started.

"That's not my name," he said, and there were gasps from the other fey.

Kaye looked him in the eye and put every bit of fury into her voice. "You can't stop me." She pushed Ethine toward Luis and Cornelius. "Try, and I *will* command you."

A muscle in his jaw twitched. His eyes were as cold as lead.

They marched past, making their way to the edge of the island. As they climbed into the ice boat they had beached among the reeds, Ethine made a soft sound that was not quite a sob.

They paddled to the far, snow-covered shore, past a young man standing as stiffly as a Christmas nutcracker, his gold and red scarf tucked into a toggle coat. His lips and cheeks were blushed with blue, and frost covered his chin like stubble. His pale, sunken eyes still stared at the waves. Even in death, he waited to serve the Seelie Queen.

Kaye could never run far enough or fast enough to escape them all.

10

The car was still parked in the ditch by the side of the high-way, the windows on the passenger side coated with spattered slush that had frozen to ice. The door made a cracking sound when Luis opened it.

"Get in," Kaye told Ethine. Kaye's heart beat like a rattle and her face was as cold as her fingers; all the heat in her body had been eaten up by panic.

Ethine looked at the car dubiously. "The iron," she said.

"Why aren't they following us?" Luis asked, looking back over his shoulder.

"They are," said a voice.

Kaye shrieked, raising the blade automatically.

Sorrowsap stepped out onto the road, black clothes loose and boots crunching on the gravel as he strode toward them.

"My Lord Roiben was displeased with me for letting you go across the water." There was a threat in his voice. "He will be even more displeased if you do not depart immediately. Go. I will hold whatever comes. When you cross the border into the Unseelie Court, you will be safe."

"You must see that it would be madness to keep me against my will," Ethine said, touching Kaye's arm. "You are away from the court. Allow me to return and I will speak on your behalf. I will swear to it."

Luis shook his head. "What is going to keep them from hurting my brother if we let you go? I'm sorry. We can't. We all have people we love that we have to protect."

"Do not let them take me," Ethine said, throwing herself to her knees and taking Sorrowsap's bony hand. "My brother would want me returned to my people. He seeks me, even now. If you are loyal to him, you will give me succor."

"So I guess Roiben's not such a villain anymore?" Kaye asked her. "Now he's your loving brother?"

Ethine pressed her mouth into a thin line.

"I have no orders to help you," Sorrowsap said, pulling his fingers from Ethine's grip. "And little desire to help anyone. I do as I am commanded."

Ethine rose slowly and Luis grabbed her arm. "I know that you are a great lady and all that, but you have to get in the car now."

"My brother will hate you if you hurt me," she told Kaye, her eyes narrowed.

Kaye felt sick, thinking of the last, terrible look he had given her. "Come on, we're just going on a road trip. We can play I Spy."

"In. Now," Luis told her.

Ethine climbed into the backseat and skooched over the cracked vinyl and the crumbling foam. Her face was stiff with fear and fury.

Corny drew a swirl along the hood that turned almost immediately to rust. He didn't seem to notice that he was standing barefoot on snow. "I'm a murderer."

"No, you're not," said Luis.

"If I'm not a murderer," asked Corny, "how come I keep killing people?"

"There's plastic bags here," said Kaye. She reached into the well of the backseat and fished them out from the piles of empty cola cans and fast-food wrappers. "Put these on until we get gloves."

"Oh, very well," Corny said with a lunatic half smile. "Don't want to wither the steering wheel."

"You're not driving," Luis said.

Kaye wrapped Corny's hands in the bags and steered him to the passenger side. She jumped into the back, beside Ethine.

Luis started the car and, finally, they were moving. Kaye looked through the rear window, but no faeries seemed to follow. They did not fly overhead, did not swarm down and stop the vehicle.

The hot, iron-soaked air of the heater dulled Kaye's thoughts, but she forced her eyes open. Each time dizzy slumber threatened to overtake her, terror that the Host were almost upon them startled her awake. She kept her eyes on the windows, but it seemed to her that the clouds were dark with wings and all the woods they passed were full of hungry wet mouths.

"What are we going to do now?" Luis asked.

Kaye thought of Roiben's long fingers knotted in Silarial's red hair, his hands pulling her down to him.

"Where are we even going?" Corny asked. "Where's this safe place that we're in such a rush to get to? I mean, I guess we have a better chance with Roiben than Silarial, but what happens when we give Ethine back? Do you really think Silarial's going to leave us alone? I killed Adair. I *killed* him."

Kaye paused. The enormity of how isolated and helpless they were settled into her bones. They had taken a hostage that both of the courts wanted back, and Silarial needed something that only Kaye knew. There was no secret weapon this time, no mysterious faerie knight to keep her safe. There was only a crappy old car and two humans who hadn't deserved to get dragged into this. "I don't know," she said.

"No such thing as safe," said Corny. "Just like I said. Not for us. Not ever."

"There's no safe for anyone," Luis said. Kaye was surprised at how calm he sounded.

Ethine moaned in the backseat.

Luis glanced at her in the rearview mirror.

"It's the iron," said Corny.

Luis nodded uncomfortably. "I knew it bothered them."

Corny smirked. "Yeah, watch out. She might puke on you."

"Shut up," Kaye said. "She's sick. She's not even as used to it as I am."

"'Last exit in New York,'" Corny read off the sign. "I guess we can pull over at the next rest stop. Get her some air. We should be in Unseelie land by now. "

Kaye scanned the skies behind them, but there was still no sign that they were being followed. Were they going to be bargained with? Shot with arrows that would burrow into their hearts? Were Silarial and Roiben working together to get Ethine back? They had left the map of what Kaye knew, and she felt as though they were about to fall off the edge of the world.

A gust of fresh, icy wind woke her from her miserable reverie.

They had pulled into a gas station and Luis was getting out. He headed toward the station while Corny started filling the tank. His bag-covered hands slipped, thin plastic tearing. He staggered back in surprise, gasoline splashing the side of the car.

Kaye stumbled out. The air was heady with vapors.

"What happened back there?" she asked him quietly. "You killed Adair? Why?"

"You don't think I just did it because I could? I killed Nephamael, didn't I?" Corny shoved the nozzle back into the car.

"Nephamael was already dying," Kaye said. Her head hurt. "Because of me, remember?"

He pushed bag-covered fingers through his hair, hard, like he wanted to tear it out. Then he held his hand out in front of him. "It all happened so fast. Adair was talking to me, being scary, and I was trying to be scary back. Then Luis walked up. Adair grabbed him—he was going on about how Silarial made no promise about *Luis* being unharmed. He said he should put out Luis's other eye, and he put his thumb right up against it. And I just—I just grabbed his wrist and shoved him. Then I grabbed his throat. Kaye, when I was in middle school, I got my ass kicked pretty regularly. But the curse—I didn't have to press very hard. I just held on to him and then he was dead."

"I'm so—" Kaye started.

Corny shook his head. "Don't say you're sorry. I'm not sorry."

She leaned her head against his shoulder, breathing in the familiar smell of his sweat. "Then I'm not sorry either," she said.

Luis walked back from the small store with a pair of lemon yellow dishwashing gloves and flip-flops. Kaye looked down and realized that Corny's feet were still bare.

"Put these on," Luis told him, avoiding looking either of them in the face. "There's a diner across the street. We could get something to eat. I called Dave and he's going to hide out with a friend in Jersey. I told him to get out of Seelie territory—even if the city is mostly just full of exiles."

"You should call your mom," said Corny, pulling out his cell. "Battery's dead. I can charge it in the diner."

"We have to get some other clothes at least," said Kaye. "We're all dressed crazy. We're going to stand out."

Luis peered into the car. Ethine watched him with her knife gray eyes.

"Can't you guys use glamour?" he asked.

Kaye shook her head. The world swam a little. "I feel like shit. Maybe a little."

"I don't think some T-shirts are going to make up for the fact that you're green," Luis said, turning around. "Get her out. We'll take our chances with the diner crowd."

"Do not presume that you may give orders." Ethine stepped carefully onto the asphalt and immediately turned to vomit on the wheels. Corny grinned.

"Watch her—she could try to run," Luis said.

"I don't know." Corny frowned. "She looks pretty sick."

"Wait a minute," Kaye said. She leaned over to Luis and reached into the pocket of the purple plaid coat he wore—her coat. She pulled out fuzzy handcuffs lined in fur. After slapping one on Ethine's wrist, she clasped the other one onto her own.

"What is this?" Ethine objected.

Luis laughed out loud. "You do *not.*" He looked at Corny. "She does *not* have a pair of handcuffs handy in case she happens to take a prisoner."

"What can I say?" Corny asked.

Ethine shivered. "Everything reeks of filth and iron and rot."

Corny shouldered off his leather jacket and Ethine took it gratefully, sliding it on over her free arm. "Yeah, Jersey pretty much blows," he said.

Kaye concentrated, hiding her wings, changing her eyes and the color of her skin. That was all she had energy for. The car ride and the Queen's ripping off of the human glamour had left her sapped. Ethine had not even bothered to make her own ears less pointed or her features less elegant or inhuman. As they climbed the steps, Kaye considered saying something, but bit her tongue when Ethine shrunk back from the metal on the door. If Kaye felt bad, Ethine probably felt worse.

The outside of the diner was faux stone and beige stucco with a sign on the door proclaiming TRUCKERS WELCOME. Someone had sloppily painted the windows with reindeer, Santas, and large wreaths. Inside, they were seated without a second glance by a stout older woman with carefully groomed white hair. Ethine stared at her lined face with undisguised fascination.

Kaye slid into the booth, letting the familiar smell of brewed coffee wash over her. She didn't care that it stank of iron. This was the world she knew. It almost made her feel safe.

A cute Latino boy handed them their laminated menus and poured their water.

Luis drank it gratefully. "I'm starving. I ate my last protein bar yesterday."

"Do you really have more power over us if we eat your food?" Corny asked Ethine.

"We do," Ethine said.

Luis gave her a dark look.

"So I—" Corny started, but then he opened his menu, hid his face, and didn't finish.

"It fades," Ethine said. "Eat something else. That helps."

"I have to make a call," Kaye told Corny.

Corny leaned down to plug the cord into an outlet sitting underneath a painting of happy trees and a moose. He sat back up and handed the slim phone to Kaye. "As long as you don't jerk it out of the wall, you can use it while it's charging."

She dialed her mother's number, but the phone just rang and rang. No voice mail. No answering machine. Ellen didn't believe in them.

"Mom's not home," Kaye said. "We need a plan."

Corny put his menu down. "How can we make a plan when we don't know what Silarial's scheming?"

"We need to do something," Kaye said. "First. Now."

"Why?" Luis asked.

"The reason that Silarial wanted me to come to the Seelie Court is because I know Roiben's true name."

Ethine looked over at Kaye, eyes wide.

"Oh," Corny said. "Right. Shit."

"I managed to deceive her about what his name is for a while, but now she knows I played her."

"What a typical pixie you are," Ethine said.

She might have said more, but at that moment the waitress walked over, taking her pen and pad out of her apron. "What can I get you kids? We have an eggnog pancake special still going."

"Coffee, coffee, coffee, and coffee," Corny said, pointing around the table.

"A strawberry milkshake," said Luis. "Mozzarella sticks and a deluxe cheeseburger."

"How would you like that cooked?" the waitress asked.

Luis looked at her strangely. "Whatever. Just on a plate in front of me."

"Steak and eggs," Corny said. "Meat, burnt. Eggs, over easy. Dry rye toast."

"Chicken souvlaki on a pita," Kaye said. "Extra tzatziki sauce for my fries, please."

Ethine looked at them all blankly and then looked at the menu in front of her. "Blueberry pie," she said finally.

"You kids been to that Renaissance Faire up in Tuxedo?" the woman asked.

"You guessed it," said Corny.

"Well, you all look real cute." She smiled as she gathered their menus.

"How horrible to be dying all your life," Ethine said with a shudder as the waitress walked away.

"You're closer to death than she is," Luis told her. He poured a line of sugar on the table, licked his finger, and ran it through the powder.

"You're not going to kill me." Ethine lifted her cuffed hand. "You don't know what to do. You're all just frightened children."

Kaye tugged abruptly against the other end of the cuff, pulling Ethine's hand back down to the vinyl-covered booth seat. "I heard something about a duel. Silarial agreed to give you her kingdom if Roiben won. What's up with that?"

Ethine turned to look at Kaye in confusion. "She agreed?"

"Well, maybe she got distracted during all the kissing that preceded it."

"Whoa," Corny said. "What?"

Kaye nodded. "It wasn't like he had her right there in front of me, but there was some definite pitching and catching of woo." Her voice sounded rough.

Ethine smiled down at the table. "He *kissed* her. That pleases me. He does have feelings for her, even still."

Kaye tried to think of an excuse to tug on the cuff again.

"Back to what you know about the duel," prompted Luis.

Ethine shrugged. "It is to take place in neutral territory—Hart Island off of New York—a day from tonight. At best, my brother could win the Unseelie Court a few years of peace, perhaps long enough to build up a larger legion of fey or a better strategy. At worst, he could lose his lands and his life."

"Doesn't sound worth it," Corny said.

"No, wait," said Kaye, shaking her head. "The problem is that it sounds totally worth it. It sounds *possible* for him to win. I bet Roiben thinks he can beat Talathain. Silarial didn't want them to go at it today, but Roiben didn't seem to mind. Why would she give him even a chance to win?"

Luis shrugged. "Maybe it's no fun if it's too easy to take over the Unseelie Court?"

"Maybe she's got some other plan," Kaye said. "Some way to give Talathain an advantage."

"What about cold iron bullets?" Corny said. "Fits in with her use of that big rig. She's on a whole mortal tech kick."

"Is any bullet really more terrible than an arrowhead that burrows through your skin to strike your heart?" Ethine asked. "No mortal weapon will kill him."

Luis nodded. "Then Roiben's name. That's the most obvious, right? Then the whole duel becomes a smoke screen because she can force him to lose."

"Whatever my Queen's plan, I imagine it is beyond your ken," said Ethine.

The waitress came and poured coffee into their cups. Corny raised his in one yellow-gloved hand. "Here's to us." He looked at Ethine. "Brought to this table by friendship or fate—or because you're a prisoner—and here's to the sweet balm of coffee, by the grace of which we shall accomplish the task before us and ken what we need to ken. Okay?"

The three of them lifted their cups of coffee and clinked them together. Kaye clinked her cup against Ethine's.

Corny closed his eyes in bliss as he took his first sip. Then he sighed and looked over at them. "Okay, so what were we talking about?"

"The plan," Kaye said. "The plan we don't have."

"It's hard to come up with a scheme to thwart some other scheme you don't even know about," Luis said.

"This is what I think we should do," said Corny. "Lay low until after the duel. We surround ourselves with iron and keep her for insurance." He gestured toward Ethine with his coffee spoon, and a few drops spattered on the table. One hit the faerie woman's gown, soaking into the strange fabric. "So, Kaye, if you're the linchpin of Silarial's plan, the plan won't happen. The duel will go fairly. May the best monster win."

"I don't know," said Kaye. The waitress set a steaming plate in front of her. Her mouth watered at the smell of the cooked onions. Across the table, Luis picked up a mozzarella stick and dredged it through a dish of red sauce. "I feel like we should be doing something more. Something important."

"Do you know what fairy chess is?" Corny asked.

Kaye shook her head.

"It's what they call it when you change the rules of the game. Usually it's just a single variation."

"They really call it that?" Kaye asked. "Like in chess club?"

He nodded. "I was the president. I should know."

"There were absolutely no blueberries in that pie, were there?" Ethine asked as she climbed into the car beside Kaye, the hand-cuffs taut.

"Dunno," said Corny. "How was it?"

"Barely edible," said Ethine.

"Right there, that is the great thing about diners. The food is much tastier than you would think. Like those mozzarella sticks."

"*My* mozzarella sticks," Luis said as he started the car.

Corny shrugged, a wicked grin spreading across his features. "Worried about getting my germs?"

Luis looked panicked, then abruptly angry. "Shut it."

Kaye poked Corny in the back of his neck, but when he turned to her, his expression was hard to decipher. She tried to mouth a question. He shook his head and turned back to the road, leaving her more puzzled than before.

She leaned against the cushions of the seat, letting her glamour slip away with relief. She was coming to hate the weight of it.

"Once more, I ask you to release me," said Ethine. "We're well away from the court, and my continued captivity will only draw them to you."

"No one likes being a hostage," said Luis, and there was some satisfaction in his voice. "But I think they're coming whether you're tagging along or not. And we're safer with you here."

Ethine turned to Kaye. "And you are going to let the humans speak for you? Will you side against your people?"

"I would think you'd be glad you're here," Kaye said. "At least you don't have to watch your beloved Queen kill your beloved brother. Who she's probably in love with." As she said it, her stomach clenched. The words echoed in her ears, as if she'd doomed him.

Ethine pressed her mouth into a thin, pale line.

"Not to mention the pie," said Corny.

Exits streamed by as Kaye stared out the window, feeling sick and helpless and guilty.

"Do we need to pick up Dave somewhere?" Corny asked softly, his voice pitched so that Kaye knew she wasn't included in the conversation.

Luis shook his head. "I'll call from your place. My friend Val said she'd pick him up at the station and keep an eye on him. She could probably even drop him off if we need her to." He sighed. "I just hope my brother actually got on the train."

"Why wouldn't he?" Corny asked.

"He doesn't like to do what I say. About a year ago, Dave

and I were living in an abandoned subway station. It was shitty, but the iron kept away the faeries, and this bargain I'd struck with the faeries kept away most everyone else. Then Dave found this junkie girl and brought her down to live with us. Lolli. Things were tense between me and my brother before that, but Lolli just made everything worse."

"You both liked her?" Corny asked.

Luis gave him a quick look. "Not really. Dave followed her around like a puppy dog. He was obsessed. But she . . . Inexplicably, she liked me."

Corny laughed.

"I know," said Luis. He shook his head, clearly embarrassed. "Hilarious, right? I hate this girl's guts and am blind in one eye and . . . Anyway, Dave never really forgave me. He used this drug, Never—it's magic—to make himself look like me. Got really strung out. Killed some faeries to get more."

"And that's why you have to work for Silarial?" Corny asked.

"Yeah. Only her protection really keeps him safe in New York." Luis sighed. "It barely works. The exiles are sworn to nobody and they were the ones he was killing. If he would just straighten himself out . . . I know things could be better. Next year he'll be eighteen. We could get loans from the state on account of both our parents being dead. Go to school."

Kaye thought about what Dave had said when they were in New York, about having some fun before he died. She felt awful. He wasn't thinking about getting an education.

"Go to school for what?" Corny asked.

Luis sighed. "It's going to sound dumb. I thought about being a librarian—like my ma—or a doctor."

"I want to stop at my house," Kaye said loudly, interrupting them. "If you turn here, we're really close."

"What?" Corny turned around in his seat. "You can't. We have to stick together."

"I want to make sure my grandmother's okay and get some clothes."

"That's stupid." Corny turned around farther in his seat to look back at her. "Besides, you're handcuffed to our prisoner."

"I have the key. You can cuff her to yourself. Look, I'll meet you at your house after I get my stuff." She paused, fishing around in her pocket. "I need to feed my rats. They've been alone for days and I bet their water bottle is getting low."

"You'll never feed them again if you get *carried off by faeries*!"

"And I don't wish to be left alone with two mortal boys," Ethine said softly. "If you won't let me free, then you are charged with my comfort."

"Oh, please," Kaye said. "Corny's *gay*. You don't have to worry about—" She stopped as Corny glowered at her, and she sucked in her breath. He liked Luis. And he thought Luis knew, but didn't like him. That was what all the defensiveness about the mozzarella sticks and the germs had been about.

"Sorry," she mouthed, but it only made him glare more. "Turn here," she said finally, and Luis turned.

"You misunderstand my concern," said Ethine, but Kaye ignored her.

"I know you want to check on your grandma and your mother." Corny's voice was low. "But even if your grandmother

knows something about what's going on with your mom—
which is a long shot—I really doubt you are going to like what
you hear."

"Look," Kaye said, and her voice was as soft as his, "I don't
know what happens next. I don't know how we fix things. But
I can't just disappear forever without saying good-bye."

"Fine." He pointed for Luis. "Stop there." He looked at
Kaye. "Be quick."

They pulled up in front of Kaye's grandmother's house.
She uncuffed her wrist, handed the key to Corny, and got out.

Luis cranked down the window. "We'll wait for you."

She shook her head. "I'll meet you guys at the trailer."

All the lights on the second floor were on, glowing like jack-
o'-lantern eyes. No holiday lights trimmed the front steps,
although all the neighboring houses were bright and twinkling.
Kaye climbed up the tree in front of her bedroom, the frozen
bark rough and familiar under her palms. As she stepped onto
the snow-covered asphalt of the shingles, she could see figures
in her bedroom. Crouching, she scooted closer.

Ellen stood in the hallway, talking to someone. For a
moment, Kaye touched her hand to the window, ready to throw
it open and call to her mother, but then she noticed her rat cage
was missing and her clothes had been piled in two garbage bags
on the floor. *Chibi-Kaye*, Corny had said, joking. Chibi-Kaye
came into the room, wearing Kaye's Chow Fat T-shirt. It hung
to her scabby knees.

The little girl did look like Kaye in miniature—dirty blond
hair in tangles over her shoulders, brown eyes and a snubbed

nose. Looking through the window was like seeing a scene out of her own past.

"Mom," Kaye whispered. The word clouded in the air, like a ghost that could not quite manifest. Her heart hammered against her chest.

"You need anything, Kate?" Ellen asked.

"I don't want to sleep," the little girl said. "I don't like to dream."

"Try," said Kaye's mother. "I think—"

Lutie flew down from the branch of a tree, and Kaye was so startled that she fell back, sliding a little ways on the roof. From inside, she heard a high-pitched shriek.

Ellen walked to the window and looked out at the snowy roof, her breath clouding the glass. Kaye scuttled back, out of Ellen's line of sight. Like a monster. Like a monster waiting for a child to fall asleep so she could creep in and eat it up.

"There's nothing," Ellen said. "No one to steal you away again."

"Who's *she*?" Lutie whispered, alighting on Kaye's lap. Lutie's wings brushed Kaye's fingers like fluttering eyelashes. "Why is she sleeping in your bed and wearing your clothes? I waited and waited like you said. You have taken a long time coming back."

"She's the baby who got taken to make room for me. She's who I thought I was."

"The changeling?" Lutie asked.

Kaye nodded. "The girl who belongs here. The real Kaye."

The cold of the snow seeped through her faerie gown. Still, she sat on the roof, peering at the girl inside as Ellen shut off everything but the night-light.

It was a simple thing to wait until the hallway light went dark, climb a little ways, then push open the window to the attic. Kaye ducked inside, swinging her feet over the ledge and slithering through.

Her feet touched grime-covered floorboards, and she pulled the switch to turn on the single bulb.

Her hip hit a box, sending the contents spilling out. In the sudden light, she saw dozens and dozens of photographs. Some of them were stuck together while others were chewed at the edges, but they all featured a little girl. Kaye bent low. Sometimes the girl was a swaddled-up baby sleeping on a patch of grass, sometimes she was a skinny thing dancing around in leg warmers. Kaye didn't know which photos were of her and which ones were of the other girl—she had no memory of how old she'd been when the switch occurred.

Kaye traced her fingers through the dust. *Impostor*, she wrote. *Fake*.

A gust of wind blew through the open window, scattering the photographs. With a sigh, she started gathering them up. She could smell the droppings of squirrels, the termite-eaten wood, the rotted sill. In the eaves something had made a nest of pink insulation, garish against the planks. Looking up at it, she thought again of cuckoos. She shoved the pictures into a shoebox and headed for the stairs.

No one was inside the second-floor bathroom, but another night-light glowed beside the sink. Kaye felt empty in this familiar space, as though her heart had been scraped hollow. But she had guessed right; no one had packed away her dirty clothes.

Picking through the hamper, she pulled out T-shirts,

sweaters, and jeans she'd worn the week before, balled them up, and tossed them out the window onto the snowy lawn. She wanted to take her records and notebooks and novels too, but she didn't want to risk going into her bedroom to get them. What if the changeling screamed? What if Ellen walked in and saw her there, clutching the stupid rubber necklace she'd five-fingered at a street fair?

Carefully, Kaye opened the door and stepped out into the hallway, straining for the sound of her rats. She couldn't just leave them to get dumped out in the snow or given to a pet store like her grandmother threatened whenever their cage was particularly filthy. She felt panicky at the thought of not being able to find them. Maybe someone had put them on the enclosed porch? Kaye crept down the staircase, but as she snuck into the living room, her grandmother looked up from the couch.

"Kaye," she said. "I didn't hear you come in. Where were you? We were very worried."

Kaye could have glamoured herself invisible or run, but her grandmother's voice sounded so normal that it rooted her to the spot. She was still in the shadows, the green of her skin hidden by the darkness.

"Do you know where Isaac and Armageddon are?"

"In your mother's room—upstairs. They were bothering your sister. She's afraid of them—has quite an imagination. She says they're always talking to her."

"Oh," Kaye said. "Right."

A Christmas tree sat near the television, trimmed with angels and a glitter garland. It was real—Kaye could smell the crushed pine needles and wet resin. Underneath sat a few boxes wrapped in gold paper. Kaye couldn't remember the last time they'd put up a tree, never mind bought one.

"Where have you been?" Her grandmother leaned forward, squinting.

"Around," Kaye whispered. "Things didn't go so well in New York."

"Come on, sit down. You're making me nervous, standing there where I can't see you."

Kaye took another step back, into deeper darkness. "I'm fine here."

"She never told me about Kate. Can you imagine that? Nothing! How could she not tell me about my own flesh and blood? The spitting image of you at that age. Such a sweet little girl, growing up robbed of a family to love her. It hurts my heart to think of it."

Kaye nodded again, stupidly, numbly. *Robbed*. And Kaye was the robber, the shoplifter of Kate's childhood. "Did Ellen say why Kate is here now?"

"I'd thought she'd have told you—Kate's dad checked himself into a rehab. He had promised not to bother Ellen, but he did and I'm glad. Kate's a strange child and she's clearly been raised terribly. Do you know that all she'll eat is soybeans and flower petals? What kind of diet is that for a growing girl?"

Kaye wanted to scream. The disconnect between the normalcy of the things her grandmother was saying and what she knew to be true seemed unendurable. Why would her mother tell her grandmother a story like that? Had someone enchanted her to believe that was the truth? Magic choked Kaye, the words that would conjure silence sharp in her mouth. But she swallowed them, because she also wanted her grandmother to keep talking, wanted everything to be normal for one more minute.

"Is Ellen happy?" Kaye asked quietly instead. "To have . . . Kate?"

Her grandmother snorted. "She was never really ready to be a mother. How will she manage in that little apartment? I'm sure she's happy to have Kate—what mother wouldn't be happy to have her child? But she's forgetting how much work it all is. They're going to have to move back here, I'm sure."

With growing dread, Kaye realized that Corny had been right all along. Giving her mother a changeling child had been a terrible plan. Ellen had just been getting ahead with her job and the band, and a kid completely derailed that. Kaye'd screwed up, really screwed up in a way she had no idea how to fix.

"Kate's going to look up to you," her grandmother said. "You can't be running around anymore, missing important family things. We don't need two wild children."

"Stop! Stop!" Kaye said, but there was no magic in her words. She put her hands over her ears. "Just stop. Kate isn't going to look up to me—"

"Kaye?" Ellen called from the top of the stairs.

Panicked, Kaye headed for the kitchen door. She yanked it open, glad for the cold air on her burning face. Right then she hated everyone—hated Corny for being right, Roiben for being gone, her mother and grandmother for having replaced her. Most of all, she hated herself for making all those things happen.

"Kaye Fierch!" Ellen shouted from the doorway in her

seldom-used "mom" voice. "You get back in here right now."

Kaye stopped automatically.

"I'm sorry," Ellen said, and Kaye turned toward her, saw the distress in her face. "I handled things badly, I admit that. Please don't leave. I don't want you to leave."

"Why not?" Kaye asked softly. Her throat felt tight.

Ellen shook her head, walking out into the yard. "I want you to explain. What you were going to tell me last time, at my apartment—tell me now."

"Okay," Kaye said. "When I was little, I got switched with the—the human—and you raised me, instead of the—the human girl. I didn't know until we moved back here and met other faeries."

"Faeries," Ellen echoed. "Are you sure that's what you are? A faerie? How can you tell?"

Kaye held up one green hand, turning it over. "What else would I be? An alien? A green girl from Mars?"

Ellen took a deep breath and let it out all at once. "I don't know. I don't know what to make of any of this."

"I'm not human," Kaye said, those words seeming to cut to the thing that was the most terrible and incomprehensible about the truth.

"But you sound—" Ellen stopped, correcting herself. "Of course you sound like you. You are you."

"I know," Kaye said. "But I'm not who you thought I was, right?"

Ellen shook her head. "When I saw Kate, I was so afraid. I figured you did something dumb to get her back from whatever had her, didn't you? See, I know you. *You.*"

"Her name's not Kate. She's Kaye. The real—"

Ellen held up one hand. "You didn't answer my question."

"Yeah." Kaye sighed. "I did something pretty dumb."

"See, you're exactly who I think you are." Ellen's arms went around Kaye's shoulders and she laughed her deep, cigarette-rough laugh. "You're my girl."

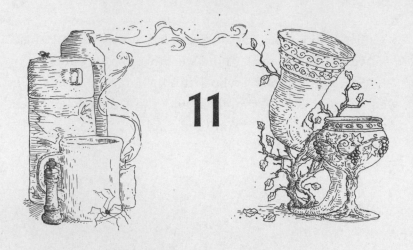

11

though i have closed myself as fingers,
you open always petal by petal myself as Spring opens
—E. E. CUMMINGS, "SOMEWHERE I HAVE NEVER TRAVELLED,
GLADLY BEYOND"

The lawn in front of Corny's trailer was decorated with
a giant inflated penguin wearing a green scarf and hat
and a red *Star Trek* shirt complete with an insignia on the left
breast. It sat on the lawn, glowing erratically. As Luis pulled
into the gravel drive, multicolored lights strobed from the
roof of the trailer next door, turning the whole lot into a
disco.

"Aren't you going to tell me what a beautiful home I have?"
Corny said, but the joke felt forced, lame.

Ethine leaned forward, her fingers on the plastic seat.

Luis shut off the car. "Is that penguin dressed as—"

"Tip of the iceberg," said Corny.

Leading Ethine by the fur-lined handcuff, Luis waited as
Corny unlocked the front door. Inside, the rainbow fiber-optic

tree illuminated a pile of dirty dishes. Framed needlepoint samplers hung on the wall next to signed pictures of Captain Kirk and Mr. Spock. A cat jumped down with a thud and started to wail.

"My room's down that hall," Corny whispered. "Home sweet home."

Luis padded over the worn carpet, leading Ethine behind him. There was a musty smell that Corny hadn't noticed before. He wondered if he'd just gotten used to it.

Corny's mother opened the hall door. There was something sad about her thin nightgown, her tangled bed-hair and bare feet. She hugged him before he spoke.

"Mom," Corny said. "This is Luis and . . . Eileen."

"How can you just walk in here like this?" she said, stepping back and looking him over. "You missed Christmas, this year of all years. The first Christmas since your sister's funeral. We thought you were dead too. Your stepfather cried like I've never seen him."

Corny squinted, as though some problem with his vision could explain her words. "I missed Christmas? What day is it?"

"It's the twenty-sixth," she said. "What are you three wearing? And your hair's black. Where have you been?"

Five days gone. Corny groaned. Of course. Time ran differently in Faerieland. It had seemed like two days when it had been twice that. Crossing to that island had been like crossing another time zone, like flying to Australia, except there was no way to gain that time on the way back.

"What is wrong with you? What have you been doing that you don't know how long you've been gone?"

Corny plucked at his tunic with a yellow-gloved hand. "Mom—"

"I don't know if I can ever forgive you." She shook her head. "But it's the middle of the night and I'm too tired to listen to your excuses. I'm exhausted from worrying."

She turned toward Luis and Ethine. "There's some more blankets in the closet if you get cold; remind Corny to turn on the space heater."

Ethine seemed ready to say something, but Luis spoke first. "Thank you for letting us stay." He looked almost shy. "We'll try not to be any trouble."

Corny's mom nodded absently, then squinted her eyes at Ethine. "Her ears are . . ." She turned to Corny. "Where *have* you been?"

"A sci-fi convention. I'm so sorry, Mom." Corny opened the door to his bedroom and switched on the light, letting Luis and Ethine walk past him, inside. "Seriously, I don't know how I lost track of so much time."

"A convention? ChristmasCon? I expect to hear a much more convincing story in the morning," she said, and went back into her own room.

A computer hummed on his desk, the screen fading between a series of screen shots from *Farscape*. A poster of two angels hung above his bed, one with black wings and one with white, their hands twined together by a cord of thorns, their blood the only color on the large glossy paper. Piles of books were stacked where he dropped them right before he fell asleep. Manga volumes sat on top of graphic novels and paperbacks. He kicked a few under the bed, embarrassed.

He had always thought of his room as an extension of his interests. Now, looking around the room, he thought it looked as dorky as the penguin on his lawn.

"You can sleep here," Corny told Ethine, nodding toward his bed. "The sheets are pretty clean."

"Gallant," she said.

"Yeah, I know it is." He walked over to his dresser, where a white King and a black King stood side by side. He liked to signal his moods by which one was in front, but he'd stopped doing that after Janet died; there was no annoying sister to signal to. And besides, it made him think about just how much he missed her. Opening the drawers, he pulled out a T-shirt and boxers and tossed them onto the bed. "You can wear these, if you want. To sleep in."

Luis unlaced his boots. "Can I grab a shower?"

Corny nodded and rummaged for the shirt that had the least pathetic logo. He found a faded navy blue one that said, I CAN DRINK MORE COFFEE THAN YOU CAN. Looking up, ready to hand it to Luis, he froze as Ethine stripped off her dress with complete nonchalance. The blades of her shoulders were covered with what looked like the buds of wings, pink against the handkerchief white of her skin. As she slid his boxers up her thin legs, she looked over at him and her eyes were chilling in their emptiness.

"Thanks," Luis said too loudly, taking the cloth out of his hands. "I'm going to borrow jeans, if you don't mind."

Corny nodded toward a few pairs stacked on a basket of clean clothes. "Take whatever."

Ethine sat on the edge of the bed, the unnaturally long toes of her bare feet scrunching in the rug as Luis left the room.

"I could enchant you," she said.

He stepped back, looking away from her face. "Not for long. Luis or Kaye would come in, and you can't enchant them." But, of course, Kaye was at her grandmother's house and Luis was in the shower. A quick glance told him that he hadn't bothered to lock her other cuff to anything. She'd have plenty of time.

"Even with the sound of my voice, I could make you do my bidding."

"You wouldn't tell me that if you were going to." He thought about the little faerie he'd captured the night of the coronation, and slid his hand behind the dresser, to where the iron poker was leaning. "Just like if I say that I could make your skin wrinkle like the old waitress at that diner, you can be pretty sure I'm not planning on it."

"And your sweet mother, I could enchant her, too."

He turned around, whipping the brand through the air, toward her throat. "Lock the other cuff. Do it right now."

She laughed, high and bright. "I only meant that you should not forget that by bringing me here, you are putting those you love in danger."

"Lock the cuff anyway."

She leaned over and cuffed herself to the support on his headboard, then twisted so that she was lying on her stomach. Her gray eyes flashed as they caught the light of the side table. They were as inhuman as those of a doll.

Crossing to the window, Corny took the key out of his jacket, opened the window, and tossed it out into a leaf pile. "Good luck ordering me around now. Enchanted or not, it's going to take someone a while to find that key."

He watched her, poker in hand, until Luis came back wearing Corny's jeans and a bleached towel wrapped around his braids. The mahogany skin of his chest was still flushed with the heat of the shower.

Corny looked down quickly at his gloved fingers, at the thin layer of rubber that protected him from ruining everything he touched. It was better, looking down, instead of taking the chance that his eyes might stare too long at all that bare skin.

Luis unwrapped the towel from his head and seemed to suddenly notice the poker and the locked cuff. "What happened?"

"Ethine was just messing with me," Corny said. "No big deal." He set down the metal rod and stood, going into the hall and leaning against the wall for a moment, eyes closed, breathing hard. Where was Kaye? Almost half an hour had passed; if she was quick about getting her stuff and if she walked fast, she could show up at any minute. He wished she would. She always came through for him, saving his ass when he'd thought he was beyond saving.

But they had a creepy hostage and no idea what the next attack would be or when it would happen, and he didn't think even Kaye could get them out of this one.

She could be in a lot of danger.

She was too upset to be thinking straight.

And he'd let her get out of the car. He hadn't even thought to give her his phone.

Pushing himself off of the wall, he gathered up a bunch of blankets and old pillows from a shelf over the the water heater in the hall closet. Everything would work out—things would be okay. Kaye would come back here and she'd have a clever plan. They'd trade Ethine for the promise of safety for their families and themselves—something like that, but smarter. Kaye wouldn't give up Roiben's name. Without Silarial knowing his name, he'd win the duel against the Seelie Court champion. Roiben would apologize to Kaye. Things would go back to normal, whatever normal was.

And Corny would wash his hands in the same ocean that had killed his sister, and the curse would be gone.

And Luis would ask him out on a date, because he was so cool and collected.

Walking back into the bedroom, Corny dumped the pile of blankets onto the bed. "Kaye can take the bed with Ethine when she shows. We can just spread out a few of these on the floor. I think it'll be bearable."

Luis had the borrowed T-shirt on and was sitting on the floor, flipping through a dog-eared copy of *Swordspoint*. He looked up. "I've slept on much worse."

Corny unfolded an afghan with a zigzag pattern of yellow and neon green and arranged it, then rolled out another layer of a slightly stained baby blue comforter on top. "Here," he said, and started to prepare his own bed beside that one.

Luis settled himself, pulling a blanket up to his neck and stretching luxuriously. Corny tucked himself into his makeshift pallet. His room looked different from the floor, like an alien landscape full of discarded paper and dropped CDs. Leaning his head back, he stared up at the water stains on the ceiling, spreading from a dark center like the rings of an old tree.

"I'll get the light," Luis said, getting up.

"We're still waiting for Kaye. And your brother, right?"

"I tried to call again, but I couldn't get him. I left your address with Val in case he calls her or shows up. I hope he did what he said he would and got on a train."

Luis stopped. "You know, though, Val said something else. She's got a friend among the exiled fey in the city. He'd been paid a visit from your Lord Roiben a couple of days ago. *Before* Roiben's visit to the Seelie Court."

Corny frowned. His tired brain couldn't make any sense of that. "Huh. Weird. Well, I guess now all we do is wait. Kaye knows her way in. Maybe your brother can tell us more about Roiben's visit. We'd all be better off if we could get some real sleep."

Luis hit the switch, and Corny blinked, letting his eyes adjust to the room. Lights trimming nearby trailers made it bright enough to see Luis kneel back down on the blankets.

"You're gay?" Luis whispered.

Corny nodded, although Luis might not see that in the dim light. "You knew, didn't you? You acted like you knew. You kissed me like you knew."

"I figured it didn't matter."

"*Nice*," Corny whispered.

"No, I don't mean it like that," Luis said, kicking his feet out from under the afghan. He laughed softly. "I mean, you were bespelled. Girls, boys, you didn't care. If it had a mouth, you were kissing it."

"And you had a mouth," said Corny. He could feel the close proximity of their bodies, noticed every movement of his thighs, the clamminess of his hands inside the gloves. His heart beat so loudly he was afraid that Luis could hear it. "It was smart, though. Quick thinking."

"Thanks." Luis's voice seemed slowed somehow, like he couldn't quite get his breath. "I wasn't sure it would work."

Corny wanted to lean in and taste those words.

He wanted to tell him it would have worked, even if he hadn't been bespelled.

He wanted to tell him that it would work right now.

Instead, Corny flipped over, so that Luis couldn't see his face. "Good night," he said, and shut his eyes against regret.

Corny woke from a dream where he'd been paddling, doggy-style, through an ocean of blood. His legs would tire, and when he missed a kick, he would drop under and glimpse, through the red, a city under the waves, full of friendly beckoning fiends.

He woke as his leg kicked ineffectually at the blankets. He saw a figure near the window and for a moment thought that it was Kaye, sneaking in so as not to disturb his mother and stepfather.

"Brought us right to your hidey spot, he did," a voice hissed. "For just a lick of nectar."

Cold air drifted down to chill Corny.

"I get it," he heard Luis whisper. He was the figure, but Corny couldn't see who he was speaking with. "I'll trade. Ethine for my brother. I'll bring her to the front door."

Corny's whole body tightened with betrayal.

Metal flashed in the moonlight as the creature passed the discarded handcuff key through the open window. Corny felt like an idiot. He'd thrown it right to them.

He stayed very still as Luis walked toward the bed, then grabbed his leg. Luis fell and Corny rolled on top of him. He ripped off the glove with his teeth and brought down his fingers, spread like a net, to inches above Luis's face.

"Traitor," Corny said.

Luis bent his head back, as far from Corny's hands as he could get. He swallowed, his eyes wide. "Oh, shit. Neil, please."

"Please what? With sugar on top? Pretty please, let me fuck you over?"

"They have David. My brother. He didn't get on the train—he went to them instead. They'll kill him."

"Ethine is the only thing keeping us safe," Corny said. "You can't trade away our safety."

"I can't let them have him," Luis said. "He's my *brother*. I thought you'd understand. You said yourself that there was no safe for us."

"Oh, come on. You thought I'd understand? That's why you're sneaking around in the dark. You seem *real sure*." His bare hand clenched in a fist just inches from Luis's throat. "Oh, I understand all right. I understand you'd sell us out."

"That's not it—" Luis started. *"Please."* Corny could feel Luis's body tremble beneath him. "My brother is a fuckup— but I can't stop wanting to save him. He's my brother."

Roiben's words came back to him. *The more powerful you become, the more others will find ways to master you. They'll do it through those you love and through those you hate.*

Corny hesitated, bare hand shaking. He thought of Janet, drowned after following a boy out onto the pier. He thought of being under the hill, kneeling at the feet of a faerie Lord while his sister gulped lungfuls of ocean. He thought of water closing over his head.

Whatever you loved, that was your weakness.

That didn't stop Corny from wishing he'd saved his own sister. He imagined her sinking deeper and deeper, only this time as he reached out, her fingers rotted away in his hands.

If he'd had a chance, he hoped he'd have done whatever it took to save her. But he *knew* Luis would have. He looked down at the boy underneath him, at the scars and the piercings and the way his braids had started to fray. Luis was *good* in a way that Corny wasn't. He didn't have to force himself to be good. He just was.

Corny pushed himself off Luis, his cursed hand fraying the acrylic of the carpet. He felt cold all over, thinking what he'd almost done. What he'd become. "Go ahead. Take her. Make the trade."

Luis remained wide-eyed, his breathing ragged. He stood hastily. "I'm sorry," he told Corny.

"It's what you have to do," Corny said.

The key caught what little light there was, gleaming like one of the steel rings piercing Luis's skin, as he uncuffed Ethine. She gasped, pushing herself up onto her knees and holding out her arms as if she expected to have to fight.

"Your people came for you," Luis told her.

She rubbed her wrist and said nothing. The shadows made her face look very young, although Corny knew she wasn't.

He bundled up her clothes with his glove-covered hand.

"I really am sorry," Luis whispered.

Corny nodded. He felt a hundred years old, tired and defeated.

They crept down the hallway, to the front door. It opened with a creak to reveal three creatures standing in the dirty snow, their faces grave. The foremost of them had the face of a fox and long fingers that tapered into claws.

"Where's Dave?" Luis asked.

"Give us the Lady Ethine and you shall have him."

"And you'll leave us unharmed once we hand her over?"

Corny asked. "Dave and Luis and me and Kaye and all our families. You'll go away and leave us alone."

"We will." The fox faerie spoke in a monotone.

Luis nodded and let go of Ethine's arm. She darted out in her bare feet and boxers, standing between the other faeries. One removed a cloak and spread it over Ethine's shoulders.

"Now give us Dave," said Luis.

"He is hardly worth your bargaining," one said. "Do you know how we found you? He led us here for a bag of powder."

"Just give him to me!"

"As you desire," said another. He nodded to someone behind the side of the trailer and two more of them stepped out, holding a body between them with a bag over its head.

They set him down on the step. He flopped, head lolling.

Luis took a step forward. "What did you do to him?"

"We killed him," said a fey with scales along his cheekbones.

Luis froze. Corny could hear his own heartbeat thundering in his blood. Everything seemed very loud. The cars on the road roared by and the wind made the leaves crackle.

Corny crouched and pulled off the cloth bag. Dave's ashen face looked as though it were made from wax. Dark circles ringed his sunken eyes, and his clothes were wrinkled and filthy. His shoes were gone and his toes looked pale, as if frostbitten.

"My Queen wishes to inform you that your brother lived so long as you were her servant," said the fox faerie. "That was her promise to you. Consider it kept."

A fierce gust of wind tore the fabric from Corny's hand and whipped at the cloaks. He closed his eyes against the sting of snow and dirt, but when he opened them, the faeries were gone.

Luis screamed, running out to where they had been, turning. His screaming was raw, terrible. His hands were fists, but there was nothing to strike.

Lights flashed on in the windows of two of the trailers. Corny reached out his gloved hand to touch Dave's cold cheek. It seemed impossible that they hadn't saved him. Dead like Janet. Just like Janet.

Corny's mother came to the door. She had the portable phone in her hand. "You woke up half the—" Then she saw the body. "Oh my god."

"It's his brother," Corny said. "Dave." That seemed important. Across the street, Mrs. Henderson came to the door and looked out through the glass.

Corny's stepfather came to the door. "What the hell's going on?" he demanded. Corny's mother started punching numbers into the phone. "I'm calling the first aid squad. Don't move him."

Luis turned. His face looked blank. "He's dead." His voice was hoarse. "We don't need an ambulance. He's *dead*."

Corny stood and stepped toward Luis. He had no idea what to do or say. There were no words that could make things better. He wanted to wrap his arms around Luis, comfort him, remind him he wasn't alone. As his bare hand moved toward Luis's shoulder, he looked at it in horror.

Before he could snatch his hand back, Luis caught him around the wrist. His eyes sparkled with tears. One streaked down his face. "Yes, good," he said. "Touch me. It doesn't fucking matter now, does it?"

"What?" Corny said. He reached up with his other hand, but Luis seized that, too, fingers scrabbling to pull off the rubber glove.

"I want you to touch me."

"Stop it," Corny shouted, struggling to move away, but Luis's grip was unyielding.

Luis pressed Corny's palm to his cheek. His tears wet Corny's fingers. "I really did want you to touch me," he said softly, and the longing in his voice was a surprise. "I couldn't tell you that I wanted you. So now I get what I want and it kills me."

Corny fought him. "Stop it! Don't!"

Luis's fingers were stronger, pinning Corny's hand in place. "I want to," he said. "There's no one to care what I do anymore."

"Stop! I fucking care!" Corny shouted, then abruptly went still. The skin of Luis's face wasn't bruised or wrinkled where his bare hand touched it. Luis let go of Corny's wrists with a sob.

Corny ran his finger reverently over the curve of Luis's cheekbone, painting with his tears. "Running water," Corny said. "Salt."

Their eyes met. Somewhere in the distance a siren wailed closer, but neither of them looked away.

12

Kaye saw the flashing lights from a block away. She sprinted onto the gravel street of the trailer park just as the ambulance pulled out. Neighbors stood on their patchy snow-covered lawns in robes or coats hastily thrown over nightclothes. The door to Corny's trailer was shut, but the lights were on inside. Lutie hovered above Kaye, darting back and forth, her wings beating as fast as Kaye's heart.

It seemed to Kaye that there were no right decisions anymore, only endless wrong ones.

She pulled open the door to the trailer and stopped, seeing Corny's mother pouring hot water out of a kettle. Her husband sat on one of the armchairs, a cup balanced on his leg.

His eyes were closed and he was snoring faintly.

"Kaye? What are you doing here?" Mrs. Stone asked. "It's the middle of the night."

"I—" Kaye started. A slight breeze signaled Lutie's blowing into the room. The little faerie alighted on top of a Captain Kirk bust, causing one of the cats to take a swipe at it.

"I called her," Corny said. "She knew Dave."

Knew Dave. Knew. Kaye turned to Luis, who was gripping his cup so tightly that his fingers looked pale. Papers rested on the floor beside him, a scattered stack of photocopied forms. She noticed his reddened eyes. "What happened?"

"Luis's brother overdosed on our steps." Mrs. Stone shuddered, looking like she might be sick. "They couldn't pronounce him dead because they're just volunteers, but they took him to the hospital."

Kaye looked toward Corny for an explanation, but he just shook his head. She sank down on the linoleum floor until she was sitting with her back to the wall.

Mrs. Stone put down her mug in the sink. "Corny, can I talk to you for a minute?"

He nodded and followed her down the hall.

"What really happened?" Kaye asked Luis, her voice low. "He didn't overdose, did he? Where's Ethine?"

"I bargained with a faerie to save Dave's life a long time ago. After my dad shot him. I tried to take care of him, like a big brother's supposed to—keep him out of trouble—but I didn't do such a good job. He got into more trouble. That meant more bargains for me."

Dread settled into the marrow of Kaye's bones.

"When I called at that rest stop, he went right to them,"

Luis said. "He traded where I was at for more Never. Even though he's burnt up his insides with it. Even though I'm his brother. And you know what? I'm not even surprised. It's not even the first time. So now he's dead and I should feel something, right?"

"But how did he die—?" Kaye started.

"I'm *relieved*." His words were a lash turned on himself. "Dave's dead and I feel relieved. Now, what does that make me?"

Kaye wondered if everyone felt like there was a monster underneath their skin. It was obvious that the relief wasn't the largest part of what he felt. It was obvious that he was in pain, that he'd been crying. And yet it was what he was dwelling on, an imperfect mourning.

Corny and his mother walked back into the room. He had his arm around her and was speaking softly. Kaye cried out at the sight of his bare hand on her arm, but the cloth under his hand was neither unraveled nor discolored.

"Sorry," she said, realizing how loud she'd been.

Luis looked around as though he'd just woken from a dream. He got awkwardly to his feet.

Corny's mom rubbed her face. "I'm going to wake up Mitch. You three go on and get what sleep you can."

Kaye stopped Corny in the hallway. "Is she okay?"

He shook his head. "We missed Christmas, you know. My mom's been going crazy thinking about Janet and not knowing where I was. I feel like an ass. And now this."

Kaye thought back to the handful of unopened presents sitting under the tree at her grandmother's and realized they must have been for her. "Oh," she said, and caught his warm, dry fingers. He didn't pull away from her. "What about the curse?"

"Later," he said. "War council in my room."

Kaye flopped on top of the tangled sheets of his bed, kicking her feet off one end. Luis sat on the floor and Corny sprawled beside him, close enough that their legs touched.

Lutie flew in, landing on Corny's computer. Luis must not have noticed her before, because he jumped up like a snapped cord.

"It's just Lutie-loo," Kaye said.

Luis looked at the little faerie with suspicion. "Fine, just . . . just keep it—her—away from me right now."

"Kaye, here's the summary-in-ten-seconds version of what you missed," Corny said quickly. "The Seelie Court wanted to trade Luis's brother for Ethine. We traded, but Dave was already dead. They'd killed him."

"And the curse?" Kaye asked.

"It got . . . accidentally removed," said Luis. He looked down at the threads of the carpet, and Kaye could see a worn patch that she didn't remember.

She nodded, since clearly neither of them wanted to talk about it. Lutie was perched on a cell phone cradle.

"It's weird," Corny said, resting his head on his knee. "Silarial was looking for Ethine but not you. She could have sent her people to swoop down out of the sky and grab you, or at least try."

"Maybe Sorrowsap is still watching over Kaye," said Luis.

Corny made a face. "Okay, but if you were the Seelie Queen and your plan was to use Roiben's name, would you waste your time getting one of your courtiers back?"

"He's right," Kaye said. "It doesn't make any sense. Killing Dave . . ." She glanced quickly at Luis. "It's like she'd already gotten everything she wanted. She had time for pettiness."

"So Silarial needs Ethine? What for?" Corny asked.

Luis frowned. "Didn't you say that Ethine would get the throne if Roiben won the duel?"

Kaye nodded. "He said something about how his sister would probably just hand back the crown, since she's so loyal. Maybe Silarial needs her to do that? I mean, it was odd that Silarial agreed to that bargain in the first place."

"I don't know," Corny said. "If there was even a chance I had to forfeit my crown, I'd be pretty happy if the person I had to give it to went missing. Of course, my crown would have lots of rhinestones spelling out 'tyrant' so not everyone would want to steal it either."

Kaye snorted. "Idiocy aside, you're right. You'd think she'd *want* Ethine dead."

"Maybe she does," Luis said.

"So, what, Silarial kills her and puts the blame on us? I don't know. . . ."

They sat in silence as the moments ticked by. Corny yawned while Luis stared at the wall, bright-eyed. Kaye imagined Talathain dueling Roiben, his sister grim-faced on the sidelines, the Queen smiling as though she'd eaten the last tart off the tray, Ruddles and Ellebere watching. There was something she was missing, something that was right in front of her.

She stood up with a gasp. "Wait! Wait! Who is Roiben fighting?"

Luis squinted up at her. "Well, we're not sure. I guess Silarial's knight or whatever courtier she thinks can kick his ass. Whoever's going to wield her secret weapon."

"Remember what we were talking about in the diner—how it seemed like Roiben had a good chance at beating Talathain? How it all seemed too simple?" Kaye shook her head, the thrill of discovery fading to a jittery nausea.

Corny nodded.

"I don't think there is a secret weapon," Kaye said. "No armor, no unbeatable swordsman. Getting his true name out of me—she never needed it."

Luis opened his mouth and then shut it again.

"I don't get what you're saying." Corny said.

"Ethine." Kaye said, feeling like the name was a slap. "Silarial's going to make Roiben fight Ethine."

"But . . . Ethine's not a knight," Luis said. "She couldn't even get away from us. She can't fight."

"That's the point," said Kaye. "There is no contest of skill. If he doesn't murder his own sister, Roiben dies. He has to choose between killing her and killing himself."

She wanted to stay angry with Roiben, to hang on to the feeling of betrayal so that it pushed back all her hurt, but at that moment she couldn't help pitying him for loving Silarial. Maybe more than she pitied herself for still loving him.

"That's . . ." Corny stopped.

"And if he's gone, there'll be no one to stop Silarial from doing whatever she wants to whomever she wants," Luis said.

"And charm an endless army of people," Kaye said. "Scores of frozen sentries."

"You were a distraction," Luis said. "A red herring. Keep Roiben looking at you, wondering if Silarial's going to get his true name, so he doesn't notice what's right in front of him."

"Neither fish nor fowl," Kaye said softly. "Good red herring.

That's right, isn't it? Kind of funny. That's what I was. A good red herring."

"Kaye," Corny said. "It's not your fault."

"We have to warn him," she said, pacing the room. She didn't want to admit that it bothered her that she wasn't going to be carried off for the Tithe, she wasn't the key, she wasn't even important. She'd just made things worse for Roiben, distracted him. Silarial had played them both.

"We don't even know where he is," said Corny. "The hollow hill in the graveyard isn't even hollow anymore."

"But we know where he *will* be," she said. "Hart Island."

"Tomorrow night. At this point, basically later today." Corny walked to his computer and jiggled the mouse, then typed in a few words. "It's an island off of New York, apparently. With a giant graveyard. And a prison—although I don't think it's in use. And—oh, perfect—it's completely illegal to go there."

All three of them slept squished into Corny's bed, with him in the middle, his arm over Kaye's back, and Luis's head pillowed on his shoulder. When he woke, it was late in the afternoon. Kaye was still curled up beside him, but Luis sat on the rug, speaking softly into Corny's cell phone.

Luis said something about "ashes" and "afford," but he shook his head when he saw Corny watching, and then turned to the wall. Padding past, Corny went out to the kitchen and turned on the coffeepot. He should have been worried. They were hours from heading into danger. Still, as he measured out the grounds, a smile spread over his face.

He immediately felt guilty. He shouldn't be so happy when Luis was mourning his brother. But he was.

Luis liked him. Luis. Liked. Him.

"Hey," Kaye said, scrubbing her hand through her tangled hair. She'd stolen one of his T-shirts and it hung on her like a dress. She grabbed a blue cup out of the cabinet. "Here's to the sweet balm of coffee."

"By the grace of which we'll accomplish the task before us."

"Do you think we will?" Kaye asked. "I don't know if Roiben will even listen to me."

The coffeepot gave a death rattle, and Corny poured three cups. "I do. He will. Honest. Drink up."

"So . . . you and Luis?" Her mug almost hid her grin.

He nodded. "I mean, not now with everything happening, but yeah, maybe."

"I'm glad." Her smile faded. "You don't have to go tonight. I'm not trying to be a martyr; it's just that with Luis losing his brother . . . This is my problem. They're my people."

He shrugged and put his arm around her shoulder. "Yeah, well, you're my problem. You're my people."

She leaned her head against him. Even just risen from bed, she smelled like grass and earth. "What about your fear of megalomaniacal fiends? I didn't think our recent trip was the ticket to getting over that."

He felt crazy with confidence. Luis liked him. His curse was gone. Everything seemed possible. "Let's get the fiends before the fiends get us."

Luis came out of the bedroom, closing the phone against his chest. "I saw your mom this morning. She said that she wanted to talk to you when she got home from work. I didn't tell her anything."

Corny nodded, reminding himself to seem calm. Reminding himself not to kiss Luis. He hadn't brushed his teeth and it didn't seem like great timing anyway.

"I'll leave a note. Then we'd better go. Luis, if you have to stay here and sort out stuff—"

"What I need is to stop Silarial from hurting anyone else." He looked Corny dead in the eye, as if daring him to pity him.

"Okay," Kaye said. "We're all in. Now what we need is a map and a boat."

"Hart Island is in Long Island Sound, off of City Island, which is off of the Bronx. Not exactly within paddling distance." Corny held out a mug to Luis. When he took it, their fingers brushed, and he felt the opposite of cursed.

"So we need a boat with a motor," Kaye said. "There's a nautical goods store on Route 35. I could turn a pile of leaves into money. Or we could find a marina up there to filch from."

Luis busied himself adding sugar to his coffee. "I've never steered a boat or read a navigational chart. Have you?"

Kaye shook her head, and Corny had to admit that he hadn't either.

"There's mermaids in the East River," said Luis. "Probably in the Sound, too. I don't know much about them, but if they don't want us to get to Hart Island, they could pitch us into the water. They've got vicious teeth. The good news is that they're part of the Undersea, not any of the courts of the land."

Corny shuddered at the thought. His mind went to Janet, held underneath the waves by a delighted kelpie. "We could

trade them something, maybe," he said. "They might take us there for a price."

Kaye looked over at him warily. He figured she was remembering how they'd traded an old carousel horse to that same kelpie for information. Before they knew how dangerous the kelpie was. Before it murdered Janet.

She nodded slowly. "What do mermaids like?"

Luis shrugged. "Jewelry . . . music . . . sailors?"

"They eat people, right?" Corny asked.

"Sure. When they're done with them."

Corny smiled. "Let's bring them a couple of big steaks."

They bought an inflatable green raft and two oars at the boat store. The clerk looked at Kaye strangely when she counted out hundreds of curled and tattered dollars, but her smile charmed him into silence.

They got back into the car.

Luis rode shotgun and Kaye rested in the back with her head on the raft's cardboard box. As Corny changed lanes on the highway, he looked over at Luis, but Luis looked out the window, his eyes not focused on anything. Whatever he saw, it wasn't something Corny could share. Silence filled up the car.

"Who was it?" Corny asked finally. "On the phone?"

Luis looked toward him too quickly. "It was the hospital. They were upset about me not having a credit card or a landline phone and him being under eighteen. And even though they didn't know if I'd be allowed to claim him, they started talking about my options. Basically, I have to come up with the money for cremation."

"Kaye could—"

Luis shook his head.

"We could sell the boat when we're done with it."

Luis smiled, a small lift of his lip. "I want him to have a good burial, you know."

At Janet's funeral there had been a coffin and a service, flowers and a stone. Corny had never asked about the cost, but his mom wasn't rich. He wondered how much she'd gone into debt for his sister to be buried in style.

"My parents—they're out where we're going." Luis's finger turned his lip ring.

"Hart Island?"

He nodded. "That's where potter's field is. Where they bury the 'friendless' dead. Which basically means the dead with no living relatives, who are renters and in credit card debt. My parents. I was underage, so I couldn't claim them. If I'd even tried, they'd probably have hauled Dave and me off to child services."

The possible replies scrolled in front of Corny's eyes. *Wow. Are you okay? I'm so sorry.* All of them inadequate.

"I've never been there," Luis said. "It'll be good to go."

They drove over the drawbridge, to the very edge of City Island, and parked the car behind a restaurant. Then, sitting in the snow, they took turns blowing up the raft, like they were passing around a joint.

"How are we going to attract those mermaids?" Corny asked, while Luis huffed into the little tube.

Kaye picked up a receipt from the floor of his car. "You got something pointy?"

Corny searched through his backpack until he came up with a discarded safety pin.

She poked her finger and, wincing, smeared her blood onto the paper. Walking to the edge of the water, she dropped it in. "I'm Kaye Fierch," she said firmly. "A pixie. A Seelie Court changeling on a quest for the King of the Night Court. I come here and ask for your help. I ask for your help. Three times I ask for your help."

Corny looked at her, standing in front of the water, her green hair pulled back from her glamoured face, her battered purple coat blown by the wind. For the first time, he thought that even in her human guise she had somehow grown formidable.

Heads bobbed in the black water, pale hair floating around them like sea grass.

Kaye went down on her knees. "I ask that you bring us three to Hart Island safely. We have a boat. All you have to do is pull it."

"And what will you give us, pixie?" they answered in their melodious voices. Their teeth were translucent and sharp, like they were made of cartilage.

Kaye walked back to the car and brought out the ShopRite plastic bag full of meat. She held up a raw and dripping shank. "Flesh," she said.

"We accept," said the mermaids.

Kaye, Corny, and Luis dragged the boat onto the water and pushed off. The mermaids swam around them, pushing the boat and singing softly as they went, their voices so beautiful and insistent that Corny found himself dazed. Kaye appeared tense, sitting at the prow like a ship's figurehead.

Looking over the side, Corny saw a mermaid coming up through the water, and for a moment it seemed like she wore his sister's face, blue with cold and death. He looked away.

"I know who you are," one of them said to Luis, her white, webbed hand reaching up onto the side of the boat. "You brought the troll's potion."

He nodded, swallowing.

"I could teach you how to heal better," the mermaid whispered. "If you came with me. Under the water."

Corny put his hand on Luis's arm, and Luis jumped as if he'd been stung.

The mermaid turned her head toward Corny. "What about vengeance? I could give you that. You lost someone to the sea."

Corny choked. "What?"

"You want it," she said. "I know that you do."

The mermaid reached up, her webbed hand settling on the side of the raft, near Corny. Scales skived off, shining on the rubber. "I could give you the power," she told him.

Corny looked down at her gelatinous eyes and her thin, sharp teeth. Envy curled in his gut. She was beautiful and terrible and magical. But the feeling was distant, like being envious of a sunset. "I don't need any more power," he said, and was surprised to find he meant it. And if he wanted vengeance, he'd get it on his own.

Kaye made a soft noise. Corny looked up.

There on the far shore, behind heaps of mussel shells, a great crowd of beings had gathered. And beyond them, abandoned buildings stood near rows and rows of graves.

13

"Thou art the unanswered question;
Couldst see thy proper eye,
Alway it asketh, asketh;
And each answer is a lie. . . ."
—RALPH WALDO EMERSON, "THE SPHINX"

Kaye pushed through the crowd with Corny and Luis, shoving lavender-skinned bodies and batting aside clouds of pin-size sprites. A phooka with a goat head and dead white eyes called to her as she passed, licking its teeth with a cat's tongue. "Licksy tricksy pixie!"

Ducking beneath the arm of an ogre, Kaye leaped onto a grave marker to avoid three spindly hobmen locked in an embrace in the dirt.

From the top of the marker, she surveyed the court. She saw Ruddles drinking from a bowl and passing it to a number of other animal-headed beings. Ellebere stood beside him— hair fading from wine to gold as it fell over his shoulders, his armor a deep and mossy green.

Roiben himself was talking animatedly to a woman as slim as a wand, her long black hair knotted into a jeweled cape that draped over her back to match the twitching tail also hung with jewels. From where she stood, Kaye couldn't tell whether or not they were arguing. The woman was gesturing broadly with her hands.

Then, abruptly, Roiben turned and looked in Kaye's direction. Kaye was so surprised that she fell. She forgot to flap her wings. Her head hit a stone, and tears sprung to her eyes. For a moment she just lay there, resting her head against the ground and listening to the Folk milling around her. It was awful to be so near him, awful how her heart leapt.

"You shouldn't eat the bones if you chew them like that." She heard someone say nearby. "They're too sharp. Cut up your insides."

"Haven't you become a little beetleflower?" said another voice. "Marrow's better than meat, but you've got to go through the bones to get it."

Corny reached out a hand to pull Kaye to her feet. "I don't think he saw you."

"Perhaps not, but I did." A woman, her wings so tattered that only the veins hung from her back, looked down at Kaye. She held a knife that curved like a snake, and her armor gleamed the same shining purple as the carapace of a beetle.

"Dulcamara," Kaye said, standing. "My friends need to talk to Roiben."

"Perhaps after the duel," she said. Her pink eyes regarded Kaye with contempt.

"They have to talk to him *now*," said Kaye. "Please. He can't duel. He has to call it off."

Dulcamara licked the edge of her blade, painting it with her mouth's blood. "I will play messenger. Give me your words and I will carry them to him with my own tongue."

"They have to tell him themselves."

Dulcamara shook her head. "I will allow no more distractions from you than he has already borne."

Corny stepped up. "Just for a moment. It'll only take a moment. He knows me."

"Mortals are liars. They can't help it," said the faerie knight. Kaye could see her teeth were as sharp as the knife in her hand, and unlike the mermaids', hers were bone. She smiled at Corny. "It's your nature."

"Then let me go," Kaye said. "I'm no mortal."

"You can't." Luis put his hand on her shoulder. "Remember? He's not allowed to see you."

Mortals are liars. Liars.

"Indeed," Dulcamara said. "Get close to him and I will run you through. No more of the glamoured games you played in the Seelie Court."

Over and over Kaye heard the words repeat: *Liars. Untruth. Lie. Lying. Dying. Dead.* She thought about Corny's fairy chess. She had to change the rules of the game. She had to solve the quest. She had to be the single variation. But how could she lie without lying?

Kaye looked over at where Roiben stood, his armor being strapped onto his back. His long hair had two plaits braided in the front, each one wrapped with a sharp silver clasp at the end. He looked pale, his face pinched, as though with pain.

"Oh," Kaye said, and then she leaped into the air.

"Stop!" Dulcamara shouted, but Kaye was already flying,

her wings flapping frantically. For a moment, she had a view of the lighthouse on the far shore of City Island, and the glimmering city lights beyond. Then she half landed, half fell at Roiben's feet instead.

"You," he said, and she couldn't parse the tone of his voice.

Ellebere grabbed her wrists and wrenched them behind her back. "This is no place for a Seelie Court pixie."

Ruddles pointed at her with a clawed hand. "To stand before our Lord and King, you must have completed your quest. If not, custom allows us to rend you—"

"I don't care what custom dictates," Roiben pronounced, waving off his chamberlain. When he looked at Kaye, his eyes were empty of any emotion she knew. "Where is my sister?"

"Silarial's got her," Kaye said in a rush. "Ethine's what I came to talk to you about." For the first time since the Tithe, she was afraid of him. She no longer believed that he would not hurt her. He looked as though he might relish it.

Lick the Queen of the Seelie Court's hand, Rath Roiben Riven. Lick it like the dog you are.

"My Lord," said Ruddles, "though I would not choose to contradict you, she may not remain in your presence. She hasn't completed the quest you bestowed on her."

"I said leave her!" Roiben shouted.

"I can lie," Kaye choked out, her heart beating like a drum against her skin. The ground tilted under her feet and everyone around her went silent. She had no idea if she could pull this off. "I can lie. I am the faerie that can lie."

"That's nonsense," said Ruddles. "Prove it."

"Are you saying that I can't?" Kaye asked.

"No faerie can tell an untruth."

"So," Kaye said, letting out her breath in a dizzy rush. "If I say I can lie and you say I can't, then one of us must be telling an untruth, right? So either I am a faerie that can lie, or you are. Either way, I have completed my quest."

"That reeks of a riddle, but I see no fault," the chamberlain said.

Roiben made a sound, but she couldn't tell if it was an objection.

"Clever." Ruddles's grin was full of teeth, but he patted her on the back. "We accept your answer with pleasure."

"I suppose you have succeeded, Kaye," said Roiben. His voice was soft. "From this moment forward your fate is tied to the Unseelie Court. Until the time of my death, you are my consort."

"Tell them to let me go," Kaye said. She'd won, but her victory felt as hollow as a blown egg. After all, he didn't want her.

"Since you're my consort, you may tell them yourself," said Roiben. He did not meet her eyes. "They ought not deny you now."

Ellebere dropped Kaye's arms before she could speak. Stumbling, she turned to glare at him and Ruddles. "Go," she said, trying to sound commanding. Her voice broke.

They looked to Roiben and moved at his nod. It was still hardly privacy, but it was the closest she was likely to get.

"Why have you come here?" he asked.

She wanted to beg him to be the Roiben she knew, the one who said she was the only thing he wanted, the one who hadn't betrayed her and didn't hate her. "Look at me. Why won't you look at me?"

"The sight of you is a torment." His eyes, when he raised them, were full of shadows. "I thought if I kept you out of this war, it would be the same as keeping you safe. But there you were in the middle of the Seelie Court as though to prove me a fool. And here you are again, courting danger. I only wanted to save one thing, just one thing, to prove there was some good in me after all."

"I am not a *thing*," Kaye told him.

He closed his eyes for a moment, covering them with long fingers. "Yes. Of course. I shouldn't have said that."

She caught his hands and he let her draw them from his face. They were as cold as the falling snow. "What are you *doing* to yourself? What's going on?"

"When I became King of the Unseelie Court, I thought we could not win the war. I thought that I would fight and I would die. There is a kind of mad glee in accepting death as an inevitable cost."

"Why?" Kaye asked. "Why bind yourself to such a miserable fate? Why not just say 'screw this, I'm going make birdhouses' or something?"

"To kill Silarial." His eyes glittered like chips of glass. "If she isn't stopped, no one will be safe from her cruelty. It was so hard not to crush her neck when I kissed her. Could you tell it from my face, Kaye? Did you see my hand tremble?"

Kaye heard her own blood pounding at her temples. Could she really have confused loathing with longing? Recalling the blood on Silarial's mouth, she thought of the way his eyes had seemed glazed over with passion. Now it seemed closer to madness. "Then why did you kiss—"

"Because they're my people." Roiben swept his hand over

the field, taking in the graveyard and the prison. "I want to save them. I needed her to believe I was in her power so she might agree to my terms. I know it must have seemed—"

"Stop." Kaye felt a cold finger of dread shiver up her spine. "I came here to tell you something," she said. "Something I figured out about the battle."

He raised a single silvery brow. "What is it?"

"Silarial's going to choose Ethine as her champion."

His laugh was almost a sob, short and terrible.

"Call off the duel," Kaye said. "Find some excuse. Don't fight."

"I wondered what terrible thing she might set against me, what monster, what magic? I forgot how clever she is."

"You don't have to fight Ethine."

He shook his head. "You don't understand. Far too much is at stake tonight."

Coldness spread from her heart to freeze her body. "What are you going to do?" Her voice came out sharper than she'd intended.

"I'm going to win," he said. "And you would do me a great service if you told Silarial that I said so."

"You wouldn't hurt Ethine."

"I think it's time that you went, Kaye." Roiben swung a strap with his scabbard attached over his shoulder. "I won't ask you to forgive me, because I don't deserve it, but I did love you." He looked down as he said the words. "I do love you."

"Then stop doing this. Stop not telling me shit. I don't care if it's for my own good or whatever stupid reason—"

"I *am* telling you shit," Roiben said, and hearing him swear made her laugh. He smiled back, just a little, like he got the joke. In that one moment he seemed heartrendingly familiar.

He reached out, still smiling, as though he were going to touch her face, but he traced the shape of her hair instead. It was not even a real touch, feather-light and never coming to rest, as though he were afraid to dare more. She shivered.

"If you really can lie," he said, "tell me this will end well tonight."

Icy air blew up a thin flurry of snow and tossed back Roiben's hair as he strode past graves to the area marked for the duel. The Night and Bright Courts waited restlessly in a loose circle, whispering and chittering, pulling their cloaks of skin and fur and cloth closer. Kaye hurried behind the edge of the crowd to where the Bright Queen's courtiers stood, their shimmering gowns blown by the wind.

Ellebere and Dulcamara walked beside Roiben, their insect-like armor glittering against the frost-covered landscape and the stone markers. Roiben dressed as gray as the overcast sky. Talathain and another knight flanked Silarial. They wore green-stained leather with gilt studding their shoulders and their arms like the markings on a caterpillar. Roiben bent in so deep a bow that he might have touched his lips to the snow. Silarial made only a shallow bob.

Roiben cleared his throat. "For decades there has been a truce between the Seelie and the Unseelie Courts. I am both proof of and witness to that old bargain, and I would broker it again. Lady Silarial, do you agree that if I defeat your champion, you will concede a concord between our two courts?"

"If you deal my champion a mortal blow, I so swear,"

Silarial said. "If my champion lies dying on this field, you will have your peace."

"And do you have a further wager in this battle?" he asked her.

She smiled. "I will also give over my throne to the Lady Ethine. Gladly I will set the crown of the Seelie Court upon her head, kiss her cheeks, and step down to be her subject should you win."

Kaye could see Roiben's face from where she stood, but she could not read his expression.

"And if I die on the field of battle," Roiben said, "you shall rule over the Unseelie Court in my place, Lady Silarial. To this I agree."

"And now I must name my champion," said Silarial, a smile slitting her face. "Lady Ethine, take up arms for me. You are to be the defender of the Bright Court."

There was a terrible silence among the gathered throng. Ethine shook her head mutely. The wind and the shifting snow came down as the tableau held.

"How you must hate me," Roiben said softly, but the wind seemed to catch those words and blow them out to the audience.

Silarial turned in her frosting-white dress and strode from the field to her bower of ivy. Her people clad Ethine in a thin armor and placed a long sword in her limp grip.

"Go," Roiben told Ellebere and Dulcamara. Reluctantly, they left the field. Kaye could see the doubt in the faces of the Unseelie Court, the tension as Ruddles ground his teeth together and watched Ethine with gleaming black eyes. They had thrown in their lot with Roiben, but his loyalties were uncertain and never more so than at this moment.

Hobmen paced the outside edge of the ring, scattering herbs to mark its boundaries.

At the center of the snowy bank, Roiben made a stiff bow and drew his sword. It curved like a crescent moon and shone like water.

"You don't mean to do this," Ethine said, but in her mouth it was a question.

"Are you ready, Ethine?" Roiben brought his sword up so that the blade seemed to bisect his face, casting half into shadow.

Ethine shook her head. *No.* Kaye could see Roiben's sister shiver convulsively. Tears ran down her pale cheeks. She dropped her sword.

"Pick it up," he said patiently, as if to a child.

Hurrying, Kaye walked to where the Bright Lady of the Seelie Court sat. Talathain raised his bow, but did not stop her. The sound of blades crashing together made her turn back to the fight. Ethine staggered back, the weight of her sword clearly overbalancing her. Kaye felt sick.

Silarial looked down from her perch, coppery hair plaited with deep blue berries knotting a golden circlet atop her head. She smoothed the skirt of her white gown.

"Kaye," she said. "What a surprise. Are you surprised?"

"He knew it was going to be Ethine before he went out there."

Silarial frowned. "Oh?"

"I told him." Kaye sat down on the dais. "After I figured out his stupid quest."

"So you're consort to the King of the Unseelie Court?"

Silarial raised one eyebrow. Her smile was pitying. "I'm surprised you still want him."

That stung. Kaye would have protested, but the words twisted in her mouth.

"But then, you will only be his consort as long as he lives." The Bright Lady turned her gaze to the two figures fighting in the snow.

"Oh, come on," Kaye said. "You act like he's the same kid you sent away. Do you know what he did when I told him about Ethine? He laughed. He laughed and said he'd win."

"No," said Silarial, turning too quickly. "I cannot believe he would play cat and mouse first if he intended to kill her."

Kaye squinted. "Is that what he's doing? Maybe it's just not easy to murder your own sister."

Silarial shook her head. "He craves death, just as he craves me, though perhaps he wishes he didn't want either. He will let her stab him and perhaps tell her some sweet thing with a mouth full of blood. All this taunting is to make her angry, make her swing hard enough for a killing blow. I know him as you do not."

Kaye closed her eyes against that thought, then forced them open. She didn't know. She honestly didn't know if he would kill his sister or not. She didn't even know what to want, both choices were so terrible. "I don't think so," she said carefully. "I don't think he wants to, but he's killed a lot of people he didn't want to kill."

As if on cue, there was a great cry from the audience. Ethine lay in the snow, struggling to sit up, the tip of Roiben's curved blade at her throat. He smiled down at her kindly, as if she had merely fallen and he was about to help her up again.

"Nicnevin forced him to kill," Silarial said quickly.

Kaye let the anger she felt bleed into her voice. "Now you're forcing him."

Roiben's words carried over the field. "Since it seems that the crown of the Bright Court will come to you *after* your death, tell me upon whom you wish to bestow it. Let me do this last thing for you as your brother."

Relief flooded Kaye. There was a plan. He had a plan.

"Hold!" Silarial shouted, leaping up from her makeshift throne and striding out onto the field. "That was not part of the bargain." As she passed through the ring of herbs, they caught with greenish fire.

Wailing rose from the Unseelie Folk while the Bright Court went deathly silent. Roiben stepped back from his sister, taking the blade from her throat. Ethine fell back in the snow, turning her head so that no one might see her face.

"Neither was your interrupting this fight," he said. "You may not reconsider our bargain now that it no longer favors you." His words silenced the Unseelie Court's cries, but Kaye could hear the rest of the crowd murmur in confusion.

Ethine stumbled to her feet. Roiben extended his hand to help her, but she didn't take it. She looked at him with hate, but there was no less hate when she looked upon her mistress. She picked up her sword and held it so tightly her knuckles went white.

"My oath was that the crown would go to Ethine if you killed my champion. I did not promise that she could choose a successor." Silarial's voice sounded shrill.

"That was not yours to promise," Roiben said. "What is hers in death, she may give with her last breath. Perhaps she will even pass it back to you. Unlike the Unseelie crown that is won by blood, the Seelie successor is chosen."

"I will not have my crown bestowed by one of my own handmaidens, nor will I be lessoned by one who once knelt at my feet. You are not one part what Nicnevin was."

"And you are too much like her," said Roiben.

Three Seelie knights strode onto the field, clustering close enough to Roiben that were he to move toward Silarial, they might be faster.

"Let me remind you that my forces overwhelm yours," said Silarial. "Were our people to fight, even now, I would win. I think that gives me leave to dictate terms."

"Will you void our agreement, then?" Roiben asked. "Will you stop this duel?"

"Before I let you have my crown!" Silarial spit.

"Ellebere!" Roiben shouted.

The Unseelie knight drew a little wooden flute from inside the wrist of his armor and brought it to his mouth. He blew three clear notes that traveled over the suddenly quiet crowd.

At the edges of the island, things began to move. Merfolk pulled themselves onto shore. Faeries appeared from the abandoned buildings, stepped from the woods, and rose out of graves. An ogre with a greening beard crossed a pair of bronze sickles over his chest. A thin troll with shaggy black hair. Goblins holding daggers of broken glass. The denizens of the parks and the streets and the shining buildings had come.

The exiled fey.

The crowd's murmuring became shouts. Some of the assemblage scrambled for arms. The solitary fey and the Night Court moved to surround the Seelie Court gentry.

"You planned an ambush?" Silarial demanded.

"I've been making some alliances." Roiben looked as though he were swallowing a smile. "Some—many—of the exiled fey were interested to know that I would accept them into my court. I would guarantee their safety even, for a mere day and night of service. Tonight. Today. You are not the only one with machinations, my Lady."

"I see you have played to some purpose," said Silarial. She looked at him as though he were a stranger. "What is it? For what do you scheme? Ethine's death would weigh on you and the stain of her blood would seep into your skin."

"Do you know what they wish for you when they give you the Unseelie crown?" Roiben's tone was soft, like he was telling a secret. Kaye could barely catch his words. "That you be made of ice. What makes you think it matters what I feel? What makes you think I feel anything at all? Surrender your crown to my sister."

"I will not," said Silarial. "I will never."

"Then there will be a battle," Roiben said. "And when the Unseelie Court is victorious, I will snatch that crown from your head and grant it as I see fit."

"All wars have casualties." Silarial nodded to someone in the crowd.

Talathain's hand came down hard over Kaye's mouth. Fingers dug into the soft pad of her cheek and the flesh of her side as she was dragged onto the field.

"Make one move, make one command," said Silarial, turning to Kaye with a smile, "and she will be the first."

"Ah, Talathain, how you have fallen," Roiben said. "I thought you were her knight, but you have become only her woodsman—taking little girls to the forest to cut out their hearts."

Talathain's grip on Kaye tightened, making her gasp. She tried to tamp down her terror, tried to convince herself that if she stayed very still, she could figure a way out of this. No ideas came.

"Now give up your crown, Roiben," Silarial said. "Give it up to me as you should have when you got it, as fit tribute to your Queen."

"You're not his Queen," Ethine said, her voice numb. "And neither are you mine." Silarial spun toward her, and Ethine plunged her blade into the Bright Queen's chest. Hot blood pocked the snow, melting dozens of tiny craters as though someone had scattered rubies. Silarial stumbled, her face a mask of surprise, and then she dropped.

Talathain shouted, but he was too late, much too late. He pushed Kaye out of his arms. She fell on her hands and knees, near the Bright Queen's body. Stepping over them both, he swung his golden sword at Ethine. She waited for the blow, not moving to defend herself.

Roiben stepped in front of her in time to catch the sword with his back. The edge sliced through his armor, opening a long red line from his shoulder to his hip. Gasping, he fell with Ethine beneath him. She shrieked.

Roiben rolled off of her and into a crouch, but Talathain had knelt beside Silarial, turning her pale face with a gloved hand. Her ancient eyes stared up at the gray sky, but no breath stirred her lips.

Roiben stood stiffly, slowly. Ethine's body shook with shallow sobs.

Talathain looked over at her. "What have you done?" he demanded.

Ethine tore at her dress and her hair until Kaye caught her hands.

"He did not deserve to be used so," she said, her voice thick with tears and mad faerie laughter. Her sharp nails sank into Kaye's flesh, but Kaye didn't let go.

"It's done," Kaye soothed, but she was frightened. She felt as though she were onstage, performing a play, while the hordes of the Unseelie Court and the exiled fey waited uneasily for a signal to crash down upon the Seelie Court they surrounded. "Come on. Stand up, Ethine."

Roiben cut the golden circlet from Silarial's hair. Chunks of braided coppery strands and berries hung from it as he held it aloft.

"That crown is not yours," said Talathain, but his voice lacked conviction. He looked from the Unseelie Court to the exiled fey. Behind him, the champions of the Bright Court had moved to the edge of the dueling grounds, but their expressions were grave.

"I was just getting it for my sister," Roiben said.

Ethine shuddered at the sight of the circlet, caught with hair and ice.

"Here," Roiben said, picking it clean with quick fingers and shining it against the leather of his breastplate. It came away red as rubies. His brows knitted in confusion, and Kaye saw that his armor was wet with blood, that it seeped down his arm to cover his hand in a dripping glove of gore.

"Your . . . ," Kaye said, and stopped. *Your hand,* she'd almost said, but it wasn't his hand that was hurt.

"Put your puppet on the throne," said Talathain. "You may make her Queen, but she won't be Queen for long."

Ethine trembled. Her face was pale as paper. "My brother needs his attendants."

"You brought her flowers," Roiben said. "Don't you remember?"

Talathain shook his head. "That was a very long time ago, before she killed my Queen. No, she won't rule for long. I'll see to that."

Roiben's face went slack, stunned. "Very well," he said slowly, as though he were puzzling out the words as he said them. "If you would not swear loyalty to her, perhaps you will kneel and swear your loyalty to me."

"The Seelie crown must be given—you cannot murder your way to it." Talathain pointed his sword at Roiben.

"Wait," Kaye said, pulling Ethine to her feet. "Who do you want to get the crown?"

Talathain's sword didn't waver. "It doesn't matter what she says."

"It does!" Kaye shouted. "Your Queen made Ethine her heir. Like it or not, she gets to say what happens now."

Ruddles strode out onto the field, giving Kaye a quick smile as he passed her. He cleared his throat. "When one court ambushes and conquers the gentry of another court, their rules of inheritance are not applicable."

"We'll be following Unseelie custom," Dulcamara purred.

"No," Kaye said. "It's Ethine's choice who gets the crown or if she keeps it."

Ruddles started to speak, but Roiben shook his head. "Kaye is correct. Let my sister decide."

"Take it," Ethine told him hollowly. "Take it and be damned."

Roiben's fingers traced over the symbols on the crown with his thumb. He sounded distant and strange. "It seems I will be coming home after all."

Talathain took a step toward Ethine. Kaye dropped her hand, wanting to be ready, although she had no idea what she'd do if he swung.

"How can you give this monster sovereignty over us? He would have paid for his peace with your death."

"He wouldn't have killed her," Kaye said.

Ethine looked away. "You have all turned into monsters."

"Now the price of peace is merely her hatred," said Roiben. "That I am willing to pay."

"I will never accept you as King of the Seelie Court," Talathain spat.

Roiben set the circlet on his brow. Blood smudged his silver hair.

"It is done, whether you accept it or no," said Ruddles.

"Let me finish the duel in your sister's place," said Talathain. "Fight me."

"Coward," Kaye said. "He's already hurt."

"Your Bright Lady broke her compact with us," said Dulcamara. She turned to Roiben. "Let me kill this knight for you, my Lord."

"Fight me!" Talathain demanded.

Roiben nodded. Reaching into the snow, he lifted his own sword. It was cloudy with cold. "Let's give them the duel they came for."

Kaye wanted to scream, but she thought she understood.

Roiben won his crown in blood. If he backed down now, there would be a target on his back in the Court of Termites. By contrast, if he killed Talathain, the rest of the Seelie Court would fall in line.

Talathain and Roiben circled each other slowly, their feet careful, their bodies swaying toward each other like snakes. Both their blades extended so that they nearly touched.

Talathain slammed his blade down. Roiben parried hard, shoving the other knight back. Talathain kept the distance. He stepped in, swung, then retreated quickly, staying just outside Roiben's range as if he were waiting for him to tire. A single rivulet of blood ran like sweat down Roiben's sword arm and onto his blade.

"You're wounded," Talathain reminded him. "How long do you really think you can last?"

"Long enough," Roiben said, but Kaye saw the wetness of his armor and the jerkiness of his movements and wasn't sure. It seemed to her that Roiben was fighting a mirror self, as though he were desperate to cut down what he might have become.

"Silarial was right about you, was she not?" said Talathain. "She said you wanted to die."

"Come find out." Roiben swept the sword in an arc so swiftly that the air sung. Talathain parried, their blades crashing together, edge to flat.

Talathain recovered fast and thrust at Roiben's left side. Twisting away, Roiben grabbed the other knight's pommel, forcing Talathain's sword up and kicking against his leg.

Talathain fell in the snow.

Roiben stood over him, pointing the blade at the knight's throat. Talathain went still. "Come and get the crown if you want it. Come and take it from me."

Kaye wasn't sure if she heard a threat or a plea in those words. Talathain didn't move.

A faerie with skin like pinecones, rough and cracked, took Talathain's golden sword from his hands. Another spat into the grimy snow.

"You'll never hold both courts," Talathain said, struggling to his knees.

Roiben teetered a little, and Kaye ran out to put her arm under his. He hesitated a moment before leaning his weight against her. She nearly staggered.

"We'll hold the Bright Court just as your mistress would have held us," Dulcamara purred, squatting down beside him, a shining knife touching his cheek, the point pressing against the skin. "Pinned down in the dirt. Now tell your new Lord what a fine little puppy his cleverness has bought him. Tell him you'll bark at his command."

Ethine stood stiff and still. She closed her eyes.

"I will not serve the Unseelie Court," Talathain said to Roiben. "I will not become like you."

"I envy you that choice," said Roiben.

"I'll make him bark," Dulcamara said.

"No," Roiben said. "Let him go."

She looked up, surprised, but Talathain was already on his feet, pushing his way though the crowd as Ruddles called out, "Behold our undoubted Lord Roiben, King of both the Unseelie and the Seelie Courts. Make your obeisances to him."

Roiben swayed slightly, and Kaye tightened her grip. Somehow he remained standing, although his blood slicked her hand. "I'll be better than she was," she heard him say. His voice was all breath.

14

*In a certain faraway land the cold is so intense that
words freeze as soon as they are uttered, and after
some time then thaw and become audible so that
words spoken in winter go unheard until the next
summer.*

—PLUTARCH, MORALIA

When Kaye and Corny walked into the small apartment,
Kate was lying on an air mattress in the middle of the
floor. She was drawing in a magazine. Kaye could see that
the little girl had blacked out Angelina Jolie's eyes and was in
the process of drawing bat wings over Paris Hilton's shoulder
blades.

"Cute kid," said Corny. "Reminds me of you."

"We got lo mein and veggie dumplings." Kaye shifted the
bag in her arms. "Grab a plate; it's leaking on my hand."

Kate scrambled to her feet and pushed back a tangle of
dirty blond hair. "I don't want it."

"Okay." Kaye set the cartons on the kitchen counter. "What
do you want?"

"When's Ellen coming home?" Kate looked up, and Kaye could see her brown eyes were rimmed with red, as though she'd recently been crying.

"When her rehearsal's over." The first time Kaye had met Kate, the girl had hidden under the table. Kaye wasn't sure if this was better. "She said she wouldn't be that late, so don't freak out."

"We don't bite," Corny put in.

Kate picked up her magazine and climbed up on Ellen's bed, scooching over to the far corner. She tore off tiny pieces and rolled them between her fingers.

Kaye sucked in a breath. The air in the apartment tasted like cigarettes and human girl, at once familiar and strange.

Kate scowled ferociously and threw the balled-up paper at Corny. He dodged.

Opening the refrigerator, Kaye took out a slightly withered orange. There was a block of cheddar with mold covering one end. Kaye chopped off the greenish fur and put the remaining lump on a piece of bread. "I'll grill you some cheese. Eat the orange while you wait."

"I don't want it," Kate said.

"Just give her bread and water like the little prisoner she is." Corny leaned back on Ellen's bed, cushioning his head with a pile of laundry. "Man, I hate babysitting."

Kate picked up the orange and threw it against the wall. It bounced like a leather ball, hitting the floor with a dull thud.

Kaye had no idea what to do. She felt paralyzed by guilt. The girl had every reason to hate her.

Corny switched on the tiny television set. The channels were fuzzy, but he finally found one that was clear enough to show Buffy staking three vampires as Giles clocked her with a stopwatch.

"Rerun," Corny said. "Perfect. Kate, this should teach you everything you need to know about being a normal American teenager." He looked up at Kaye. "There's even the sudden addition of a sister in it."

"She's not my sister," the girl said. "She just stole my name."

Kaye stopped, the words like a kick to the gut. "I don't have a name of my own," she said slowly. "Yours is the only one I've got."

Kate nodded, her eyes still on the screen.

"So what was it like?" Corny asked. "Faerieland?"

Kate tore off a larger chunk of the magazine, crushing it in her fist. "There was a pretty lady who braided my hair and fed me apples and sang to me. And there were others—the goat-man and the blackberry boy. Sometimes they would tease me." She frowned. "And sometimes they would forget me."

"Do you miss them?" he asked.

"I don't know. I slept a lot. Sometimes I would wake up and the leaves would have changed without me seeing them."

Kaye felt cold all over. She wondered if she'd ever get used to the casual cruelty of faeries, and hoped she wouldn't. At least here, among humans, Kate would wake up each day until there was no more waking.

Kaye fidgeted with the sleeves of her sweater, worming her thumbs through the weave. "Do you want to be Kaye and I'll be Kate?"

"You're stupid and you don't even act like a faerie."

"How about I make you a deal," Kaye said. "I'll teach you

about being human and you teach me about being a faerie." She winced at how lame that sounded, even to her.

The frown hadn't faded from Kate's face, but she looked like she was thinking things through.

"I'll even help," Corny said. "We can start by teaching you human curse words. Maybe we could skip the faerie curses, though." Corny took a deck of cards out of his backpack. Printed on the back of each was a different cinema robot. "Or we could try poker."

"You shouldn't bargain with me," the girl said, as though by rote. She looked smug. "Mortal promises aren't worth the hair on a rat's tail. That's your first lesson."

"Noted," Kaye said. "And, hey, we could also teach you the joys of human food."

Kate shook her head. "I want to play the cards."

By the time Ellen walked in, Corny had beaten them both out of all the spare change they'd found in their pockets or under Ellen's bed. *Law & Order* was playing on the television, and Kate had agreed to eat a single fortune cookie. Her fortune had read: "Someone will invite you to a karaoke party."

"Hey, one of the guys on the street was selling bootleg movies for two bucks," Ellen said, throwing her coat onto a chair and dumping the rest of her stuff onto the floor. "I got a couple for you kids."

"Bet the back of someone's head blocks the screen," Kaye warned.

Ellen picked at the noodles on the counter. "Anyone eating these?"

Kaye walked over. "Kate didn't want them."

Ellen lowered her voice. "I can't tell if she's just a picky eater

or if it's some *thing*—doesn't like sauces, barely can stand cooked food at all. Not like you. You used to eat like you had a tapeworm."

Kaye busied herself packing up what was left of the food. She wondered if every memory would snag, like wool on a thorn, making her wonder if it was a symptom of her strangeness.

"Everything okay?" Ellen asked her.

"I guess I'm not used to sharing you," Kaye said softly.

Ellen smoothed Kaye's green hair back from her head. "You'll always be my baby, Baby." She looked into Kaye's eyes a long moment, then turned and lit a cigarette off the stove. "But your kid-sitting days are just beginning."

Luis didn't want enchantments or glamours to pay for his brother's funeral, and so he got what he could afford—a box of ashes and no service. Corny drove him to pick them up from an ancient funeral director who handed over what looked like a cookie tin.

Although the sky was overcast, the snow on the ground had turned to slush. Luis had been in New York since the duel, dealing with clients and trying to hunt up enough paperwork to prove that Dave really was his brother.

"What are you going to do with the ashes?" Corny asked, climbing back into the car.

"I guess I should scatter them," said Luis. He leaned against the cracked plastic seat. Someone had tightened up his herringbone braids, and they shone like ropes of dark silk when he tilted his head. "But it freaks me out. I keep thinking of the ashes like powdered milk. You know, if I just add water, they'll reconstitute into my brother."

Corny rested his hands against the steering wheel. "You could keep them. Get an urn. Get a mantel to put it on."

"No." Luis smiled. "I'm going to take his ashes to Hart Island. He was good at finding things, places. He would have loved an entirely abandoned island. And then he'll be resting near my parents."

"That's nice. Nicer than some funeral home with a bunch of relatives who don't know what to say."

"It could be on New Year's. Like a wake."

Corny nodded, but when he moved to put the key in the ignition, Luis's hand stopped him. When he turned, their mouths met.

"I'm sorry . . . that I've been," Luis said, between kisses, "distracted . . . by everything. Is it morbid . . . that I'm talking . . . ?"

Corny murmured something that he hoped sounded like agreement as Luis's fingers dug into his hips, pushing him up so they could crush their bodies closer together.

Three days later they brought another package of meat to the mermaids for a ride to Hart Island. Corny had found a vintage blue tuxedo jacket to put on over a pair of jeans, while Luis slouched in his baggy hoodie and engineer boots. Kaye had borrowed one of her grandmother's black dresses and had pinned her green hair up with tiny rhinestone butterflies. Lutie buzzed around her head. The mermaids insisted on taking three of the hairpins along with the steak.

Corny looked back at the city behind them, shining so brightly that the sky over it looked almost like day. Even this far out, it was too light for stars.

"Do you think the coast guard is going to spot us?" Corny asked.

Luis shook his head. "Roiben said not."

Kaye looked up. "When did you talk to him?"

Touching the scar beside his lip ring, Luis shrugged. "He came to see me. He said that he formally extended his protection. I can go wherever I want and see whatever I see in his lands and no one can put out my eyes. I got to tell you, it's more of a relief than I thought it would be."

Kaye looked down at her hands. "I don't know what I'm going to say to him tonight."

"You're a consort. Shouldn't you be consorting?" Lutie asked. "Or maybe you can send him on a quest of his own. Make him build you a palace of paper plates."

Kaye's mouth quirked at the corner.

"You should definitely ask for a better palace than that. Reinforced cardboard at least." Corny poked her in the side. "How did you solve his quest, anyway?"

She turned and opened her mouth. Someone shouted from the shore.

A girl with a head full of gingery stubble was calling to them as she dragged her canoe up onto the island. Beside her, a golden-eyed troll unpacked bottles of pink champagne and a package of snap-together plastic glasses. Another human girl danced on the sand, her paint-stained trench coat whirling around her like a skirt. She turned to wave when she spotted them.

Even Roiben was already there, leaning against a tree, his long woolen coat wet at the hem.

Kaye jumped out, grabbing the rope and splashing through

the shallow water. She held the raft still enough for Luis and Corny to follow her.

"That's Ravus," Luis said, nodding in the direction of the troll. "And Val and Ruth."

"Hey!" The stubble-headed girl—Val—called.

Luis squeezed Corny's hand. "Be right back."

He walked over to them just as the stubble-haired girl popped a bottle of champagne. The cork shot out into the waves and she yelped. Corny wanted to trail after Luis, but he wasn't sure he was welcome.

Especially when both girls wrapped Luis in their arms.

Kaye tucked a strand of hair behind her ear and looked out at the waves. "You can see the whole city from here. Too bad we can't see the ball drop."

"This reminds me of something in a fantasy novel," Corny told her. "You know, mysterious island. Me, with my trusted elven sidekick."

"I'm your trusted elven sidekick?" Kaye snorted.

"Maybe not trusted," Corny said with a grin. Then he shook his head. "It's dumb, though. The part of me that loves this. That's the part that's going to get me killed. Like Dave. Like Janet."

"Do you still wish you weren't human?"

Corny frowned, glanced toward Luis and his friends. "I thought those were our *secret* wishes."

"You showed me it!"

"Even so." He sighed. "I don't know. Right now, being human is actually working out for me. It's kind of a first. What about you?"

"I just realized that I don't have to do normal things, being a faerie," Kaye said. "No need to get a job, right? I can turn leaves into money if I need it. No need to go to college—what would be the point? See above, no need for a job."

"I guess education isn't its own reward?"

"You ever think about the future? I mean, you remember what you and Luis were talking about in the car?"

"I guess." He remembered that Luis had hoped Dave would go to school with him.

"I was thinking about opening a coffee shop. I thought that maybe we could have it be a front, and in the back there'd be a library—with real information on faeries—and maybe an office for Luis to break curses out of. You could work on the computers, keep the Internet running, make some searchable databases."

"Yeah?" Corny could picture green walls and dark wood trim and copper cappuccino machines hissing in the background.

She shook her head. "You think it's crazy, right? And Luis would never go for it, and I'm probably too irresponsible anyway."

He grinned hugely. "I think it's genius. But what about Roiben? Don't you want to go be the Faerie Queen or whatever?"

Across the field, Corny saw the troll rest a massive, monstrous hand on Luis's shoulder. Luis relaxed against the creature's bulk. The girl with the dark hair—Ruth—said something and Val laughed. Roiben stepped away from the trees and started toward them. Lutie sprung off Kaye's shoulder, launching herself into the air.

"I thought Luis hated faeries," Kaye said.

Corny shrugged. "You know us humans. We talk an enormous amount of shit."

The funeral was simple. They all stood in a semicircle around Luis as he held up the metal tin of ashes. They'd dug a shallow pit near the edge of the numbered grave markers and passed out champagne.

"If you knew my brother," Luis said, his hand visibly shaking, "you probably already have your own opinions about him. And I guess they're all true, but there doesn't have to be only one truth. I'm going to choose to remember David as the kid who found the two of us a place to sleep when I didn't know where to go, and as the brother that I loved."

Luis opened the tin of ashes and dumped them. The wind caught some and lifted them into the air, while the rest filled the hole. Corny wasn't sure what he'd thought they would look like, but the dust was gray as an old newspaper.

"Happy New Year, baby brother," Luis said. "I wish you could drink with us tonight."

Roiben stood by the water, swigging out of a bottle of champagne. He'd loosed his salt white hair and it covered most of his face.

Kaye walked over to him, pulling out a noisemaker from her pocket and sticking it in her mouth. She blew and the long checkered paper tongue unfurled with a squeak.

He smiled.

Kaye groaned. "You really are a terrible boyfriend, you know that?"

He nodded. "A surfeit of ballads makes for odd ideas about romance."

"But things don't work like that," Kaye said, taking the bottle from his hand and drinking from the neck. "Like ballads or songs or epic poems where people do all the wrong things for the right reasons."

"You have completed an impossible quest and saved me from the Queen of the Faeries," he said softly. "That is very like a ballad."

"Look, I just don't want you to keep hiding things from me," Kaye said, handing him back the bottle, "or hurt my feelings because you think it's going to keep me safe, or sacrifice yourself for me. Just tell me. Tell me what's going on with you."

He tipped the champagne so that the liquid fizzed on the snow, staining it pink. "I taught myself to feel nothing. And you make me feel."

"That's why I'm a weakness?" Her breath came out like a cloud in the icy air.

"Yes." He looked out at the black ocean and then back at her. "It hurts. To feel again. But I'm glad of it. I'm glad of the pain." He sighed. "Most of the time I'm glad of it."

Kaye took a step closer to him. The bright sky silvered his face with light and highlighted the way the points of his ears parted his hair. He looked both alien and utterly familiar.

"I know I failed you," Roiben said. "In the stories when you fall in love with a creature—"

"First I'm a thing, now I'm a creature?" Kaye said.

Roiben laughed. "Well, in the stories it is often a creature. Some kind of beast. A snake that becomes a woman at night, or someone cursed to be a bear until they can take off their own skin."

"How about a fox?" Kaye asked, thinking of Silarial's story of the thornbushes.

He frowned. "If you like. You're crafty enough."

"Yeah, let's say a fox."

"In those stories, one is often asked to do something unimaginably terrible to the creature. Cut off its head, say. A test. Not a test of love, a test of trust. Trust lifts the spell."

"So you think that you should have cut off my head?" Kaye grinned.

He rolled his eyes. "I should have accepted your declaration, whether I thought it was wise or no. I loved you too much to trust you. I failed."

"Good thing I'm not really a fox," Kaye said. "Or a snake or a bear. And good thing I'm sneaky enough to figure out a way around your dumb quest."

Roiben sighed. "Once more I mean to save you, and yet you come to my rescue. If you hadn't warned me about Ethine, I would have done just what Silarial expected."

She looked down so he wouldn't see her cheeks go pink with pleasure. She stuck her fingers into the pockets of her coat and was surprised to feel a circle of cold metal.

"I made you something," Kaye said, pulling out the bracelet of green braid wrapped in silver wire.

"This is your hair?" he asked.

"It's a token," Kaye said. "Like from a lady to a knight. For when I'm not around. I was going to give it to you before, but I never quite got around to it."

He ran his fingers over it and looked at Kaye, astonished. "And you made it? For me?"

She nodded, and he held out his hand so she could clasp it on him. His skin felt hot to the brush of her fingers.

Across the water, along the shore, fireworks went off. Streaks of fire ballooned into carnations of light. Golden explosions rained around them. She looked over at him, but he was still looking at his wrist.

"You said it was for when you're not around. Will you not be around?" he asked her when he looked up.

She thought about the owl-eyed faerie in Silarial's court and what he'd told her. *They say that nameless things change constantly—that names fix them in place like pins.* Kaye didn't want to be fixed in place. She didn't want to pretend to be mortal when she wasn't, nor did she want to have to leave the mortal world. She didn't want to belong to one place or be one kind of thing.

"How will you rule both courts?" she asked instead of answering his question.

Roiben shook his head. "I'll try to keep one foot on each side, balance on the knife edge between both courts for as long as I can. There will be peace so long as I can hold them. Provided I don't declare war on myself, that is."

"Is that likely?"

"I must confess to a good deal of self-loathing." He smiled.

"I was thinking of opening a coffee shop," Kaye said quickly. "In Ironside. Maybe help people with faerie problems. Like Luis does. Maybe even help faeries with faerie problems."

"You know I just made a very advantageous bargain predicated on the fact that no faerie wants to live in the city." He sighed and shook his head as if he'd just realized that arguing with her was useless. "What will you call your coffee shop?"

"Moon in a Cup," she said. "Maybe. I'm not sure. I was thinking that maybe I could move out of my grandmother's— spend half my time working in the shop and half my time in Faerie, with you. I mean, if you don't mind me being around."

He smiled at that and it seemed like a real smile, with no shadows at the edges. "Like Persephone?"

"What?" Kaye leaned in and skimmed her hand under his coat, tracing the vertebrae of his back. His breath hitched.

Roiben let his hand fall lightly, hesitantly, across the wings of her shoulders. He sighed like he'd been holding his breath. "It's a Greek story. A human one. The King of the underworld— Hades—fell in love with a girl, Persephone. She was a goddess too, the daughter of Demeter, who controlled the seasons and the harvests.

"Hades stole Persephone away to his palace in the underworld and tempted her with a split-open pomegranate, each seed shining like a ruby. She knew that if she ate or drank anything in that place she would be trapped, but somehow he persuaded her to eat a mere six seeds. Thereafter, she was doomed to spend half of each year in the underworld, one month for one seed."

"Like you're doomed to spend half your time dealing with the Bright Court and half with the Night Court?" Kaye asked.

Roiben laughed. "Very like."

Kaye looked at the far shore, where fireworks still heralded the new year above the jagged teeth of buildings, and then toward where Corny and the others blew noisemakers and drank cheap champagne from plastic goblets.

She slid out of Roiben's arms and whirled on the sand of the beach. The wind blew off the water, numbing her face.

Kaye laughed and spun faster, gulping the cold briny air and smelling the faint firework smoke. Pebbles crunched under her boots.

"You still haven't told me," he said softly.

She stretched her arms out over her head, then came to an abrupt halt in front of him. "Told you what?"

He grinned. "How you managed to complete the quest. How you claimed to be able to lie."

"Oh. It's simple." Kaye lay down on her back on the snowy beach, looking up at him. "This is me," she said, her voice full of mischief as she reached out with one long-fingered hand. "I'm a faerie that can lie. See? This is me lying."

TURN THE PAGE TO READ

THE LAMENT OF LUTIE-LOO

A NEW SHORT STORY SET IN THE REALM OF FAERIE

Lutie was about the height of a large mug of tea. Or a pencil that had been sharpened a few times. Or a paperback book that could be tucked into a purse.

Small enough to hide in Kaye's hair. Small enough to not quite fit in fashion doll clothes unless she altered them with needles the length of her arm. Small enough to be thought of as utterly, completely inconsequential. Because of her size, from the moment she was born, tumbling from a flower and still slightly fuzzy with pollen, Lutie-loo was never given an *important* job. Just one silly errand after another.

When Silarial had sent her to the Unseelie Court with Spike and Gristle and the Thistlewitch, Lutie thought her fortunes were changing. The way the Lady had spoken of the task, it had seemed so important! But watching over Kaye, a child ignorant of her own magic, was barely even babysitting. It certainly wasn't a quest.

And sure, Kaye had turned out to be wild as her pixie blood, twice as clever, and three times as headstrong. She'd wound up responsible for the death of Silarial . . . and the overturning of two courts. But that definitely hadn't been part of the *plan*. And it wasn't because of anything Lutie had done.

Now Lutie was an honored member of Roiben's Court. She wanted for nothing. And nobody wanted her to do anything either. She was just expected to sit on her duff, drink dew from petals, and overlook how no member of the Gentry saw her as anything more than an oversize and slightly more intelligent bug. And, of course, most mortals didn't see her at all.

"I just need to *find* Ethine, and then I can ask her what her problem is," Kaye said. She was sitting on a stool in the back kitchen of her coffee shop, Moon in a Cup, looping glittery green laces through the eyelets of a pair of Doc Martens. "I guess I can understand why she was angry—but it wasn't his fault! She has to have realized that by now."

Lutie buzzed sympathetically, alert to the possibility that maybe finding Ethine was something she'd be good at. After all, Lutie could talk to people. She could ferret out information. And she wasn't likely to get into as many arguments as Kaye would. This would be a good job for her. "Maybe *I* could find her. Maybe."

But Kaye wasn't paying attention. "*Silarial ordered* her to fight Roiben. Even though Ethine had no idea how to use a sword and was going to *die* if Roiben fought back. And if Silarial *had* gotten her way and Roiben decided to sacrifice himself, Ethine would have had to *kill her own brother*. Maybe she would have blamed him for that too." Kaye shoved her foot into the boot, slamming it against the tiled floor with the force of her anger.

Kaye lived in New York, despite the iron and the iron sickness that came with it. The last time she visited Roiben, she'd redecorated his throne room, throwing out a dozen hideous and doubtless treasured Unseelie objects over the protests of his councillors, including many bloodstained textiles and a mouse-skin rug. Kaye didn't understand leaving things well enough alone. She never had. Once, Lutie had watched the Thistlewitch instruct Kaye not to take off a protective glamour. Kaye immediately went and did exactly the thing she'd been forbidden from doing.

Lutie loved her, but Kaye was not a reasonable creature. She certainly couldn't understand someone like Ethine, who seemed like she just wanted all her problems to go away.

"Ethine is proud," Lutie said. "Proud and sad and dull."

Kaye made a face. "If I just explained . . ."

Lutie could picture Kaye running around Faerieland, accidentally overthrowing governments and causing one huge scene after another. Lutie was sure Roiben would not like that, especially if it got his sister even angrier with him. But maybe Lutie could find Ethine herself and arrange the meeting. It was true that a great court lady like Ethine was probably no more interested in what a sprite had to say than a pixie, but all the Gentry loved protocol. And a messenger would make everything more formal. Besides, if Ethine was totally against speaking to Kaye, at least Kaye would go in forearmed. Or be persuaded not to go at all.

Lutie cleared her throat to make her suggestion again. "I could look for her."

Kaye gave her an evaluating look. Lutie flew in place, attempting to look competent. And larger.

"No," Kaye said finally, shaking her head. "It's too much of a bother for you."

"I can do it!" Lutie said, rather more sharply than she'd intended.

Kaye appeared surprised. "I am sure you *could*."

"It will be my mission," said Lutie. "I will do deeds of daring!"

Kaye's green eyebrows rose. "I hope not. But if you really want to go, then fine. I bequeath this annoying quest to you. Find Ethine and bring word to me of her whereabouts, and possibly news of what crawled up her ass to make her such an awful—"

"Yes!" Lutie said, zooming through the air joyfully. "I will find the sister. I will arrange everything!"

Kaye grinned up at her. She said she believed Lutie could do it, and Kaye could no more lie than any of the Folk. Lutie felt a burst of hope. If she could pull this off, not only would it make Kaye happy, but Lord Roiben would be pleased too. Perhaps the gloomy King of the Court of Termites would cheer up and grant her a medal or a hollow tree to call her own. And perhaps he'd send her on an even more important quest.

It took her all day to assemble and pack the things she thought she might need—a long steel pin tucked into a leather sheath, to serve as a sword; doll gowns and a few other items filched from a dollhouse, jammed into a velvet gift bag she was using for a rucksack; and three organic single-origin chocolate-covered coffee beans, for energy.

Then she realized she had no idea how to find Ethine. She was sure she could. But that didn't mean she had the first idea how. So she pondered and she pondered and she ate one of the chocolate-covered coffee beans.

It was very late when she found herself flying above the stump of a tree beneath the Manhattan Bridge. She tried to find something optimistic in the way the roots had cracked up through the pavement before humans had chopped the tree down, but it was hard.

She slid through a window and flew inside, to the waiting room of the potion-maker and alchemist for the solitary fey of New York. Ravus the troll lived here. She knew him because he'd once been part of Silarial's court and because he had a human companion who'd been one of Kaye's roommates. As she recalled that, she also realized she wasn't sure how much time had passed since then. What had happened to the girl? Lutie couldn't remember.

Ravus had been exiled from Silarial's court, she knew that. He'd been at court when she had, although their paths hadn't crossed. He was just so *huge* that being around him scared Lutie. He could crush her easily, absentmindedly, in the swat of one giant hand.

But because he was the maker of a powder that allowed the Folk a resistance to iron, many solitary fey and even Gentry visiting the cities came to see him. Everyone used the powder, even Lutie. It made living near the iron bearable. Maybe Ethine had been one of them. Or maybe he'd heard a rumor.

Lutie was hoping. And she was further hoping he'd be friendly about it. And not ask for too much in exchange for the information.

There was a little bell near the door to Ravus's chambers. She rang it and waited nervously as the tinkling sound echoed through the dark.

A few minutes later, a large wooden door creaked open, a sliver of light spilled out, and there was a heavy tread on the floor. Ravus appeared, his skin a green that looked a bit sickly in the gloom. Lutie's tiny heart sped like the whir of humming-bird wings.

"Welcome," he said in his deep voice. "What is it you seek?"

"A courtier," Lutie told him, darting past and into his workroom. "Lord Roiben's sister." A long wooden table was laden with ingredients—dry snakeskins; tiny pale bones; and stoppered and waxed glass bottles of many different shapes, bearing labels in the troll's looping hand. The first tag read: LAST HOPE OF A HEART.

The room she'd entered was very tall, with a loft suspended above her. She could see a bed with disarranged sheets and one pale leg sticking out, bare to the thigh. Too pale, Lutie thought. Was it a dead body? Lutie rose a little without quite meaning to. Then the person on the bed turned over in sleep. For a moment, Lutie was relieved. The paleness was only moonlight. But a moment later she noticed the distorted shape of the girl, with an abdomen like that of an enormous spider.

What had he done to her? Was it some kind of alchemical experiment?

"I don't have your courtier hidden among my poultices," Ravus said, pitching his voice low. "But come have some tea and I will see what I can recall."

He already had a cup for himself poured, she realized when he freshened it. Then he took down a thimble from one of his shelves and filled it with tea from the same steaming pot. "There are biscuits around here as well, if Val hasn't eaten them all."

Val. Valerie. That was the girl's name. She remembered now. With hair like a copper penny.

Ravus brought a plate over to the table, along with a cup,

which he turned over to make a sprite-size stool. Lutie sat, holding her thimble much as one might hold a pail. The scent that wafted up to her nose was a delicious blend of elderflower and nettle. The cookies piled on the plate appeared to be studded with rosemary. But Lutie couldn't help a nervous glance toward the loft.

"Ethine left," she said, trying to focus on her mission.

Ravus nodded. "Stomped off in a huff, isn't that right?"

"Yes, and Kaye wants her back." Lutie took a sip of the tea. "She thinks Roiben is sad."

Ravus grinned, showing too-long canines. "The fearsome Lord of Termites? I never imagined him anything so ordinary."

Lutie buzzed in understanding. Sometimes it did seem like when Kaye talked about Roiben, she was attributing nuanced emotions to a handsome murder-loving murderer. "But you do know where she is?"

"I do, as a matter of fact," he said. "Ethine came to a friend of mine for a potion to change her hair. She didn't want to glamour it because she was going to the High Court, where they'd be very likely to see through any magic. And the silver is so distinct. After all, it's the same as his."

"The High Court?" Lutie squeaked. She didn't like that, not one bit.

"No one wants to storm off to serve a lesser court," Ravus observed mildly.

Lutie finished her tea disconsolately. The High Court of Elfhame, where High King Eldred ruled, had been collecting lower courts since the time of Queen Mab. It was said that they made you swear not to the royals themselves, but to a crown that never broke. So far, they hadn't marched on Roiben, but she was sure they would very much like for him to pledge his fealty to the High Court and bring a large chunk of the East Coast into their fold. They were scary.

And it meant that Lutie would have to fly over the sea to the isles of Elfhame. She hated flying great distances, especially over water. There was nowhere to land when her wings got tired, and birds and fish often thought she'd make a delicious snack until she showed them otherwise. But that was an obstacle—and all quests had obstacles. She could overcome them, she was sure of it.

There was a creak on the stairs. The girl—no, a woman now, with the same copper penny hair that Lutie remembered—was coming down, in what appeared to be an oversize band shirt stretched over her enormous abdomen and fuzzy slippers. "Is someone there?" Val called.

"I better be off," Lutie squeaked. Kaye wasn't going to like to hear what had become of her friend.

"Did we wake you?" Ravus asked Val, smiling warmly at her. Surely he wouldn't look at her like that if he was the cause of her suffering.

The woman shook her head and yawned. One hand went to her belly. "Heartburn."

And something about the gesture made Lutie finally recognize what was wrong with Valerie. Or not wrong at all. She was *pregnant*.

Faeries didn't reproduce often or easily, not like mortals. And while Lutie had seen pregnant human women before, there was something somewhat shocking about thinking that a mortal was carrying a faerie child. But it was still embarrassing that she'd thought all those things about Ravus.

Lutie fled.

At Fisherman's Wharf, she stared out at the water, reassuring herself. Her quest was going well, she thought. Once she got to Elfhame, it wouldn't be hard to find Ethine in the High Court, and then no matter what she said, Lutie could come right back—job complete! Really, it wasn't even that hard of a job. She could handle much worse. With that happy thought in mind, she snuck into a dollar store, where she filched both a plastic saddle for a toy horse and a ball of yarn. Then she startled a seagull awake. It snapped its beak in her direction immediately. Jumping back, she lifted her hands and spoke in the language of birds. "Do my bidding. Bear me on your back and fly me wheresoever I say."

It stopped attacking, and Lutie threw her makeshift harness onto its back.

She could totally handle this job! Everything was going just fine.

The gull hurtled up toward the stars with a great cry. On its back, the journey was swift and sure, carrying her away from the lights and metal stink of Manhattan, out over the waves. It wasn't long before she spotted the three isles— Insmear, Insmire, and Insweal—shrouded in fog, their hills and valleys an emerald green never to be found in the mortal world. Despite herself, her heart gave a little leap. Here was a place only for the Folk, thick and heavy with enchantment. As the gull flew closer, even the scent of the air made her giddy. It was a feeling she'd only had before at Silarial's court, the feeling of coming home.

The seagull landed on one of the black rocks of near the shore. Lutie climbed down off its back, untied the saddle, and waved the creature off. It looked around in confusion, as though unsure of how it came to be there, and then began grooming its feathers.

"Silly thing," Lutie said, petting its head with some affection. From there, Lutie headed toward the palace, pausing only to alight on the branch of a tree and change into a strapless red-and-gold Barbie ball gown that gave her the shape of a bell.

Guards were stopping those that approached the towering knowe, but as usual, no one bothered with Lutie. As a sprite, she flew right over the guards' heads. They gave her as little notice as a mortal might give a lightning bug.

Inside, the hollow hall was bustling with activity. There appeared to be no revel that night, and instead courtiers sat around the room, a few trailing between groups. Lutie looked for other sprites and found a clump of them among a particularly thick knot of trailing roots. They wore fanciful little gowns of petals and scraps of velvet, lit to fine effect by the glow of their bodies. Lutie was suddenly very conscious of the fact that she was wearing the dress of a doll, even it if was very nice. She wasn't sure if she felt provincial or very modern.

"Um, hello," said Lutie.

One of the other sprites—a boy—stepped away from the others. He looked her over with some disdain, and she gave him an equally haughty look back. "You're not of the High Court," he said. "Where do you hail from?"

"West of here," she told him. "East of elsewhere. I am looking for a courtier." Lutie was not enormously skilled with glamour, but she could draw an image in the air. She swept her hand in the space between them, and a picture of Ethine formed, an Ethine with dark hair. It held a moment and then faded into shimmers.

The boy frowned. "And for what reason should I help you?"

"That's easy." Lutie fished around in her rucksack and came up with a chocolate-covered coffee bean. "I will trade you a rare treat from the mortal world, which will please your tongue and work upon your blood, filling it with joy."

He looked skeptical, but after a moment, reached for the bean. "I will make this trade, strange one. The courtier is known as Ethna, one of the Princess Elowyn's ladies. She belongs to the Circle of Larks, who love music and art above all other things. Look for a woman with golden skin and you will find her close by. I would try that group there." He pointed. "Where Edir is about to embarrass himself with his poor playing."

Lutie squinted. Then she nodded, pleased with herself. Another obstacle overcome! And all because of her good planning.

The sprite boy bit the edge of the chocolate bean. As she flew off, she saw more sprites had gathered around him, taking bites of their own. One looked a little confused, having clearly bit through the chocolate layer and into the bean itself.

She discovered Ethine close to where the boy had pointed, serving herself a goblet of lilac wine near where poetry was being recited. Her dyed-black hair was drawn up into combs. She wore a gown in the pale blue of the morning sky with rose dusting the edges.

"Excuse me," Lutie said, hovering in the air in front of her.

Ethine looked at Lutie in surprise, but not recognition. She was probably unused to being addressed by a sprite. "Yes?" she said, not at all encouragingly.

"I am from the Court of Termites, sent here by your brother's consort. Kaye wishes a meeting with you." Lutie hoped that sounded formal enough. It was certainly a longer sentence than she usually spoke.

"No one knows me here," Ethine's voice dropped to a harsh whisper. "And I do not wish to be known."

"Maybe we could talk alone." Lutie was unwilling to be dismissed. After all, she was on the verge of her first successful mission.

Ethine looked toward the other court ladies and the Princess Elowyn. "I suppose," she said, seeming to realize that arguing with Lutie in the middle of the brugh was going to make the scene she'd been attempting to avoid. "Follow me."

Ethine led her into the hall, then to a room off of it, a parlor thick with the scent of earth and flowers. "So Kaye sent you?"

Lutie nodded. "Yes, she wants to talk. She wants you to reconcile with Lord Roiben."

"*Lord Roiben,*" Ethine scoffed, turning his title into the focus of her contempt. Lutie fluttered in astonishment, wondering if she would be so foolish as to say something like that to his face. Not many would and expect to survive it.

"You're still angry with your brother," Lutie said, then regretted it when Ethine turned her glare upon her.

"If he'd only put his pride aside," Ethine said. "I know he was angry. The Unseelie Court treated him poorly. But he and Silarial could have united the courts without any bloodshed."

Lutie looked at her with bafflement, but then, she didn't understand much about politics. Nor did she understand the point of imagining how things could have been had everything happened differently. "Will you meet with Kaye? Just to talk."

Ethine shook her head. "No. Her coming here will just draw attention—and to no purpose. I do not intend to see my brother again."

"She might come anyway," Lutie warned. "If you pick the time and place—"

"Tell her not to come," Ethine said, her voice rising. "Tell her I won't see her, no matter what she says and no matter to whom she says it."

Lutie sighed. This was not the sort of success that would get her medals and praise and trusted with important tasks in the future. She'd found Ethine and she'd gotten an answer, but it wasn't the answer anyone wanted.

"Yes," said Lutie, wings drooping. "I will."

Ethine left the parlor without looking back. After a moment, Lutie decided to follow her. She had to find another seabird to take her home. But perhaps first she would have a bit of oatcake and a gossip with the sprites she'd met. That would make her feel better and fortify her for the journey. And if it made Ethine a little nervous that she was still around, well, that might be a little bit satisfying.

With those thoughts running through her mind, she flew out of the parlor. She was moving fast enough that she didn't notice the man.

At least not until his gloved hands closed around her. Lutie screamed in her tiny voice. She struggled and bit and kicked, but that only made him grip her more tightly.

"Got you." He wore a crown on his brow and a scowl on his face. "You should be honored. It's not everyone who can be the prisoner of the eldest prince of Elfhame. And you're going to help me get my father's crown."

Those ominous words made Lutie struggle harder. He gave her an amused look and then tossed her into a sack, drawing it tightly around her. There was a strange scent on the cloth.

Within minutes, Lutie was asleep.

She woke in a cage made of woven gold. It had the shape of a birdcage, but the bars were much narrower and the things inside were clearly intended for a sprite. She was lying across a cushion. Beside her sat half of a plum and a miniature blown-glass goblet of watered wine.

She went to the edge and looked down. The cage hung up in the corner of a room, the rest of which appeared to be filled with revelers. Clearly, a party was going on.

Lutie had to get out of the cage. Now was a good time, while there was so much noise that no one was likely to notice. There was a clasp on the door, twisted tight with thick wire. She set to work on that, sticking her arm through the bars, pushing on it as hard as she could.

"Look," said a girl's voice. "The sprite's awake. What does your brother want it for?"

Outside of the cage, two of the Folk stood: One, a girl from the Undersea, with the characteristic webbed ears and that strange translucence to her teeth. The other was apparently related to the prince who'd captured her. Lutie might have guessed, even without the girl's words. He had the same features, with spilled-ink hair and a sneer to rival his brother's. Another prince, then.

"Debauchery, I'd wager," said the young prince. "He grows easily bored."

The girl wrinkled her nose fastidiously.

"Let me out," Lutie said, although she had little hope. "Please."

The girl gave a tinkling laugh, but the boy drew closer. His eyes glittered with something Lutie didn't like.

"We're all trapped in cages, little sprite," he told her. "How can I free you when I can't even free myself?"

"Get away from there, Cardan." Lutie raised her eyes to see that the elder prince, the one who captured her, had come into the room. The boy—Prince Cardan, she supposed—and the girl retreated. He swiped a bottle of wine from the table and they headed toward a set of stairs.

Lutie watched them go with regret as her cage was taken off its hook. "Awake at last," he said. "Allow me to introduce myself. You may address me as Prince Balekin, or if you prefer, my lord."

"Yes, my lord," said Lutie, accustomed to the Gentry and their love of pomp and ceremony.

"Now you will give me your name," he said. Without his gloves, his knuckles seemed to have thorns growing from them, thorns that ridged his wrists, disappearing up under his clothes.

"Lutie," she told him.

"A mere scrap of one," he told her, although he could hardly expect her to give him the whole thing.

When she didn't answer, he carried the whole cage out of the room, sending it swinging so that the wine spilled, the goblet shattered, and the plum went hurtling around like a boulder. Lutie clung to the side, looking out at all the rooms they passed through.

It turned out that questing was terrible and that she was terrible at questing.

The party went on with people drinking and singing, in

various states of undress. Eventually, Prince Balekin came to a door and passed through into an office, where he set the cage down heavily on a desk.

"Now admit it, you're from the Court of Termites," he said.

Lutie was startled. "How did you—"

"I have spies," he said. "They overheard that you were looking for a courtier. Ethna? Isn't that right? I never gave her much notice before, but I have now. In particular, I noticed that the roots of her hair are a rather startling silver."

Lutie's heart thudded in her chest. This wasn't how the mission was supposed to go. She'd considered what would happen if she didn't manage to complete the job—if she couldn't find Ethine and had to go home in disgrace. But she'd never considered causing harm.

"What do you want?" Lutie demanded.

"Just confirmation that I was right. And now I have that." He smiled, smug. "She's on her way here. I imagine that the three of us will have a lot to discuss."

Lutie fumed in her cage. She kicked the plum, although it bounced back at her and she had to jump out of its way.

Prince Balekin called for servants to bring a tray with wine and figs. He called for another servant to bring him Ethna, from his sister's circle, who would be arriving any minute.

When she did come, she looked out of sorts. She wore the same gown she'd had on before, but over it was a cloak that she waved off a servant's attempt to take. "My lord," she said, with a curtsy. "Your invitation was very kind. And your messengers were very insistent, but—" She bit off her words as she noticed the cage with Lutie in it. "*You*. What are you doing here?"

"You were once called Ethine of the Court of Flowers, isn't that right?" Prince Balekin asked, ignoring her question to Lutie.

"A long time ago," she said, stiffly.

"So, you're really his sister." Balekin grinned the kind of slow malicious grin that signaled something really bad was going to happen.

"We are estranged," Ethine said. "The last time I saw my brother, we were at swords drawn."

Balekin's gaze went to Lutie. "True," she said. "All true. She hates him."

"Ah," said Balekin. "But she will invite him here, nonetheless. You see, Prince Dain would take my rightful place as my father's heir. He has worked at that goal, to make High King Eldred trust only him. You know that Princess Elowyn has been pushed out of the line of succession in much the same way."

"Princess Elowyn doesn't care to play politics," Ethine said.

"Well I do!" Prince Balekin shouted, and she took a nervous step back. He held up his hands consolingly. "And if the mighty Lord of the Court of Termites agrees to join the High Court, I can show my father that I am worthy of being his heir."

"If you believe that I can make my brother do anything, you are much mistaken." Ethine sighed. "He might come here for me, but he wouldn't bow his head to his own beloved. Not for her sake, not for mine or for the sake of the people who were once those he loved best in the world."

Oh, this was all her fault, Lutie thought. If Roiben came and made a bad bargain for Ethine's sake, it was because of her. Because of her failure. Back in Ravus's workroom, Lutie had worried that Roiben was a handsome murder-loving murderer with no heart. Now she hoped that was true. If he had a heart, he was going to get in a lot of trouble.

"Write and invite him," urged Balekin. He took a piece of paper and set it on his desk, beside an inkwell and a feather, the end cut into a fresh nib.

"Yes, and then I will take the message!" Lutie said. Perhaps if they sent her with it, she could go to Kaye. Kaye would have a plan.

Balekin shook his head. "You will stay in your cage and tell me all you can of the Court of Termites. Once the Lady Ethine composes her correspondence."

Ethine stared at the pen as though it was a snake that might turn upon her at any moment and bite. "I will not write to him. And your sister would not like to see one of her ladies so ill-used."

"I am the eldest prince of Elfhame and I will do what I like with you," Prince Balekin said. "And if Elowyn doesn't like it, more's the pity."

"Let me," Lutie said.

He turned a scowl on her. "You're an eager little thing, aren't you?"

"Yes!" Lutie said. "Very eager. I was on an important mission to arrange a meeting. And now a meeting will be arranged."

At that, Balekin threw back his head and laughed. "I suppose it is no bad thing that you have your own priorities, especially since they don't conflict with my own."

"Do not do this," Ethine cautioned, but Lutie ignored her.

Balekin untwisted the wire on her cage. Lutie considered attempting an escape. He might grab her, but if he missed, she was very hard to catch once she got going. She could be out the window and then away from Elfhame entirely.

But if she left Ethine behind, then Balekin would make her write to Roiben. And he might be able to get the message there faster than Lutie flew. And it wasn't really doing a job well if you made everything worse for all the people you were supposed to be helping. With a sigh, Lutie remained motionless as Balekin took out the plum, mopped up the spilled wine and plum juice, and placed the writing materials on the floor of the cage.

Kaye was clever. Now Lutie just had to be clever too.

She began to write:

> Kaye,
> Wonderful news! Everyone will be happy
> to hear that I found Ethine in the Court
> of Elfhame. All it took was asking around.
> Roiben ought to come and meet with her.
> Ending the enmity between them seems
> possible. Have him come as soon as he is able.
> Obviously, he is very busy. Still, he should
> come. The sooner the better. Alone. Go
> and tell him as soon as you can. Every day is
> another day without them speaking.
>
> > Sincerely,
> > LUTIE

Balekin took the note out of the cage when she was done writing. He snorted, reading it over. "Laying it on a bit thick, no?" he asked.

Lutie gave him her best blank look, and he shook his head.

"It'll do," he said finally. "So long as he comes. If not, it will be you who suffers. Do you understand?"

She nodded, torn between relief and fresh worry.

"You will remain here," Balekin told Ethine. "Hardly the first of the Court of Larks to slip into the Court of Grackles for a little fun. Come, make merry. Drink deep. Drown your sorrows."

Ethine gave him a scandalized look, but she let him escort her out. That left Lutie alone in the cage. She retrieved the wet cushion from the side of the cage and threw herself down on it. She tried to consider this as just another obstacle to the successful completion of a quest, but it didn't work. She was too worried. Would Kaye understand her message? Kaye was clever, but would she remember to be clever just then? It was hard to think of anything else.

Time passed. Enspelled human servants came, first to hang her cage in the hall, and then at strange hours to shove scraps into it from whatever food was being served elsewhere. Bits of fat and gristle. Hard ends of cheese. Shriveled grapes. Lutie ate them and drank the stale, warm water too. Who knew when they might forget her entirely.

She saw the young Prince Cardan argue with the Undersea girl. "Betrayer, do not believe you won't be betrayed in turn," he told her. "And don't think it won't give me pleasure when you are. Maybe more pleasure than your company ever did."

When the girl stalked off, he noticed Lutie looking. "You know what my brother usually does to sprites? He traps them under glass to use as lights until they die. Because that's all they're good for."

Lutie pushed herself against the bars on the opposite side of the cage. "He won't be High King," she said, because that's all she knew Balekin wanted.

Prince Cardan laughed. "You think Dain would be better? Or me, prophesied to be a monster?"

Lutie stayed pressed against the bars until he went away, hating the High Court and everyone in it.

Another time, she saw Ethine staggering, too sick with drink to stand, her body thudding into a wall as she passed. Lutie called down to her, but she didn't seem to hear.

Then one of the servants took Lutie's cage down from the hook and brought her into a parlor, where Lord Roiben was sitting, drinking a cup of tea. He was dressed entirely in black, his shining hair spilling over his shoulders in a cascade, like mercury from a broken thermometer. Balekin stood nearby, with Ethine beside him. She looked tired, dressed in a gown embroidered with lavender stalks. Her hair was silver again, and short.

Lutie's heart sank. Kaye wasn't there. Kaye wasn't coming to save her.

"Lutie," Roiben said, peering into her cage with his wintry gray eyes. "I got your message."

Lutie nodded glumly. He'd come as soon as he could, just like she'd said, but had no idea what he was walking into. Still, she couldn't be sorry when he began unwinding the clasp on her cage. She'd prefer not to be a prisoner a moment more.

"What are you doing?" Balekin asked him, moving closer.

Roiben didn't pause in his unwinding of the wire, though, and a moment later Lutie was loose, flying up as high as she could, clinging to a bit of decorative molding on the ceiling. She didn't want to be in grabbing distance of Balekin or his creepy servants.

Or any of the rest of them, for that matter.

"I freed her," Roiben said mildly. "What else could you possibly imagine I would do, as she is a subject of mine? You ought not have kept her like that."

Balekin stared at him. Perhaps he'd thought a sprite would be beneath Roiben's notice. Perhaps Roiben's bloodthirsty reputation gave the prince some reason to believe the Lord of the Court of Termites would be amused by cruelty.

Roiben went on. "It is a kindness to be able to see my sister again. But I would speak with her alone."

Balekin nodded with a half smile that this was part of his plan. He gave Ethine an encouraging push toward Roiben. "I hope that, whatever the outcome, you will consider swearing fealty to the High Court. I am sure Ethine will speak well of her time here. She's pledged herself already, you see."

Lutie startled. She hadn't considered that, although it was obvious that living at the High Court, as a courtier in a princess's inner circle, Ethine would have been asked to make a vow of loyalty. But it meant that Roiben had no claim on protecting her, even if he'd known she was in danger.

"I do see," said Roiben.

Balekin went out, closing the door behind him. Lutie was sure he was spying somehow, but she had no idea how and didn't want to risk getting grabbed again by investigating.

"You didn't want me to come, did you?" Roiben asked her when Balekin left. "You seem unhappy. I suppose you're doing this for him?"

"In a manner of speaking," Ethine said. Lutie thought that probably meant she had no choice.

"Sit beside me," Roiben said. "Tell me what I can do to fix things between us."

"You destroyed everything I loved," Ethine told him. "There was no Court of Flowers without Silarial. Talathain was lost, and worst of all, you were unrecognizable in your cruelty. I thought I knew you, but I did not. And I am not sure I knew Silarial either."

"You will not want to hear this," Roiben said. "But I felt the same, once. When I realized that she had known what it was she was sending me to endure, that she had not cared enough—"

"But she couldn't have known!" Ethine protested.

"She did." Roiben gave a long sigh. "They were sisters, for one, and more alike than not. I like to believe it stung a little to give me up. But she got Nephamael in the bargain, and he was more loyal to her than either of them pretended. And a better schemer by far. With him by her side, she brought down the Unseelie Court. Had Kaye not poisoned him, I imagine he would have passed it all over to his mistress. She very nearly had both courts."

Ethine pressed her lips together in a thin line. "You could have been the one to pass it over. You could have bowed your head and presented her with the Unseelie Court, like the greatest jewel in her crown. She would have made you her consort. Perhaps you could have even wed and ruled together."

The corners of Roiben's eyes crinkled. "You said as much, once. But it is a difficult thing to be loved for one's dowry alone."

"Don't jest!" Ethine said.

"Then let me be as frank as I can. I loved another. I love another. Do you understand me? It was not merely pride or rage or any of the other things that you accuse me of, although I felt them in the full measure. I would not have been Silarial's consort, not if I gave her the Unseelie Court. Not if I bowed my head and humbled myself. Not if she begged me."

That startled Ethine. She looked at Roiben as though once again he was utterly unknowable. "But you can't mean—"

"I do mean it. I love Kaye with my whole heart. And whether you think well of that or ill, it's the truest truth I have ever spoken. Silarial wasn't the person you thought she was, and you are angry with me that you came to know it. The only good thing bowing my head to her would have done is allow you to keep your eyes shut."

Lutie expected Ethine to protest that, but she didn't.

"I hurt you," he said. "In the duel. But that's not why you're angry, is it? What you cannot forgive me for is Silarial's death."

"You wish to remind me that I am the one who murdered her," Ethine said. "As though I can forget it."

"I wish to remind you of nothing. I am not the one who sought you out. It is Kaye who cannot leave things well enough alone."

Lutie thought that truer words were never spoken.

"Yet you say you love her!" Ethine protested.

"Yes, I love Kaye. And also, I know her." Roiben smiled faintly. "Just as I know and love you."

"Are you angry with me?" Ethine asked in a very small voice. "For taking Silarial away forever?"

He shook his head, closing his eyes, as though he couldn't bear looking at her while he spoke. "I was relieved to be spared the choice you made."

For a moment, they just sat together in silence. After a while, Ethine reached for his hand and he let her take it, then drew their clasped fingers to his heart.

Finally, he said, "So, sister. What is it I must do here? These are your people now."

"I know what you will say to bowing your head," Ethine said. "Even if it is for my sake. Let us not repeat what is past."

"What happens if I don't swear fealty to the High Court?" he asked. "Let me be more specific: What will they do to you?"

"I don't know," Ethine replied, her voice so low that Lutie understood her more from the movement of her lips than anything else.

Roiben let go of her hand and stood. "Prince Balekin," he called. "I had a visit with my sister. Now let's get to the meat of the matter. Come out. I would bargain with you."

It took a moment, but the doors opened and Balekin strode through. He was trying to look confident, but something in his manner showed that he was worried. He ought to be. Lutie had seen Roiben fight. He had come alone, just like she'd said in her stupid note, but she'd seen him cut through more guards than Balekin had in his employ.

Of course, killing the eldest prince of Elfhame would probably mean war.

"So," said Balekin. "What bargain do you propose?"

"Ah, you wish to play out the game. I will say that I wish to take my sister home with me. You will remind me that she belongs here, that you are a prince. Perhaps add a few ominous things that are meant to imply you will not be a good guardian. As though I cannot see you've treated her poorly."

"She was offered every pleasure of my household," Balekin protested.

"And now I am here to unwind the wire of her cage," said Roiben. "Let me guess. You wish the fealty of the Court of Termites."

Ethine stood up from the couch. "Wait. Roiben." She put a cautioning hand on his arm.

Lutie held her breath. What had she done? Not just ruined the mission, but stolen the sovereignty from the Court of Termites. Kaye would never forgive her. Oh, this was very, very bad.

Roiben turned to Ethine. "You think it was pride that kept me from bowing my head, but it was never that." Then he looked at Balekin. "You release all claim on her if I agree that the Court of Termites swears fealty to the High Court?"

Balekin frowned, as though trying to figure out how he'd lost control of the situation. "Yes . . ."

"Done," Roiben said, his voice clipped. He looked up. "Lutie, perhaps you'd prefer to travel in the pocket of my coat? It's velvet lined."

"Wait!" Balekin said. "We must go to my father and tell him the news. You must come and take the oath and tell him of my role. This is my triumph."

"Let us be off, then," said Roiben, offering his sister his arm. She placed her hand on his and they walked through Balekin's estate, past his guards and out through the doors. Balekin called for horses.

Lutie was sorry she'd ever thought of Roiben as a handsome

murder-loving murderer. She darted down, grateful he didn't want to squish her. Even more grateful he didn't want to leave her behind.

"This is all your fault," Ethine said to Lutie.

"I know," Lutie replied mournfully.

"Nonsense," Roiben said. "Lutie-loo sent me a very clever message. Do you know what an acrostic code is? Mortals like them very much. The children use them to write poems at school, using the letters of their names."

"What are you speaking of?" Balekin said. "I read that letter myself."

"Yes, you might well have, since I imagine you forced her to write it. But did you notice the first letter of each of the sentences?" said Roiben. "W-E-A-R-E-H-O-S-T-A-G-E-S. We are hostages. As I said, clever."

"But if you knew—then why did you come alone?" Ethine cried. "Why put yourself in his power?"

Roiben gave her a real smile. A slightly smug one. "I didn't. Dulcamara and Ellebere are both with me. And I won't be going to visit the High King Eldred with you, Prince Balekin. You see, I've already been there. With your brother Dain. I have already given him my fealty—should he become the High King, I have agreed to swear to him and to him alone."

"No," Balekin's eyes went wide. "How?" His fingers reached inside his coat, as though seeking a blade.

But as he did, out of the shadows came Roiben's knights. Dulcamara with her skeletal wings and her ruby-red hair and her fierce smile. Ellebere with his insectile armor. And behind them, knights of Elfhame.

"Brother," said a man who could only be Prince Dain.

Roiben didn't wait to hear what they would say to each other. He and Ethine moved toward Dulcamara, and minutes later they were all in the sky, on steeds made of smoke, racing through the dark. The velvet lining was soft around Lutie, the cloth warmed by the heat of the body that wore it. She looked up from Roiben's pocket and watched the stars turn over her head.

🐚 🪶 🐚 🐚

Back in New York, Kaye was putting together a party in miniature for Lutie. She'd covered two bricks to make a banquet table, set it on top of her own dining room table, and piled it with foodstuffs. A cupcake set on a silver-chased compact mirror. A single sticky sesame wing on a chipped child's saucer, as large to Lutie as a whole turkey. Three raspberries and a blueberry, stuffed into a freshly peeled lychee. And then, around that, food for everyone else.

"Congratulations!" said Kaye. "You made it out of the High Court and stopped a coup. Pretty good for a first mission."

Kaye had invited Ravus and Val, whom it turned out Kaye had known was pregnant. Corny and Luis were there too. And Roiben, who looked surprised by his own happiness. No Ethine, but that was fine. She was, apparently, traveling to the part of the Court of Termites that had once been the Court of Flowers. Maybe looking for Talathain. Maybe just going back to doing courtier things. Lutie was glad not to have her there, making things awkward.

"Will you ask a boon from me?" Roiben said.

Lutie drew herself up. She thought about what the awful prince had said to her in the cage, about sprites not being good for anything. And she thought about how hard the job had really been, way harder than she'd thought.

"I want another job," said Lutie.

His eyes crinkled in amusement and she worried he was going to laugh at her. She held her breath.

"I didn't ask you to assign yourself a punishment," said Lord Roiben of the Court of Termites. "But who am I to argue with such a generous request? Consider it done."

RETURN TO FAERIE

in the complete critically acclaimed Modern Faerie Tales trilogy from #1 *New York Times* bestselling author Holly Black.

A MODERN FAERIE TALE

★"A gripping read."
—*Publishers Weekly*, *starred review*

TITHE

#1 *NEW YORK TIMES* BESTSELLING AUTHOR
HOLLY BLACK

A MODERN FAERIE TALE

"A powerful book."
—*Tamora Pierce*

VALIANT

#1 *NEW YORK TIMES* BESTSELLING AUTHOR
HOLLY BLACK

A MODERN FAERIE TALE

BONUS
SHORT
STORY
INSIDE!

"Decadent and deadly."
—*Kirkus Reviews*

IRONSIDE

#1 *NEW YORK TIMES* BESTSELLING AUTHOR
HOLLY BLACK

"**Dark, edgy, beautifully written, and compulsively readable.**"—***Booklist***

PRINT AND EBOOK EDITIONS AVAILABLE
From Margaret K. McElderry Books
simonandschuster.com

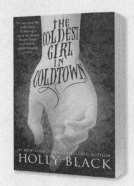